HONEST DEALING

THE
SEFWARIAN NYSS
SERIES

ERICA-JANE BATTISSON

WILD TEAZEL

Published in Great Britain 2021
by Wild Teazel Publishing
(First edition)

ISBN 978-1-7398043-0-5 (Paperback)

www.erica-janebattisson.com

Martin

Orbis Terrarum Contra Me et Te

***

Molly-Mae Emma & Jaime-Rose Erica

A d'doo, always

xxx

No legacy is so rich as honesty.

— WILLIAM SHAKESPEARE

PROLOGUE

Watching the sea crash gently onto the rocks below, she replayed the entire night's events over again in her mind. Tears streaked down her face as she sobbed uncontrollably. Her face burned with the heat of anger and disbelief. *Why?*

She swayed. Dangerously close to the edge, the white crest of the sea swirling menacingly below. *I could just fall* ... she thought.

1

Porthrosen

There were cardboard boxes everywhere. Each one labelled carefully in black marker pen with its intended destination. The removal men trudged back and forth from the large van outside carrying more boxes, sweating profusely in the searing heat. It was mid-August, and today's weather provided no exception to the almost intolerable heat which had dominated the summer so far. On any other day, the temperature would have been bearable and welcome. It was the perfect heat for the school holidays; for lazing in the garden with a good book or lying by a pool listening to your favourite music. But today was different. This day was hectic.

They had left Leicestershire when the birds had barely woken, having spent the previous few days packing up all that they owned. Merryn's dad had bounced around the house whistling and singing at the top of his voice, something he did on a regular basis in order to raise the household from its slumber.

It had been a long journey down to Cornwall. Merryn had drifted between a deep sleep and a fuzzy daze as the car swept quietly along. First the motorways: then the many smaller dark, and oh so narrow roads with high hedges and few places to pass other vehicles.

She was woken from another snooze by her younger sister's excited announcement that she could see the sea.

"I can, look Mum! There! Oh, it's lovely."

"Ssh darling, you'll wake your sister up," her mum whispered.

"Too late, Mum, I'm awake," mumbled Merryn from behind her blanket. "Where are we?"

"We're right by the sea, Merryn, look!" squealed Tamsyn.

Both girls peered out of the car window as it drove along the coastal road. The sea stretched out to their left, glistening bright blue in the warm sunshine.

"It's so beautiful," her mother said, smiling, as she touched her husband on the arm. "I can't believe we're finally here. We're finally going to live by the sea, after all those years of dreaming about it."

Merryn's mum had wanted to live by the sea since she was young. She had shared with her girls the fond memories of holidaying in Cornwall as a child. Unfortunately, Merryn had remained unconvinced of how moving to the sea would change their lives for the better. She had friends in Leicestershire. Good friends that she was going to miss. In addition, she knew that it would be difficult changing schools and starting her A-levels, but she had achieved good grades in her GCSE's so hopefully she would be ok. She had chosen to study, art, English and maths as she was quite creative, but wanted to keep her university and career options open; having no idea what she wanted to do in later life as yet. But, Merryn's main concern was not that of what subjects she would study or even the stress of finding her way around a new school or village. Her dominating worry was focussed on if she would make friends, and whether she would be able to secure the kind of strong bond she'd had with her old friends.

She stared out of the window at the gentle, lapping coastline and pondered the next few weeks ahead. How difficult was it going to be starting at a new school? How would she ever make friends? Merryn felt uncertain about so many things. Even though deep down she knew that this was a beautiful place to live, she could not convince herself that she was going to be happy here. She just wanted to go home.

MERRYN SAT cross-legged on the wooden floor of the hallway leaning against a box marked Miscellaneous. Picking at the corner of an old sticker on the top of the box, she considered what her friends were doing now. Cara was probably busy being the centre of attention. Olivia would be laughing at everything that Sarah did whilst secretly wishing she could be half as confident. Merryn felt her stomach knot. She already missed home so much. Home. This was her home now. *How long is it going to take before this place feels like home?*

"Come on, sweetheart," her mum knelt down next to her. "You look so sad. Please don't be sad. This is an adventure for all of us. I promise everything's going to be great." She pulled Merryn tightly into her chest and kissed the top of her head. "Why don't you go and start unpacking in your room? See if you can get it looking a bit more like home."

Her mum was petite and slim with blonde hair that brushed her shoulders in gentle curls. She looked younger than her forty years. Merryn was constantly in awe of how her mum seemed to be able to find the positive in everything.

Merryn's new room had a view of the harbour to the front and fields full of sheep across the back. In the distance, huge green hills and a rocky tor rose majestically and proud creating a picturesque backdrop to the small Cornish village. She hated to admit it, but in addition to the amazing view, it was the most beautiful room and deep down she knew that she was very lucky. The cast-iron fireplace gave it a homely feel. Two large windows, framed by white voile, allowed light to penetrate every corner and made the room feel large and spacious, although the scorching sun had heated the room to an uncomfortable temperature. In contrast to this, her wrought iron bed, placed in the centre of the room by her dad, looked skeletal and cold. Merryn's eyes searched the many boxes for the one marked Bedding. She found it underneath another box and opened it. Pulling the pink flowered quilt out, and shaking it vigorously, she created a much-needed breeze. Prompted by this rush of air, she realised that the windows were closed tightly. She opened them both and a much larger, generous breeze filled the room, cooling her face and lifting her long, brown hair slightly. She made the bed and arranged her many pillows at one end, carefully placing her special teddy on the top pillow. Clover had been everywhere with her. She had had him since she was a baby. He was a well-travelled bear, having been her constant companion on many holidays, and had even kept her company at Brownie Guide camp when she was younger. Merryn secretly felt that she was a bit too old for cuddly toys, but she couldn't stand the thought of parting with him or packing him away in a dusty cupboard somewhere or worse still, throwing him away.

As Merryn sat on her newly made bed she stared out of the window and her mind wandered to the boats bobbing and dipping gently in the harbour. What adventures had they experienced? Where had they sailed to? It was certainly strange looking at the boats on the water rather than seeing a tree-lined road and more houses, which was what she was used to. A small fishing boat glided smoothly across the water, skimming the harbour wall gently as it came to a stop. It looked old and slightly dilapidated. Merryn wondered how many trips the boat had taken in its lifetime and what stories the fishermen could tell of their travels and work. By contrast, a much larger, more glamorous vessel seemed in a hurry to get out to sea with a roar of engines and a swirl of waves. Merryn decided that whoever was aboard was definitely not going to work. They had much more fun in mind!

Suddenly, she felt an unusual sensation run down her body. Then another, accompanied by a shudder down her spine followed by an overwhelming feeling that someone or something was standing at the side of her bed. She shifted sharply and darted her head to the left to where she believed the presence to be. Nothing. She remained motionless for a few moments, staring; eyes unblinking. Still nothing. Taking a big breath, she shrugged it off and decided that she was tired and hot and had let her imagination run away with her. It was a new and unfamiliar house she told herself. Even so, she still felt the need to clamber off the bed and check below it; her eyes scouring the cream carpet. What she was fearful of finding she did not know, but it offered her some comfort and eased her mind to check that all was as it should be.

However, despite not seeing anything odd or unusual in her room, as she began to unpack a cardboard box full of books, Merryn still had the feeling that someone or something was watching her…

*S*ea water was lapping and splashing at the side of the tiny boat. She could feel it gently moving between her fingers as she trailed her hand in the water below. Cold and wet, sending shivers along her arm and right through her body. It was dark, so very dark. She squinted her eyes. Closed them tightly and re-opened them. No, still nothing. Wait! There! Something was moving. She couldn't see clearly, but there was definitely something there. Somewhere ahead. Then it began ... a shuffling, scraping sound that seemed to be moving closer. Like metal grinding against rock. An unpleasant, unbearable sound. Not loud, but painful in an indescribable way. She wanted it to stop. Tightening her whole body, she bowed her head and willed the terrible sound to cease; scrunching her eyes together and hunching her shoulders. Then the scraping stopped, but the shuffling continued; moving away now into the distance.

New Beginnings

Merryn stood and surveyed the corridor which was buzzing with activity as students made their way to various places. She breathed an internal sigh of relief; it felt like a huge achievement to have made it to break time relatively unscathed, apart from the minor problem of arriving at the wrong room for English. Her timetable said clearly Mr Scriven in room 106, but he had had no knowledge of her addition to his lesson, much to the amusement of the rest of the class. Having eventually found the correct room and teacher, with the assistance of a slightly over-bubbly helper, she had been seated next to Chloe, a friendly-looking girl from her tutor group who offered to 'look after' her until she had found her feet.

Chloe was still in the classroom talking to the teacher. Merryn stood in the corridor watching a group of younger boys messing around leaping on each other's backs. They seemed to think this was great fun until a very stern looking male teacher emerged from a nearby classroom, spilling a cup of tea all over the floor as he angrily opened the door with exasperated annoyance. After what appeared to be a huge lecture about behaving appropriately in corridors, the boys were dismissed and they disappeared quickly out of sight. Merryn smiled to herself. She found it reassuring that the scene could have taken place in any school across the country, and felt a tiny glimmer of hope that maybe it wouldn't take as long as she'd thought to feel like she belonged here.

Chloe appeared a few minutes later. "Sorry about that. Thanks for waiting. Are you ok?" She looked at Merryn quizzically.

Merryn nodded and smiled.

"You look stressed. It must be difficult for you to adjust. I mean starting at a new school must be so hard. I can't imagine how you must be feeling, but don't worry, I'll look after you! Come on, let's go and get something to eat from the canteen, I'm starving!" Chloe said, whilst tugging playfully on Merryn's arm. "You sure you're alright?"

"Oh, yes, it's just a lot to take in, like you said. I'm good though, thanks. It's going to take a bit of getting used to, you know, being in a new school, that's all. I was finding it hard to concentrate in English class because I was thinking about all the things that I need to find out, and where certain places are, rather than listening to the lesson. I didn't have a clue what the teacher was talking about by the end!"

"Hey, I shouldn't worry too much about that. Most of us have no idea what old Talbot is going on about ninety per cent of the time. He does like to tell his stories of when he was younger to try to make his lessons more interesting, but you'll often find that they have no relevance to anything we are studying in English, well not that I can work out anyway." Chloe pulled a face and smiled. "Come on, let's go and get something to eat before the queue is horrendously long!" They headed for the canteen, Chloe's arm linked in Merryn's.

* * *

Wow, it was loud in the canteen! Students sat at tables or leant against walls chatting and eating. Teachers patrolled the room, evicting anyone who was not sitting at a table correctly and directing students to use the bins scattered around the large room. Merryn queued and bought an apple and some juice from the counter. She sat with Chloe and was introduced to some of her friends; Amelie, a dark-haired girl with olive skin tone, and Erin who was petite and had mousey coloured hair and a pale complexion. They seemed nice and welcomed her into their group. They talked about what had happened at somewhere called Kitto's Cave on Friday night, and were discussing who fancied who; debating whether Carter Sherwood was the hottest male alive or whether Xance Cador was hotter. Merryn discovered that Kitto's Cave was the place where everyone hung out at the weekends, and sometimes straight after school on week nights. A cafe especially designed for the young, it played the latest music videos on huge screens, and had large, comfy sofas and armchairs and cool lighting. Apparently, it was *the* place to be. Merryn was reliably informed that they would all be going again this Friday and that included her.

After several minutes, a tall, slender girl with mousey hair, tied half up, half down, approached their table with three, smaller girls close behind. She stared at Merryn as she walked towards her and made her feel uncomfortable. Merryn had an idea that that was what this intruder had intended.

"Ooh! Have we got a newbie? Wonder where she's from," the girl sang in a shrill voice. She flounced past tossing her hair sideways, shooting a disapproving look in Merryn's direction.

"Take no notice of her, Merryn," Chloe reassured, "That's Emily Harper. She thinks she is the most popular girl in school and acts like she owns the place. The reality of it is that she can be an absolute bitch, and therefore most people dislike her. She's probably jealous because you're sitting with us and you haven't shown her any attention yet."

"Oh," Merryn said quietly.

That was all that she needed – for the most popular girl in school to take an instant disliking to her. She thought about it for a moment and decided that the best course of action would be to keep her head down and remain unobtrusive for at least her first half term. Merryn had been so worried about moving down to Cornwall and having to attend a new school, and knew that she didn't want to make the experience even more difficult by making an enemy of Emily and her friends. Merryn desperately wanted to make some good friends like she'd had before. At least that way she would have a chance of being happy. She wondered again what her friends back in Leicestershire were doing now. She wondered if they missed her at all. She promised herself that she would message them tonight to catch up. Her stomach lurched slightly, and she realised just how sad and lonely she felt. She seemed to have momentarily entered a bubble-like trance. The room was moving around her, but she was no longer part of it. Movement was blurred. Sound, which was once a din, was muffled and distant.

"Merryn," a voice was breaking through the fog, "Are you alright?"

Merryn blinked heavily and suddenly the noise returned in a rush of clanking cans and conversations that were shouted not spoken.

"Hey, Merryn!" Chloe yelled this time. "Are you ok?"

"Oh, yes, thanks," Merryn mustered a smile as she realised that she was back in the room with Chloe shouting in her left ear and tapping her arm.

"I told you. Don't be bothered by Emily. She's an absolute cow. I mean, she can be nice – it has been known – but she just likes to be centre of attention all the time. She won't like it that there's someone new here. She'll be worried that you may take away some of her limelight! She's only really unkind if she feels her superior status is threatened. Just keep away from her and you'll be fine."

"Right, thanks." Merryn smiled a false, but reassuring smile to Chloe.

That afternoon, Merryn had double art. She found her way to the impressive Art Suite which had huge white tables and large windows. It was light and airy in there – a pleasant contrast to some of the dingy, dark classrooms she had experienced earlier that day. The walls were filled with all different kinds of paintings on boards, paper and canvasses. In the corner, a Mod Roc sculpture sat unfinished on a bench. The teacher was Miss Starney. She floated across the room towards Merryn, in a large bright, multicoloured kaftan-style outfit that disguised a slightly plump body. Her deep plum-coloured hair was vibrant, wild and curly.

"You must be Merryn," she greeted with a smile and a welcoming arm gesture. "I was expecting you. Welcome to art. Come and sit here next to Polly." She pointed to an empty seat across from a small, friendly-looking girl with big eyes.

"Thanks, miss," Merryn said.

She sat down and tried to make herself comfortable. Glancing around the room, she noticed that many of the students had already started work, either sitting painting quietly or milling around the room collecting palettes of paint and water pots. The teacher returned with some card and various geometric shapes. She explained that Merryn was to create an abstract picture using the shapes, showing her various examples from the work of past students as inspiration. Then off she went, floating across the room, observing others in the class, and pointing out where small improvements could be made in their work.

It was at this point that Merryn noticed a boy staring directly at her. He was sitting on the other side of the room facing towards the table where Merryn sat. She looked at him briefly, then looked back at her work. After a few seconds had passed, she raised her eyes to look at the boy again. He was still staring. She stared back. He was absolutely beautiful, with large crystal blue eyes and blond hair that swept across his forehead and partly covered one eye. She noticed that he had a strong athletic build with muscular arms, and although he was sitting, she could tell that he was tall. Merryn continued with her drawing, overlapping the shapes and creating a pattern though she wasn't fully concentrating on the task. Convinced that enough time had elapsed and that it was safe to look up again, she gazed in the boy's direction. He was still staring at her. She focussed on his eyes. It was as if they were staring right into her. Deep pools of mesmerising blue, pulling her in closer and closer. A tingle went down her spine and through to the tips of her toes. She now felt that it was impossible to look away. Drawn by something unknown; captivating and controlling.

"How are you getting on, Merryn?"

Merryn jumped. Mrs Starney was standing at her side.

"Oh, good, thanks, miss," Merryn replied, slightly embarrassed.

Searching through the crowds of school children as they enthusiastically made their way out of school, Merryn scanned for Chloe, who had been in PE all afternoon. She had no idea where the sports hall was, and so was completely at a loss about which direction Chloe would appear from.

She leant back against the large silver birch tree which was providing her with shade from the blistering sunshine. She looked across to the steps leading down from the main entrance hall just as a boy was opening the large glass door. It was him – the boy from her art class! He walked casually down the steps, swinging his rucksack over one shoulder as he did so. He glanced toward the tree. He stopped abruptly; as if suddenly hitting a huge wall. His gaze fell briefly to the floor and then to his own feet before lifting back up and across to where Merryn stood. She shifted her weight slightly, still leaning on the tree. He continued to stare. Merryn felt increasingly conscious of his lengthy observation. Now it was her turn to look away. She pretended to watch a group of students walk away, noisily, down the path to her right. After a few moments, she dared to look back towards the steps. He was still looking. She noticed his thick, blond hair moving in the gentle breeze and watched as he brushed it back- wards away from his eye. She knew that she shouldn't stare back, but she felt almost bewitched by his presence. He was absolutely gorgeous, slim, but with a strong, muscular, powerful build, and for the second time today, she felt spell-bound by him. Again, a tingle shuddered through her body and drifted down towards her toes.

He removed his bag from his shoulder and allowed it to drop to his side. He stepped toward her then stopped, looking down at his bag. He remained motionless for a moment or two then looked around awkwardly. Just at this point, Chloe ran down the steps behind him and made her way across the grass. The boy looked over at Merryn and displayed what she thought was a gentle smile. He then walked away – backwards, initially, then turned and departed across the grass, swinging his bag at his side.

"I'm sorry I made you wait," beamed Chloe as she neared the tree. "I hate having PE last thing. They always make you get changed after the bell has gone."

Merryn wasn't really focussing on her new friend. Instead, she was glancing over Chloe's shoulder, desperately trying to see whether the boy had looked back over his shoulder. It seemed not.

"Merryn?" Chloe tugged at her arm.

"Oh! Sorry. I was in a world of my own," Merryn tried to look apologetic. "It's been quite a day."

"I know – it's ok. Right, as promised, let me make sure you get on the right bus. We don't want you ending up back in Leicestershire, do we?" Chloe joked.

"Erm … no. Best not. I think my dad would be slightly annoyed having to drive and fetch me!"

As the girls walked arm in arm towards the main road, Merryn smiled to herself. As much as she still desperately missed her old friends and the comfort of knowing where everything was, she had a nervous, fluttering feeling in her stomach. A feeling of excitableness. Had *he* made her feel this?

Stepping off the bus, Merryn reviewed the day's events in her head. It had not been a bad first day over all. She had made some friends, which was good, as her main concern had been that she would never meet anyone to hang out with. Of course, Emily Harper and her bitchy tone had been a low point, but she had not seen her again all day so that was a bonus. Then there was *him*. The boy from art class. The boy who stared into her very being with the most captivating blue eyes. She pondered why this boy with his blond hair and powerful stare had had such an impact on her. As she opened the garden gate, and walked along the path to her front door, she concluded that, no, it wasn't the fact that he was drop-dead gorgeous, it was more than that. Something was fascinating and beguiling about this boy. But what? She had no idea.

4

Crush

As it was a lovely warm afternoon, Merryn decided that she would go for a walk and explore some of the village. She changed into her favourite pair of denim shorts and a vest top, grabbed a quick drink from the fridge, and messaged her mum to let her know she would be back in time for dinner.

Porthrosen was a pretty, quintessentially Cornish, village. The paths and streets wound down from the hillside in between the tiny, cosy cottages and pastel-coloured houses toward the bustling, working harbour below. Roads were tiny, offering room for only one vehicle at most points. Quaint shops of every description stretched around the edge of the harbour. Merryn spotted Kitto's Cave situated on a corner in the centre of the harbour's main shopping area. Some teenagers were outside, drinking from cans of pop, watching a small group of boys show off their skateboarding skills. A variety of boats bobbed and undulated gently in the crystal-clear waters of the bay beyond the harbour wall.

Merryn made her way up a steep pathway that led directly from the harbour. Eventually, the concrete path became a natural lane that climbed up the hill and followed the cliff edge around and away from the harbour. The views were spectacular. Merryn turned around and looked back the way she had come. She could just about see her new home nestling above the other properties, high above the harbour on the opposite side. She scanned the scenery from left to right, trying to take in every aspect of this breathtaking view. Moving ahead again, she could see a large, white, painted house with elegant Georgian windows and a wide front doorway, up on the hillside above the headland to her right. It was a magnificent building. She wondered who lived there and thought that the views from the windows must be pretty stunning. As she continued along the coastal path, she noticed a small rocky tor rising from the ground across to her right. Beside it were three, huge, roughly oval-shaped stones leaning on each other as if they had been arranged that way purposefully by an artist. Merryn made her way towards them, steering herself off the marked path. As she grew closer, she realised that they were even more staggering, both in their size and magnificence. *How on earth did they get here? And why?*

Then a strange feeling overwhelmed her. She had seen these unusual stones before. She stopped and looked at them almost willing them to speak the answer to her question – *Where have I seen these stones before?*

She came to the conclusion that she must have seen a photograph on the internet or in a book, after all she had done a little bit of research on this place before the move. Merryn convinced herself that this was the solution, but despite this, something was niggling away in the back of her mind…telling her that this was not the answer. She sat down on the grass leaning against one of the large rocks, grateful for a rest. It was still warm and she hadn't realised how far she had walked. Staring out to sea, she could see a large boat sailing by, leaving a white rippling foam behind it. Merryn felt comfortable and at ease.

A few minutes had passed when she heard a rustling of grass behind her. Startled, she turned around to see a figure approaching. It was difficult to see the person's face clearly due to the bright sunshine. Her heart began to pound quickly within her chest as she wondered who the stranger approaching her was. As they came closer, she realised who it was. It was him. The boy from art class. He paused and looked out to sea briefly before sitting on the grass, and leaning on the stone opposite. He looked at her with his piercing, deep blue eyes. Merryn looked back into them. A gentle shiver went down her spine. He really was stunningly gorgeous. She surveyed his strong, shapely physique and his chiselled cheekbones. It was as if someone had carved his face; painstakingly and meticulously ensuring that every angle, every curve was in just the right place. Embarrassed, she looked out to sea, grateful that a speed boat had come into view in the distance, giving her an excuse to stare.

"I knew you would come," he said with a gentle smile, his soft voice raspy and alluring.

"Excuse me?" Merryn questioned, slightly shocked that he had actually spoken.

"I knew you would come," the boy repeated gently whilst looking down at his shoes.

"What do you mean?"

He looked deep into her with eyes that were so intense, so blue. "I knew you would come ... here."

"Why?" Merryn replied. "I ... I ... mean how could you know that I would come here when I didn't know myself?"

Ignoring her question, he continued, "I noticed you in class today. What's your name?"

"Merryn, what's yours?"

"Xance."

"Cool name ... do you live in Porthrosen?"

"Yes. My whole life. I was born here. My grandad was a fisherman until he retired, so my dad's family have always lived by the sea."

"Oh. Your dad's not a fisherman then?" Merryn was conscious that she might appear to be prying with this question as it was so early on in the conversation.

"No. He owns a shop down in the harbour. He and my mum run it together. Gifts and other stuff. They love it." He paused. "Where have you moved from?"

"Leicestershire."

"Wow, that's pretty far." He smiled.

Merryn nodded and smiled in return. A slightly awkward silence followed. Merryn looked back out to sea, spotting the speed boat returning back the way it had first travelled. Eventually, Merryn plucked up the courage to look across at Xance, who was also staring out to sea. He too had watched the speed boat return. Sweeping his blond hair away from his eye, he smiled and a slight chuckle left his lips as he glanced across at her, noticing that she was looking at him. His thick hair fell in a subtle wave down the side of his cheek, framing his face. *Even his smile is beautiful.*

"What did you mean, when you said that you knew I would come? Do you have psychic powers or something?"

"Something like that." Xance laughed, looking intensely into her eyes once more. She felt mysteriously drawn to him. Not just to his captivating and powerful eyes, but to his very being, his presence; a bewitching aura that seemed to emanate from him.

"So, how did you find school today? Was it much different to your old place?" he enquired, leaning forwards on the grass towards her.

She noticed his large forearms and tanned skin; a leather bracelet with metal rings was wrapped several times around his wrist, accentuating the muscular sinews of his lower arm. She changed her focus to the ground quickly when she realised that her gaze had lingered just a little too long. Her face felt suddenly too hot in a showy display of her embarrassment.

"School was ok," she said, still looking at the floor. "I mean, it's really tough, you know, going to a whole new place, and I won't lie to you, I was petrified first thing this morning. It was good though. I made some friends – Chloe, Erin and Amelie. They were really nice to me. Unfortunately, there was one girl who seemed to take an instant dislike to me, but I managed to steer clear of her for the rest of the day."

"Oh, right. What was this unpleasant girl's name?" Xance leant even further towards Merryn, shuffling forwards slightly on his stomach, and raising his eyebrows in jovial anticipation.

"Emily, I think."

"Emily Harper?"

"I'm not sure, why?"

"It just sounds like her that's all. Yeah, you're probably best to give her a wide berth. She can be a bit prickly sometimes."

"You know her?"

"Sort of."

They continued to chat for some time. Merryn was amazed at how quickly she felt comfortable in Xance's company. She was able to talk with him about all sorts of topics and she shared her current hobbies, and aspirations for the future. She was shocked with herself for being quite so open with someone that she had only just met, but he seemed so easy to talk to. She felt as if she had known him for ages – for her whole life. She felt intoxicated by his presence, and his eyes seemed to be able to look into her deepest thoughts, whilst never failing to send ripples of tingles down her neck and back.

An hour had passed when Xance suddenly stood up. They had been so engrossed in their talk, and each other, that they hadn't noticed the sinister mist creeping in from the sea. Eerily it had slithered in, engulfing the headland in a blanket of thick, damp grey. The sea was no longer visible. The coastal path, which Merryn had used earlier, was now shrouded in the dense fog, disappearing further as the seconds passed. She looked around her and immediately began to panic.

"What do we do? I can't see the path," she said as she stepped towards Xance.

"It's ok, don't worry," he reassured her, "It happens all the time. I'm just angry with myself for not noticing sooner! Come on, we'd better get going before it gets any worse." He began to walk towards where Merryn knew the coastal path should be. She stood frozen to the spot, seemingly unable to move with fear and dread. Then he was gone.

"Xance!" she screamed.

"It's ok. I'm here," a voice from within the thick, grey fog replied.

"I've lost you! Please ... I can't see you!"

"I'm here." His voice was calm and soothing as he appeared from out of the dense mist, one arm outstretched towards her. "Come on."

He took her hand in his and led her into the murkiness. She felt gentle waves flutter through her body at the touch of his skin on hers. Merryn willingly followed. She could barely see her own feet; stepping clumsily and shuffling out of fear of tripping over something, or worse still, losing her footing and tumbling over the side of the cliff. She tried to think rationally. *Take it steady and it will be ok. Xance knows where he is going; he knows this place.*

She continued behind him breathing heavily and clutching his hand tightly, frightened in case he should let go and she lost him again. They edged silently down the path for several minutes. Suddenly, Merryn's foot bumped something hard. She felt a sting of pain go through her toes as she lurched forwards, letting out a yelp. Xance swung round and caught her, his arms wrapping neatly around her as they both fell to the ground. He landed hard on his side, but still didn't let go of her; his body cushioning her fall. Knowing that she was on the ground, she relaxed slightly and allowed her head to fall forwards, resting it on Xance's chest. His torso was taut and warm. She breathed heavily. Breathed him in. His skin smelled clean and masculine. Ripples down her spine again. He stayed motionless, still clutching her tightly, his arms enveloping her. Relaxing slightly, she could feel the whole of his body pressing against her. She liked the way it felt. It felt good; safe; comfortable.

After several seconds, he released one of his arms and gently stroked her face with his hand, his touch was strong but tender.

"I'm so sorry, are you ok?" he asked.

"Yes, thanks. Don't apologise, it was my fault. I tripped. Are you alright? You landed pretty hard."

"Yeah, I'm fine. I'm tougher than I look," he joked.

Merryn knew that the fall must have hurt Xance, but she didn't want to push him to say it out loud; she felt guilty enough. Xance held her for a few moments longer. She placed her cheek against his chest and could hear his heart beating within. *Why does this feel so right?*

Eventually they stood. Merryn was pleased that the fog was able to shield most of her face from Xance, and hide the fact that she was embarrassed by their impromptu embrace. Xance took her hand again, leading her slowly and cautiously down the coastal path. They reached the harbour where the lights from the various pubs, shops and restaurants glowed dimly through the thinning mist. It was a welcome sight. Despite the fact that visibility had improved greatly, Xance continued to clasp Merryn's hand, but now she walked at his side rather than following behind. Again, she marvelled at how comfortable and easy this felt. She barely knew this boy, but she felt so attached to him, so contented in his company. It wasn't just that he was so beautiful – there was more to it than that. She simply didn't know what.

Merryn's phone beeped indicating an incoming message. She grabbed the phone hurriedly from her pocket and glanced at the screen.

"It's my mum, she's worried," Merryn explained.

She quickly typed an apologetic response and reassured her mum that she would be home shortly. "It's ok, Xance, you don't have to walk me all the way back. You must want to get home yourself. Where do you live?"

"Thorny Lane. It's not far from the harbour. It's alright, though, I want to walk you home. I want to make sure that you get back safely. You've had quite an experience and I feel responsible."

"Really, there's no need. Honestly, you've been so kind and you've really looked after me."

They continued walking. Side by side. No longer holding hands but close. Shoulder to shoulder.

"Where's your house?" Xance enquired as they began the gentle ascent through the winding lanes away from the harbour.

"It's Harbour View Cottage, at the top of Lark's Hill. Do you know it?"

"Yes, of course!" He smiled at her.

They reached the gate to Merryn's home. The mist had cleared mostly, but the light was beginning to fade. Night was drawing in. The harbour lights and surrounding buildings, with their many illuminations dotted randomly and hazily, painted an amazing backdrop, like an impressionist picture by Monet. For the first time this evening, Merryn felt slightly awkward. She shifted her position, resting one hand on the garden gate.

Xance broke the silence. "Well, I waited a long time, but it was worth it." His eyes looked directly into hers, warm and mysterious.

"What do you mean …waited a long time?" Merryn frowned, but did not allow her gaze to stray from the deep pools of spellbinding blue.

"Oh, nothing."

"You say some weird stuff," Merryn said, biting her lip nervously.

"Yeah, I know. You have to pay attention, otherwise you may miss something!" He took two steps backwards, smiled broadly, then turned and walked away down the lane and back towards the harbour. Merryn watched him go. She sighed loudly as she watched him disappear around the corner, pondering the evening's events and replaying some of their conversation in her head. She was embarrassed to conclude that she had, in a very short space of time, and uncharacteristically, developed a massive crush on Xance.

Huddled in a dark corner, she attempted to keep her increasingly loud breathing from giving her away. Cold, hard rock pressed against her back. It was dark, so very dark. She squinted, desperately trying to see something. Anything. A small amount of moonlight illuminated an area of the sea just ahead of her and she could just distinguish the faint outline of a little rowing boat which was knocking loudly against the shoreline.

THERE IT WAS AGAIN ... a scraping, shuffling sound. Like grating metal, its horrendous noise painful to her ears. In the distance, somewhere off to her left, someone was moving. She could make out two voices grunting then more shuffling and scraping followed.

HER OWN BREATHING was growing louder. It seemed that the harder she tried to control it, the louder and faster it became. It *seemed to be taking all of her concentration. As the scratching, grazing noise sounded again, her shoulders hunched higher as she pressed herself further back against the cold, damp rock, endeavouring to make her body as small and inconspicuous as possible. So conscious of her breathing now, that she had begun to count the breaths in and then out in and then out. Suddenly, the scraping sound ceased. The silence was thunderous. She froze. Her eyes staring hard and wide into the darkness. Her chest fully expanded as she held her breath. Not daring to allow another sound or movement to leave her body. At her side, his breaths, gentle and calm, blew warmth onto her right ear. His fingers tracing her forearm down to her wrist. Clasping her hand tightly with his own; strong, protective and caring.*

Problem

Merryn tried desperately to eat her evening meal, but all she actually managed to do was push the food from one side of the plate to the other and back again in a slow rhythmical pattern. Her dad, sitting opposite her, watched as she played with her meal. Her stomach twirled and it felt knotted. Nervous excitement embraced her whole being.

"How was school today Merryn ... did you make any new friends?" he enquired.

"It was good, thanks. I met a few people – they've invited me to go out on Friday night, if that's ok? Just down at the harbour – not until late."

Thankfully her parents agreed that she could go, if she ate some of her dinner...

* * *

SWEEPING the blusher brush across her cheeks in a large circling motion, Merryn was lost in a world of nervousness and anticipation. She stared hard at her reflection in the mirror, pausing the brush as she focussed first on her cheeks then her eyes. She added another layer of dark liner across her top lids, guiding the line to a delicate point just past the corner of her eye. She then added a final coat of mascara before adjusting her hair for the umpteenth time.

Would he be there? Would he speak to her? Would he want to spend any time with her? Merryn's thoughts were racing. She felt slightly nauseous. Since Xance had walked her home last Monday, he had been fairly elusive. It was now Friday, and she had only spotted him twice at school, and had only managed to wave politely down the corridor as he play-fought with his friends, or smile nervously across the canteen as he ate his lunch surrounded by a large group of boys.

Merryn had spent most of her week thinking about nothing but Xance. She had replayed Monday evening in her head countless times and was more than a bit angry with herself for being so taken with this person that she barely knew. Never had she felt like this before. She felt silly, but at the same time believed that it was out of her control.

* * *

33

KITTO'S CAVE was alive with the thudding of music and the chattering of voices. Young couples and friends were relaxing outside at chairs and tables on the cobbled street, drinking cola and eating nachos under a canopy draped with fairy lights. Inside, the place was adorned with a variety of coloured lights interspersed with white fairy lights giving it a cosy, inviting atmosphere. There were kids lounging on sofas or sitting in huge comfy chairs smiling and laughing with each other. Three large flat screens hung on the wall displaying music videos. Towards the back of the cafe, was a long counter featuring a selection of drinks and snacks. There were several adult staff dressed in black trousers and T-shirts embellished with Kitto's Cave in white on the reverse. Merryn was impressed. She had met Chloe, Erin and Amelie outside the cafe and was now following them as they weaved through the many bodies to find a seat in a corner next to some artificial topiary bushes. She sat down on a large squishy red sofa and removed her jacket. Erin and Amelie offered to go and get some drinks.

"So, what do you think?" Chloe smiled at Merryn.

"It's really brilliant! Is it always this busy?" Merryn asked.

"Yeah. Well, Friday night is always the busiest, but it's a popular place to come straight after school too." Chloe's attention was suddenly taken by a tall, dark-haired boy wearing blue jeans and a white T-shirt. He walked past and grinned at her, flashing perfect white teeth. Her gaze followed him as he headed across the room and towards the toilets.

"Oh shit!" she pulled a face at Merryn, raising her

eyebrows and stretching her lips wide, before breaking into a giggle. "He's gorgeous, I can't believe he just smiled at me! Did you see him?"

"Yes. Who is he though?"

"That was Carter Sherwood. He's in our year. *Very* popular – all the girls fancy him. He's totally yummy!"

"Yeah, I can see that," Merryn performed an exaggerated lean forward looking in Carter's direction before laughing.

"Hey! You're going to have to join the back of the queue, and anyway he smiled at me!" Chloe gestured to herself, and grinned widely before adding, "I know, he's a nice guy, he smiles at everyone, but I can dream, can't I?"

"Just for the record, I'm not interested, thanks," Merryn smirked.

Chloe looked at her with a questioning look and smiled.

At that moment, their conversation was interrupted by Erin and Amelie arriving back at the table with the drinks and snacks. Chloe couldn't wait to tell them what had just happened, whilst all the time keeping one eye on the toilet entrance, not wanting to miss Carter's return.

Merryn listened to the girls' conversation, but part of her attention was taken with scanning the cafe for Xance. Her eyes scoured the room in hopeful anticipation that he would be there. Then, suddenly, her view was obscured. A pair of bright red, tight trousers were now blocking it. Merryn followed the trousers up, past a white vest top and settled on a girl's face. It was Emily Harper. *Oh, crap*, she thought to herself. Emily didn't waste any time and was, or so it appeared, looking for trouble.

"Ooh, Hi, Newbie! Are you having fun with your new friends?" she screeched in a sarcastic tone, lifting her chin and looking down her nose towards Merryn, "Don't stay out too late, you don't want to get into trouble with your parents."

Merryn decided that ignoring her completely was the best course of action. She turned sideways to face Chloe and laughed loudly, making every effort to look engrossed in her friend's chatter and unperturbed by Emily's bitchy comments. Emily seemed quite irritated by this, but, fortunately for Merryn, was obviously willing to give up on the awkward situation as she turned and walked away with her two friends in tow, but not before adding one final unkind, overtly sarcastic comment,

"Nice top by the way."

After a few minutes, Merryn glanced across, just to make sure that Emily had really gone. It was then that she saw it. A sight that would crush her and ruin her evening. Emily was standing leaning against the back of a sofa, one leg raised and bent at the knee with her arms strewn leisurely around the waist of a boy. Merryn did a double take to make sure that what she thought she saw was correct. Unfortunately, it was. The boy wrapped in Emily's arms was Xance! Merryn's heart sank. A tight knot pulled uncomfortably in her chest and a sickly lump travelled up from her stomach and into her throat. Feeling as if she couldn't breathe, she excused herself from the table whilst mumbling something about going outside to get some air. Now the room was a bustling blur as she fought her way through the crowd of youths towards the door.

Once outside, she walked across the road and continued a little further until the sound from the cafe bar became distant. One or two buildings that outlined the harbour displayed pretty lights and warming glows from inside. The Run Inn was a hive of quiet activity at the end of the road, and provided a welcoming light that spread out in hazy pools along the cobbles. Merryn walked a little further along and sat down on a cast-iron bench facing the water. She could hear the gentle movement of the waves splashing delicately on the harbour wall below. She stared across the small harbour towards the coastal path. High up on the headland she could see the large white house that she had seen on her walk on Monday, its huge windows shining warm, yellow light into the extreme darkness that surrounded it. A fluttery sensation moved down her spine and through her body. Her body quivered. There was a noise to her right. Startled, she looked up. It was him.

"Xance! You startled me!" Merryn gasped.

He sat down next to her on the bench.

"Sorry. What are you doing out here on your own?" his voice was full of genuine concern.

"I was hot," Merryn lied, scared that he would see through her.

"I was worried when I saw you leave. You seemed like you were having a great time with your friends. I hadn't had chance to speak to you yet," Xance continued.

"I didn't know you were there. Well, until I saw you a few moments ago with Emily. I hadn't realised that you had a girlfriend. I mean ... the other day when we met and talked ... you never said and ..." Merryn's words broke off. She was frightened that she may reveal her true feelings and she felt stupid enough.

"Oh. I see," Xance frowned. He looked as if he didn't know what to say. He slid himself along the bench until his thigh was pressing against hers. He leant into her shoulder with his shoulder and took a deep breath. "She's not my girlfriend. Well, she's a girl, and she is a friend so she is a girl friend, but she's not my *girlfriend.*"

"Oh," Merryn said as she stared straight ahead.

"Why did you think that?" he questioned.

"Think what?"

"That she is my girlfriend?"

Merryn shifted slightly in her seat, feeling uncomfortable at visualising the thought of Emily draped around Xance earlier.

"Just what I saw … it doesn't matter anyway … it's not my business who you go out with." Merryn could feel her face growing warm as she continued to stare straight ahead at the small boats in the harbour. Why was she so bothered? She barely knew Xance. It didn't make sense.

"Well, I don't know what you saw or think you saw, but I can only tell you the truth – she's not my girlfriend. I don't have a girlfriend. The truth is I never wanted a girlfriend … I … I was waiting …" he hesitated then looked directly at her.

Merryn turned her face to look at him. He was so close to her that she could feel his breath against her cheek. She looked into his brilliant blue eyes then quickly lowered her gaze to the bench, embarrassed that he may be able to sense what she was thinking. His eyes were hypnotic. She could feel them looking at her. Her stomach lurched and she was immediately consumed by a nervous sensation throughout her body. She clasped her hands together in her lap in an attempt to compose herself. He was so beautiful but, it was more than that. She felt so drawn to him, even though it didn't make sense after such a short time.

"Emily's not part of any of this. You – us. You and me … we've … erm … got history …" he paused.

"I hardly think one conversation on the coastal path and a walk home constitutes 'history', do you?" Merryn was finding it hard to conceal her confusion.

"I didn't mean that! We …" Xance paused. He looked out across the harbour and drew a deep breath. "I can't explain. I just can't. I know I sound crazy, but I need you to give us a chance. It *will* all make sense, I promise. Please trust me."

Before Merryn had time to respond, she noticed a person moving towards the two of them in the shadows of the buildings. As the figure walked under the glow of a street lamp, Merryn could clearly see that it was Emily. *Brilliant. That's just brilliant!*

"What's going on?" Emily said in a huffy voice.

"Nothing. We were just talking," Xance offered as he stood up to face her.

"Talking? About what?" Emily's voice was louder now.

"I was just checking if she was ok."

"I wasn't feeling very well," Merryn interjected quickly.

"Oh! Poor baby!" Emily said in a bitchy tone whilst squinting her eyes at Merryn. She turned to look at Xance. "I don't see why that's your concern. Come on, you promised you'd walk me home." She grabbed his hand and pulled at his arm.

"Will you be ok getting home?" Xance asked Merryn.

"Yeah." Merryn tried to smile, conscious that it was probably more of a grimace. "I'm walking back with the others, it's fine."

Flashing a look backwards as she led Xance away, Emily shouted at Merryn, "And Newbie, stay away from Xance!"

As the pair moved further away, Merryn could faintly hear Xance chastising Emily. She watched as he pulled his arm away from Emily's grip and quickened his pace to distance himself from her. Merryn sat on the bench for a while. She felt slightly wounded that Xance had left with Emily, but she knew that she had no right to feel this way. She also knew that Emily had obviously taken a real disliking to her growing friendship with Xance, and this was a problem that would not be erased easily.

The dragging and scraping sound had disappeared off into the distance and the darkness. She breathed a loud sigh of relief, realising that she was safe. Her companion squeezed her hand. Neither of them daring to speak just yet, for fear of being caught. They remained huddled against the wall of the cave for several more minutes, leaning into each other and holding hands. When he felt enough time had elapsed, he reached to the floor and felt for the lantern. He lit it and a bright pool of light glowed across their faces. He looked at her and grinned. She looked back. His eyes were deep pools of gorgeous blue.

Confusion

Merryn had no idea why she had gone back to the ancient stone monument up on the headland. It was as if she had been compelled to return there by an unknown force. The rocks held a familiarity that Merryn couldn't make any sense of. She knew that she got a positive feeling from this place though, and she enjoyed being there as it gave her a great view of the surrounding area. She sat leaning on one of the rocks, staring out to sea. A large tanker was making its way across the horizon. While she watched, she thought about the dream she'd had last night. She didn't usually remember her dreams, but they seemed to have become increasingly regular and extremely vivid in the last week. She tried hard to remember the content. It had made her feel strange, the fact that her dream had seemed so real, so familiar. She had woken suddenly several times during the night, and was overwhelmed with a feeling that something was not right in her room. As before, when they had just moved into the house, she had a feeling that something or someone was in her bedroom. She had switched on her bedside lamp, and sat with every part of her body motionless apart from her eyes which darted frantically from one corner of the room to the other. Nothing. Merryn had concluded that the dream was responsible for her anxiousness, and she had eventually managed to return to a more peaceful sleep.

Having sat in the sunshine for about half an hour, Merryn grew hot and shifted around the rock to sit on the grass in the shade created by the largest of the three stones. She picked at the grass to her side and reflected on last night's events. She had woken that morning with a fear of dread in her stomach as she instantly recalled the previous evening. How could she have been so stupid to think that Xance liked her anyway? One of the most gorgeous, if not *the* most gorgeous boy in school! She had only known him for a week, and it was difficult to fathom why he already appeared to mean so much to her. She closed her eyes and replayed *that* moment in Kitto's Cave. She recounted seeing Emily's arms wrapped around Xance, whispering in his ear and then laughing. She pictured him walking away from her at the harbour. Merryn's insides churned. Her stomach knotted. She felt slightly queasy.

HE HAD APPROACHED unnoticed by Merryn, whose eyes were closed as she was deep in thought, only making his presence known as he lay down beside her on the grass. She physically jumped and a small squeal left her mouth.

"Sorry, I didn't mean to scare you," Xance smiled at her bearing a set of clean, white, perfectly placed teeth.

He exuded a strong smell of just-showered cleanliness, creating goose-bumps all over Merryn's body as she breathed him in.

"I had a feeling that you would be here," he added.

"I like it. It's a nice place. I feel relaxed here," Merryn said quietly. She felt uneasy and happy and nervous all at the same time as she looked into Xance's eyes. *Why did he have to be so beautiful?*

"Yes, I've always liked it here too."

There was a long pause. Neither of them spoke. Merryn shifted to lie on her back, moving to place herself into the warm sunshine once more. She stared up at the brilliant blue, cloudless sky. Xance turned onto his side so that he could look at her. Their quietness continued for several minutes.

"I'm sorry about last night. I feel I owe you an explanation." Xance broke the silence.

"No, you don't owe me anything," Merryn responded trying to sound nonchalant.

"Yes, I do. Please don't be upset with me."

"I'm not." Merryn felt slightly childish as she did not allow herself to look at him, but continued staring upwards.

"I really like you, Merryn. I can't quite believe that you're here. I can't believe that we're here, at this spot ...

together. I need things to be ok between us. I need you to understand … I just don't know how to explain – I … I can't explain."

"You barely know me," Merryn knew in her mind that her comment was silly. After all, she felt devastated about Emily's showy display of affection towards Xance last night. Merryn had only just met Xance, yet she knew she had some sort of feelings for him. She was confused about what these feelings were, and why they appeared to be so strong, but, even so, she was sure that they were real.

"You're wrong. I do know you … I …" he faltered, as if scared to say too much. "Look, I want to try to explain. We've been friends since we were small, me and Emily. Our parents are friends. She thinks she has some kind of right to be close to me. She has made it quite obvious to me that she would like our friendship to be more than just a friendship, but it's not what I want. I just don't feel that way about her. She can get very tactile, but it's mostly to warn other girls away from me." Xance let out a chuckle. "I just realised how that sounded, I'm not trying to make out that I'm anyone special or anything. It's just she's really protective over me – I hate it though – it's a massive annoyance."

"Oh," was all that Merryn could think of to say as she continued to focus on the sky.

"Honestly, it's not what I want … to be more than her friend. If I'm honest, it can be really difficult to even like her most of the time. She's a pain in the backside, and she's an absolute bitch when she wants to be. As I said, our parents are friends, and well … I'm not supposed to say, but her dad's really ill at the moment, so my parents have asked for me to keep an eye on her. They know what she can be like, and right now her emotions are all over the place."

Merryn turned to look at Xance, "Basically, what you are telling me is that Emily's not going to let any girl get near to you? She won't 'allow' you to have a girlfriend?"

"Well, it's not really quite like that. What goes on in her head is different to what is actually happening in reality," Xance playfully joked.

They both laughed, then Xance continued, "Besides, I've never been interested in having a relationship before."

Merryn scrunched up her face in disbelief. "You've never had a girlfriend?" she questioned, then felt embarrassed at how rude the query was. "I'm sorry," she quickly blurted out.

"It's ok," Xance reassured her. "But why is that so hard to believe – that I have never had a girlfriend?"

Merryn could feel her face growing hot, she looked up at the sky once more, "Because ... well, you're so ..." she couldn't say the words. She continued to keep her gaze up at the sky though she could feel his eyes staring straight at her.

"I'm so what?" Xance smiled teasingly.

Merryn broke into a smile which quickly turned into a chuckle and then a full laugh. Xance laughed with her, tapping her on the arm playfully. Once the laughter faded, they lay in the heat of the sun in comfortable silence for several minutes before Xance spoke.

"The truth is, I wasn't interested in finding anyone to be with. I knew I had to wait."

"Wait?"

"For you – I knew you would come. I just had to wait."

Merryn's face flushed pink. Surely, she would be crazy to think that Xance was interested in her? He couldn't be. Could he?

"What do you mean ... you knew I would come? You said that to me before – it doesn't make any sense."

"It makes perfect sense to me, and it will to you eventually. You just have to know what I know. Feel what I feel. Find what's hidden within you. It's there. It's always been there – right from the beginning," Xance looked away briefly.

Merryn thought she could sense frustration in his voice.

"I want to say more, but I can't. I can't risk it," he continued. "I always knew that you'd come. I didn't know when though, or even if you would ever know what you needed to know for us to be together – properly. It's hard to put your life on hold for something so certain and yet so uncertain. Only in my heart was I sure that I would have the chance to be with you."

"You're not making much sense, Xance." Merryn looked directly at him.

He looked back with deep pools of gorgeous, familiar blue, right into her. Merryn registered something in the back of her mind. The eyes in her dream. She had been dreaming about *him*! She looked away, back to the sky; scared that she would betray her thoughts. The last thing she needed was for him to know how she really felt. She panicked inwardly.

Xance reached out and stroked her arm. He traced his fingers gently down her skin, and then locked his fingers between her fingers. She liked his touch, and how confident he appeared, but she sensed a slight nervousness in his breathing.

"I know it's confusing," Xance spoke gently, "but I need you to know that I was waiting for you. I knew you would come – hoped you would find me. One day. I hoped it would be soon and then there you were, standing in my art class and I knew it was you. Straight away, I knew it was you! Your eyes looked into me and I knew! I had been watching, waiting, looking for you." He rolled onto his side to face Merryn, caressing her cheek with his hand and pulling her towards him. She quivered at his touch and a warm pulse vibrated through her whole body. He stroked her hair affectionately. Their faces were inches apart and she could feel his breath on her lips.

"I don't understand, Xance," she whispered, frightened that she may say the wrong thing again, but so confused by his explanation. "Why do you keep saying that? – 'You knew I would come.' It doesn't make sense. You couldn't know that." She looked up at him.

"I'm sorry. I've already said too much. I will find a way to help you understand. It's just going to take some time."

He stroked her arm tenderly with the back of his hand, and delicately touched the tips of her fingers with his own fingertips, stroking each one in a rhythmical pattern. His eyes moved from her hands to her face; deep blue and intense, they never failed to make Merryn's body react. He moved her hair away from her face and touched her cheek. Leaning towards her, he rested his forehead against hers briefly. She was now so conscious of her own breathing that it seemed as if her heart could be heard beating outside of her chest in a loud, flamboyant show of intense nervousness. He spoke quietly.

"I need you to trust me. I know that's going to be tough – especially after what happened last night. You will see, we belong together." For a brief moment, he leant in towards her face slightly again, his mouth so close to hers that she thought she would burst with anticipation. Merryn felt a pulsating through her body. She breathed deeply. He smelled good. Stroking her cheek tenderly, he looked deep into her eyes.

"Soon. I will help you understand," he whispered softly.

9

There was a loud splash as the body plunged into the sea. Its limbs thrashing violently in frenzied panic. She could feel the water, cold and wet, soaking into her dress and making her tremble. Sliding to her knees, she leant forwards over the edge toward the dark, cold water and the flailing body below her. She clawed and grabbed in the pitch black, trying to seize an arm or leg or even a piece of clothing. Her knees scraped roughly on the rock, sending a searing pain through her legs, and unbeknown to her, tearing her skin. If she could just reach ... just touch. She lay down now on her stomach, wincing as her bloody knees hit the damp stone again. Both arms outstretched, the water whooshing over her entire body. Then she had hold of a sleeve! Just for a split second, it was there in her hand, but all too soon snatched away again by the frantic lashing and beating of the desperate victim in the water.

THEN IT WAS quiet for just a few seconds. She stared into the darkness ahead then below. She swung her arm from side to side *and grabbed futilely at the water. Suddenly, a surge of water as a limb made one last effort. A further wave of freezing water hit her full in the face, and then there was silence ...*

10

Koyt

Merryn woke suddenly. Sweat beaded on her face; her body was damp and sticky. The dreams were becoming more frequent and growing in intensity. They felt incredibly real, and even though she was now awake, she still felt oddly uncomfortable. Her room felt cold and unwelcoming.

She lay almost motionless except for her eyes which squinted and scanned through the darkness. She was unnerved by the eerie chill that she was sensing now, because when going to sleep earlier in the evening, the room had been a little too warm for her and therefore she had placed one of the windows slightly open on its catch and switched on her desk fan for a while. It didn't seem feasible that the room could now feel so icy-cold. Something seemed to creak quietly in the corner, and Merryn held her breath and tried not to move; listening carefully for the next sound.

Nothing.

After several moments, she plucked up the courage to slide herself up the bed, and sit upright. Her eyes continued to survey the room. She switched on her bedside lamp and let out a loud breath of relief as the room – now warmly illuminated – appeared normal. At that moment, the voile curtains swung up high toward the ceiling in what seemed to be a sudden burst of air. Merryn leapt from her bed and ran to the window, grabbing the material and securing it with her hand. She checked the latch on the window, thinking that it must have slipped open to allow the wind to force the curtain into the room. However, she found the latch to be just as she had left it earlier in the evening. The inched-sized opening was not large enough to have enabled such a huge burst of air through. Merryn stood paralysed to the spot. Not able to reason how this could have happened.

Eventually, she slowly made her way back to her bed. She lay down and closed her eyes, pulling the quilt up high to her neck. After only moments had passed, she opened her eyes and checked her room again. *Just go back to sleep,* she told herself. This was easier said than done.

Each time that Merryn closed her eyes she immediately felt cold and uncomfortable. In addition, an image of the ancient stones up on the headland appeared vividly in her mind. She began to think about this monument. Why did it seem so familiar to her? Had she seen it before? If so, where? There it was again, clear as if she were standing right in front of it on a sunny day, every time she closed her eyes. She knew that she had felt mysteriously drawn to this place, having arrived there again yesterday without really knowing how or why.

After trying to go back to sleep again for what seemed like several hours, Merryn gave up. She conceded that she was not going to get any more sleep that night, and therefore she clambered out of bed and moved to sit down at her desk. She opened the lid of her laptop and pushed the button to switch it on then typed *ancient stones in Porthrosen* into the internet search box. A wealth of information appeared on the screen, detailing how the stones were an ancient Neolithic monument. The megalithic stones were thought to have been constructed into their unusual shape around 2400BC. Merryn continued to read, and found that there were many of these Quoit structures in Cornwall, and that the locals called their monument Porthrosen Koyt. There was nothing that seemed to indicate why she felt drawn or connected to these stones. She sighed loudly, and had just decided to admit defeat and stop searching, when her eyes rested on the name of an intriguing website. Why hadn't she noticed it earlier?

The website appeared unofficial; written by a handful of local enthusiasts, who merely based their fantastical theories on conjecture, hearsay and whispers, dating back hundreds of years. They claimed knowledge of many mysteries and unexplained happenings surrounding the history of Porthrosen Koyt and Porthrosen Village. Shifting on her chair and leaning forwards, as Merryn read on, her eyes grew wider and there was a nervous quiver within her chest. There were various tales of disappearances, of ghosts and spirits; of tombs and rituals and various mysterious stories based nearby or around the ancient stones. She learned about a local reverend who seemed to be at the centre of many of the tales, and who had allegedly spread rumours of supernatural occurrences and demonic entities, including a notion that the primitive stones had magical powers or paranormal properties.

There were several theories regarding the clergyman's stories; one alleged that he was merely using his fabrications to strike fear into his parishioners, and another theory purported to allude to a cover-up, suggesting that the supernatural stories he had fabricated were to camouflage the smuggling of contraband. The stories told of small boats moving to and from the tiny cove, near to the church, during the night under the cover of darkness. These mystical vessels would enter the tiny bay in the dead of night. Often, small lights could be seen blinking eerily and inexplicably high up on the headland and from the large white house up on the tor. The myths continued to suggest that, frequently, ships and large boats would be found wrecked and broken up by the rocks, just off the coast of Porthrosen, with no sensible explanation. There was an additional note regarding the white house, which stated that many of the current locals of Porthrosen believe the building to be haunted by a violent and malevolent spirit, and for this reason it remained empty and abandoned.

Merryn closed the lid of her laptop. There certainly seemed to be an abundance of mysterious and interesting stories related to the Koyt and the village of Porthrosen.

However, even with everything that she had read, she was still no wiser as to how she felt a link or such familiarity to the stone monument. She decided that she needed to find the answers. Tomorrow she would return there once more.

* * *

MERRYN GOT UP EARLY and dressed before the rest of the house had woken. She had been awake for most of the night. Having completed several hours of reading and research, she had attempted to get some rest, but the contentment of a deep sleep evaded her. Instead, she tossed and turned agitatedly; the quilt offering her a perpetual cycle of warmth or overwhelming heat which was then followed by an unsettling coldness after she threw the cover off.

She felt exhausted as she began to climb the winding route along the cliff path, but she was driven by her desire to find answers about why she was experiencing the weird visions of the Koyt. She needed to know what it was about that place that felt so familiar, and why her thoughts seemed to be so strangely obsessed by it. In the distance, the giant Koyt gradually came into view, rising majestically from the horizon; the sun creating a gentle sparkle on its granite surface. Merryn continued walking and eventually found herself in front of the Koyt. She stood still for a moment, taking in its intriguing shape and imposing size. As she stared, she thought she saw a tiny, coloured light gently emanating from the centre of the stones. She blinked. On opening her eyes, she saw that the light had gone. She closed her eyes once more, but as she did so, a vision came to her. She was standing in front of the stone monolith, and a subtle purple glow radiated from the core of the shape. She stepped forward and entered the purple iridescent glow, disappearing within its light.

Merryn opened her eyes once more. The stones stood grey and natural before her; no sign of any purple light. What on earth had she just seen? She moved towards the monument, and reached out. She traced the stones with her hands, feeling the hardness against her skin. Just then, something triggered in her mind. She *had* been here before. She *knew* these stones. The pictures in her mind were not visions, but memories! But how could this be true? It didn't make sense.

Merryn felt weak. Her limbs began to shake. Dizziness filled her head. Her mind was racing now, searching for clues, pictures, anything that would assist her in understanding what on earth was going on. How could she have been here before? She sat down on the grass, and leant backward against the Koyt, closing her eyes and taking deep breaths to try to alleviate the woozy, nauseating feeling that had overtaken her body. As she closed her eyes, she was transported to somewhere else in her mind. An image of someone's right hand. The hand bore a ring with a huge, oval, lapis lazuli stone at its centre, glistening in the light from the sun. The hand held something in its grip. The object was curved, engraved, and oblong-shaped, and appeared to be made from stone or a dark metal. The hand rotated slowly, and as it did so, a green gleam of light blazed spectacularly from the item held within. In a millisecond, the light had expanded into a large arch-shaped weapon; its beam an effervescent mixture of greens and blues. The underside of the wrist was now visible, and what looked like a tattoo of three small, delicate black dots in the shape of a triangle could be seen. Then the image disappeared – fading away slowly.

Merryn opened her eyes and blinked several times; confusion racing through her mind. The vision seemed so real. Again, she felt as if this knowledge was familiar to her, but she had no idea why this would be the case.

How could an image of what appeared to be a fantastical weapon be anything that she would remember? Whose hand was wielding this weapon? Whose finger wore the beautiful blue ring? Why was she seeing these pictures so vividly, or at all? Perhaps they were just elements of her imagination, fuelled by her lack of sleep and night-time reading of strange, mystical stories.

She sat motionless for a while, staring straight forwards and out towards the sea, but her eyes saw nothing. She could not register anything, as her mind was preoccupied with remembering the pictures of the hand and the blade and the tattoo. Over and over they played, like a film on a loop.

MERRYN MADE her way back down the cliff path towards the village. She was shaken from her experience, and it took her some time to navigate the rough path down the slope. She felt as if she was in a dream. Nothing in her peripheral vision was being acknowledged; boats traversed the sea, birds circled and swooped overhead, and her feet trampled through the tangled grass and foliage. Merryn was not aware of any of it. She walked in a trance-like state. Shocked, dazed and disorientated.

As she neared the harbour, the hubbub of activity and sound seemed to clear her mind and make her more aware of her surroundings once more. Scanning the busy scene before her, she caught sight of Xance with another person, sitting on the harbour wall. She couldn't see who it was, as the person was sitting to the other side of Xance, and they appeared to be smaller than him. Merryn stood and watched for a moment. Xance turned slightly to his side and placed his arms around the mystery person, hugging them close in to his body. Merryn's heart seemed to jump into her mouth. Her stomach twisted and lurched, and she raised her hand and covered her mouth to stop her gasps from escaping.

She began to walk nervously towards Xance, desperate to see who he was with. However, she was not prepared for what she saw next. As Xance released his arms and leant backwards, Merryn could see that the hidden figure was now clearly in view. It was Emily!

Liar, she thought. *Total liar. He told me that there was nothing between them. How could I have been so stupid?* In a mild panic, Merryn turned and half-walked, half-ran away from the harbour, taking the road that circled the long way around the harbour shops to avoid the risk of Xance seeing her.

Once at home, in the solitude of her bedroom, she sat on her bed grasping Clover tightly to her chest. Fire burned in her face – her cheeks reddening as her eyes filled with tears. Merryn sobbed. Her chest heaved and her shoulders shuddered as she cried; her tears dropping onto the bear that she clung to for comfort. *Why am I so upset?* She questioned herself. *I barely know this boy. Even if he did lie to me, why does it bother me so much?*

Merryn moved from her bed to get a tissue from the box on her desk. As she reached out to grab it, she noticed she had something on her right wrist. She wiped her eyes with the tissue before taking another one from the box and wiping her wrist with it. The marks didn't budge. She scrubbed a little harder, as she made her way back to sit back down on her bed, feeling perplexed.

She stopped the scrubbing action abruptly and froze, fixated on her wrist; eyes not moving. Her mouth fell open in shocked revelation, as she realised that the thing she had been attempting to remove from her skin was ink – tattoo ink; three small dots that formed a neat triangle. Her hands covered her mouth and she breathed heavily, closing her eyes in disbelief.

After a few moments of not daring to look, Merryn gathered enough courage to look at her wrist once more. The dots were still there. She stroked her fingers over the tiny triangle, and traced the shape several times. It was then that she had the epiphany. The vision she had had at the Koyt. The hand holding the brilliant, green-blue sword; the tattooed wrist. It was hers …

11

Guilt

It had been a fairly quiet week at school. Merryn had been preoccupied with worrying about her visions and obscure dreams, which were becoming more frequent and increasingly confusing. Plus, there was the strange phenomenon of the mysterious tattoo. The mark on her wrist was covered with a small plaster; she didn't want to risk anyone seeing it, and she definitely didn't want to have to answer questions about why she had got a tattoo – especially from her parents!

She had seen Xance a few times from afar, but he had been fairly elusive. He had waved at her at the end of morning break once, having spent the whole of the time preceding this talking with his group of friends. She had watched them from across the grass, their heads close together, deep in conversation. Like a witches' coven; plotting and scheming.

She had witnessed him leaving the building at the end of a school day – he looked like he was in a hurry to get somewhere, and he didn't seem to notice her. Merryn was convinced that he was avoiding her. And why wouldn't he? He was clearly a lot closer to Emily than he had led Merryn to believe, and he was probably running out of excuses and lies.

Friday lunchtime seemed to arrive more quickly than Merryn thought it would. As she was feeling so awful, she had felt sure that the week would drag, but she had kept herself as busy as possible with her friends and school work. She had been so stressed and upset on Monday that she had resigned herself to having a bad week. A week that dragged along and seemed never-ending. The kind of week where you just wished you could stay in bed with your head under the covers, avoiding all possible problems, and pretending life would be better next Monday.

She was in the school library searching for a new novel in an attempt to take her mind off things. She pulled books off the large, wooden shelf one at a time, scanned the covers and blurb then replaced each one systematically in its original place. She had no idea what sort of book she was looking for, and this made the task much more difficult. So far, she had managed to narrow down her selection to four novels, which she was attempting to hold precariously with one arm. As she reached up with her free arm, stretching to grab her last pick which was inconveniently situated on the top shelf, she dropped her collection of books, and they fell clattering to the floor.

"Crap!" she mumbled under her breath as she bent down to retrieve them.

One of the books had landed partly under the shelf unit, and Merryn had to almost lie flat on her stomach to reach it. Once she had stood up, she realised that the other three books had been recovered by a tall, good-looking, athletically-built boy with brown hair, who held them out towards her. She felt awkward, and tried to straighten her, now, messy hair with her free hand. Smiling, he waited patiently for her to take the books. As she did so, their hands touched accidentally causing Merryn to feel even more flustered than she already was.

"Thank you," Merryn said with a slightly self-conscious smile.

"It's a good choice," the boy gestured towards the book on top of the pile Merryn was holding. Chase Grant – he's a great author. This is the first in the series.

"You've read this?" Merryn asked.

"Yeah," he replied.

"Oh, ok."

"What? You don't believe me?" he laughed.

Merryn felt even more embarrassed now. She could feel her cheeks beginning to turn pink. "Oh, no! I … I mean, yes. Of course, I believe you."

"Hmm … but?" he continued to tease her.

"But nothing. It's just that you don't look like the type to read … well not novels anyway."

She looked up at him and their eyes met for just a second. She realised how rude the comment must have sounded and she pulled an apologetic face. There was a slight pause before they both burst into fits of giggles.

The librarian hissed "*Shh!*" from behind her desk, as they hid around the back of the bookshelf.

"You're new here, aren't you?" he enquired.

"Yes."

"I thought I hadn't noticed you before. I'm Tyler."

"Merryn." She smiled.

"You going to the cave tonight?"

Merryn scrunched her eyebrows. "Sorry?"

"The Cave – Kitto's Cave – will you be there tonight? Everyone goes on a Friday," Tyler clarified his question.

"Oh, I see what you mean! Yeah, I'm going with my friends," Merryn chuckled.

"Might see you there then."

Tyler began to walk away before adding, "See ya."

"Yeah, bye." Merryn smiled, pretending to scour the bookshelf once more.

It was noisy in Kitto's Cave. The place was heaving, with everyone ready to relax now that the weekend was finally here. Merryn sat in an alcove near the front of the cafe with Chloe, Erin and Amelie. They chatted about the past week at school, eagerly spilling juicy bits of gossip of things they had heard. Merryn was trying really hard to unwind and enjoy herself, but she was finding it tricky. Although she was listening to her friends' conversation, and nodding and laughing at all the right moments, her interest was elsewhere. She was searching for Xance in the crowded room. His friends, Luke, Bryn, Harry, Tom and Jason were seated by the bar area. Harry was sitting on the arm of a red leather armchair, whilst Bryn sat in the main seat with his leg dangling across the other arm nonchalantly. The others were sat in grey leather chairs, facing each other. There was no sign of Xance or Carter though.

Merryn excused herself, and made her way through the crowded room towards the ladies' room. She did not actually need to go to the toilet, but was using the trip as an excuse to get a better look at Xance's group of friends; double-checking for Xance's absence. She examined her hair and make-up briefly in the mirror before venturing back out into the lively cafe. As the toilet door swung closed behind her, she saw him. He was standing next to Carter by the bar, holding a can of soft drink. At that moment, he glanced across in her direction and lifted his arm in acknowledgement of her. It wasn't a wave, but more like a gesture that he had seen her. He smiled. She smiled back awkwardly, her heart drumming in her chest. Just then she came face to face with Tyler.

"Hi!" he shouted over the music.

"Hey," Merryn responded.

"How are you getting on with that book? I assume you acted on my recommendation?" he smiled.

"Yeah, I did thanks, but I haven't had chance to read any of it yet." Merryn thought that Tyler was good-looking, and he seemed kind, but she couldn't concentrate fully on their conversation because she was trying to see, without being obvious, whether Xance was watching her or not.

"Do you want to come and join us? We're just sitting over here," he gestured behind him.

"Oh, that's really kind, but I should get back to my friends," Merryn said apologetically. She started to walk away, but he called after her.

"Hey, a group of us are going bowling tomorrow afternoon, if you'd like to come."

Merryn was slightly taken aback – not expecting the question. She hesitated to answer, glancing towards Xance. He was not looking over. He was obviously not interested in what she did.

"Sure, that sounds good, thanks," she smiled.

"Great, we'll meet you by the main bus stop at two, is that ok?"

"Yeah, see you then."

Merryn returned to the table where her friends sat. As she joined them, Chloe grabbed her arm excitedly; a huge grin on her face.

"Guess who bought me this?" Chloe said, holding up a can of drink.

Merryn looked vague, raising her eyebrows and shaking her head, before breaking into a laugh "I don't know, who?"

"Carter!" Chloe squealed a little too loudly.

"Oh, that's brilliant! What did I miss?" Merryn said, trying to sound excited for her friend.

"He only got here a few minutes ago with Xance. They had something to do earlier apparently." Chloe explained still beaming and cuddling the can of fizzy pop as if it were a baby.

"Yeah, but why has he bought you a drink? Is he interested in you?"

Oh, I really, really hope so!" Chloe chuckled, "Seriously though, he just smiled at me as they walked in, then a few minutes later he came back with a drink for me. He didn't actually say anything – he just grinned," she explained.

"That's great," Merryn said.

"Anyway, I saw that you were talking to Tyler Bramley, how do you know him?"

"We met in the library today. He's really nice, and he's just asked me to go bowling with him and some of his friends tomorrow."

"Really? Are you going?"

"I said that I would."

"Fantastic!" Chloe shrieked.

"I was worried about Xance, and what he might say, but I really don't think he's that bothered about me I …" Merryn stopped herself from revealing that she had seen Xance at the harbour with Emily last weekend. She already felt like an idiot for telling Chloe that she liked Xance because she didn't really know him that well. She felt even more foolish now he had made it clear that he wasn't interested in her.

It was getting late, and Merryn's group of friends had decided to call it a night. They gathered jackets and other belongings and made their way outside, Chloe clutching her precious can of drink. At that moment, a hand grabbed Merryn's arm. She turned to see Xance standing there.

"Hi, can we talk?" He smiled at her gently.

"Erm … sorry, Xance – I … I've got to go." Merryn

stuttered awkwardly, looking back towards her friends briefly.

"I need to talk to you though," he persisted.

"I can't, not now, my friends are waiting, I'm really sorry."

Merryn knew that she was being incredibly brave. She desperately wanted to talk to Xance. Just the touch of his hand on her arm had sent gentle waves throughout her body, but she felt betrayed by his lies. She had fallen for him in such an incredibly short space of time, and now she knew that she had to break free from these feelings if she was ever going to move on.

"Tomorrow then?" he almost pleaded.

"I've got plans tomorrow," she said trying not to sound angry. Merryn's mind was racing. *How dare he do this to me? He must think I'm a complete idiot.*

"Ok, no worries. See you soon then."

Merryn turned and walked away to catch up with her friends who had waited outside the chip shop. Chloe handed her a cone of chips as they began to walk up the path away from the harbour. Merryn's stomach churned, but she tried to eat some of the chips that her friend had kindly bought for her. Why did Xance have to spoil the evening? It had been great up to that point. Merryn knew that she was lying to herself now. She knew that deep down inside, she was glad that Xance had wanted to speak to her. She knew it was wrong to feel this way, after what he was doing to her by stringing her along, but she couldn't help it. She was now dreading tomorrow's outing with Tyler. For some inexplicable reason, she was feeling guilty.

The twinkling light hovered just above the sea. Then it was gone. High up on the cliff another light danced and flickered. Twinkle. Flicker. Twinkle. Dance. Twinkle. Flicker. Twinkle. Dance. Then it was gone. A small, warm, yellow glow emanated from one corner of the large, white house, far up on the tor. The building's size dominated the cliff side. It's fortunate position over-seeing the small cove below to its right and the far side of the harbour to its left. As quickly as it had appeared, the golden radiance was gone. In the distance, a bell sounded. One singular dull chime, resonating out to sea. Blackness consumed the headland; shrouding it once more in total darkness. No shadows, no shapes, no patterns. Just black. A tiny light glinted intermittently, just out to sea, off the coast of the hidden cove. Then it was gone ...

Tattoo

Merryn lay on her bed reading her new book. It was early evening, and she had not long returned home from bowling with Tyler and his friends. Although she hadn't been looking forward to going, she had actually enjoyed herself. Tyler's friends were really kind to her. She had chatted for ages with Imogen and Katie, and had laughed almost constantly throughout the afternoon. Tyler had been kind and attentive. He made sure that she had a drink, and never allowed her to be alone – wanting her to feel at ease with his friends. She had performed shockingly badly at bowling – finishing up last in both games. Imogen had announced teasingly that she wanted Merryn to be invited every time they bowled in the future, as it meant that she was no longer the worst player. Merryn had pretended to be offended at the comment, but had to concede that her ability at bowling was severely lacking.

Tyler had walked her home from the bus stop, and had casually told her what a great time he had had, and suggested that they should do something else together soon. Merryn agreed. He had not given her any kind of indication that he was interested in her as anything more than a friend. He had been kind, polite and thoughtful throughout the afternoon, but Merryn wasn't picking up any vibes that he wanted more than friendship from her. Secretly, she was relieved. It wasn't that she didn't fancy Tyler; he was gorgeous. She simply felt that at the moment her brain could not deal with any additional boy-related stress.

MERRYN'S MUM arrived at her bedroom, announcing that there was a "young man" at the front door asking for her.

"Who is it? Is it Tyler?" Merryn asked.

"I don't know, love, I haven't met him before – come on, don't keep him waiting!" her mum replied smiling.

Merryn sat up and made her way to the mirror so that she could quickly straighten her hair. She flattened the top, and ran her hands through the ends, before hurrying along the landing. As she began to descend the stairs, she could see that her visitor was not Tyler but Xance. He was stood in the hallway dressed in black. He was always dressed in black. Black jeans that fit snugly, but not tightly, and a plain black T-shirt. Black sports trainers on his feet completed the look. Merryn's chest felt fluttery as she stood before him.

"Hi," he smiled.

"Hi," Merryn replied in a hushed voice. Knowing that her mum was more than likely listening from the other side of the kitchen door.

"Sorry to just turn up, but I tried texting you a few times earlier and you hadn't replied. I wanted to talk to you."

"Oh? I haven't seen any texts. Sorry, I've been busy."

"It's ok. Listen, do you want to come for a walk?" Merryn felt that Xance was trying to use a convincing tone, probably because she had not seemed interested in seeing him today when he had asked her last night outside the cafe.

"Sure, just let me get my things," Merryn replied, wondering why he was so keen to see her – surely he wanted to be with Emily?

They left the village along the East Road and made their way into Porthwithiel Woods. Merryn had yet to experience this place, but it was on her list of sights to see because she had heard how beautiful it was. They didn't speak much as they walked, but Merryn briefly shared her story of the bowling trip. Xance had seemed surprised that Tyler had asked her to go, or was he slightly annoyed? Merryn wasn't sure, but she definitely picked up some sort of negative vibe from the tone of Xance's voice. They were just entering the edge of the wood, when Merryn plucked up the courage to question Xance.

"I haven't seen you all week, where have you been?" As soon as she had said the words, she felt immediate regret.

It sounded awful. He didn't have to explain himself to her. She was not his girlfriend. "I'm sorry … I didn't mean it to sound like that. You don't have to explain. It's not my business," she added hurriedly.

"No, it's ok. It's been a crazy week. That's one of the reasons why I came to see you. I wanted to catch up. I've been busy with stuff and I didn't want you to think that I was ignoring you."

"But I saw you a few times at school this week, and you didn't try to come and speak to me," Merryn said tentatively. She was interested to see what he had to say, wondering if he would come clean about Emily.

"I know. I'm really sorry. It's just that I had some stuff to deal with and my friends were helping me. I … I want to be able to explain to you so that you understand, but it's difficult right now. I will though – when the time's right, I promise," Xance explained gently.

Merryn could feel anger bubbling within her. She couldn't believe that Xance would bring her all the way here to continue to lie to her, and to make ridiculous excuses about how busy he had been! It took her all that she had to not scream at him. Instead, she remained composed.

"I know you're lying to me, Xance."

"What?" Xance questioned with a confused look on his face.

"You're lying. Look, you don't owe me anything. It's just, I thought that you liked me – I thought we were friends. At least, you behaved like you wanted to be my friend. Friends don't lie to each other." Merryn stopped still.

She was trying not to cry, trying not to allow him to see just how devastated she was. Xance turned to face her. She looked directly at him. His blue eyes staring deep into her. She felt captivated by them. Like they had some sort of hold over her. She tried to look away but couldn't. A small tear formed in the corner of her eye, and she wiped it away angrily, without breaking her stare.

"Merryn, what the hell are you talking about?" said Xance, looking really perplexed. "Lied to you? About what?"

"I saw you ... with Emily."

"When?"

"Last weekend. At the harbour."

Xance frowned and tilted his head slightly, "I don't understand."

"You were hugging her. You were sat on the harbour wall, and you were hugging her," Merryn's lip quivered slightly and she looked at the floor."

"Oh, no!" Xance took her hand gently, and looked straight into her eyes, "No, she was upset, that's all. I was comforting her. She was worried about her dad. He had been at the hospital for longer than she was expecting, and she'd got herself in a state thinking the worst. There was nothing in it. I promise." Xance squeezed her hand reassuringly.

"You don't have to explain, it's ok. It's not my place to tell you who to be with ..." Merryn broke off her sentence, not really knowing what to say. She desperately wanted to believe him.

"Merryn, I'm not with Emily. I told you. We're friends, that's all. I was just trying to be kind to her, and make her feel better. I thought you knew that I liked you," he smiled tenderly.

"Why would I know that?" Merryn questioned.

"I thought it was obvious!"

"Clearly not," she grinned, feeling a wave of relief wash over her.

"Come, on. I want to show you something."

Merryn felt better that things seemed to be resolved. She hoped that Xance was being honest with her.

Xance held on to her hand, and they continued to walk further into the woods. They had followed the path for a while when he pulled her to the right, off the path and onto the grass – deeper into the woods. They had been walking for a while when Merryn noticed that she could hear running water nearby. They moved through the trees, which were much closer together at this part of the woods, until they emerged into a narrow clearing. The sound of flowing water, that Merryn had noticed moments ago, was made by a stream which now lay before her. It cascaded beautifully down a series of naturally formed stone steps. Its water formed frothy crests of white, like beautiful lace on blue silk, as it tumbled majestically over the rocks on its journey. The dense line of trees across the other side of the water formed a spectacular backdrop for the picture – standing proud, like a line of loyal soldiers guarding this body of sparkling water on its precious pilgrimage. Tiny, wild flowers created a stunning blanket of colour below the outstretched branches. A muddled rainbow; hazy purple dog violets, dark pink and white enchanter's nightshade, bright yellow common gorse, cheerful daisies and delicate blue cornflowers stretched before her, vibrant in the shards of sunlight that peeked through the full foliage above.

Merryn was overwhelmed by the beauty of this place. She had never seen anything quite like it before. Xance had stood silently, allowing her to take it all in. After a few moments of stillness, he took her hand once more and led her towards the bank of the stream where they sat down on the grass.

"I hoped you'd like it." Xance smiled at her.

"It's really beautiful," Merryn said as she glanced around again in disbelief.

Xance laid on his back and stared up at the sky through the leaves, placing his hands behind his head. As he did so, his T-shirt rode up slightly, revealing the very edge of the diagonal crease at the bottom of his torso. Merryn tried really hard not to notice, but Xance's stomach was firm and tanned, and she was unable to look away. She couldn't take her eyes off him, and was grateful that he was looking at the sky rather than at her. It was just then that she noticed what appeared to be a small tattoo just above the contoured muscular line that pointed diagonally underneath the waistband of his jeans. Merryn's mouth fell open. It wasn't shock at the beauty of his body, nor the existence of the tattoo that adorned it. It was a bewildered stupor at the realisation that the tattoo was identical to hers!

14

Realisation

"Xance, your tattoo – have you had it long?" Merryn struggled to ask the question.

This whole situation did not make any sense. She was still reeling from the reality that her own tattoo had mysteriously appeared as if by some sort of unexplained magic. She felt that this was the only probable explanation for the extraordinary occurrence. She didn't even know if she believed in magic but, she did know that it was impossible for a tattoo to simply appear on your skin out of nowhere.

Xance sat up to answer her, "A while, why?"

He looked concerned. The colour seemed to drain from his face. Merryn thought that she could see his hand shaking as it reached to rest where the tattoo lay beneath his T-shirt.

"It's probably better if I show you," Merryn said as she began to slowly and gently peel away the plaster from her wrist, revealing the three delicate inked dots below.

Xance took hold of her hand and pulled it towards him. He traced the tattoo softly with his forefinger, "When ... how did you get this?" he questioned.

"You'll never believe me," Merryn was now trembling herself. She was scared that Xance would think that she was crazy. She could feel beads of sweat forming in the crease at the centre of her back.

"You have to tell me, Merryn," Xance persisted.

"It's insane ... it ... it just appeared one day," Merryn stuttered.

She was conscious that the whole thing was unbelievable, but it sounded even more ridiculous when she vocalised it.

"Do you know what it is? Where it came from? How?" Xance questioned.

"No, I have no idea."

"Where were you when it appeared?" Xance asked.

"I was at home – in my room," Merryn answered, "Where has it come from, and why do you have the same one? Do you know, Xance?"

Merryn looked at Xance, who was staring back at her with his deep blue eyes, but he did not speak.

"How can a tattoo just appear out of nowhere on my skin? What is it? What does it mean? And now I see that you have the same mark on your skin. Is this like magic or witchcraft? I don't understand what is going on. So many strange things keep happening to me since I moved to Porthrosen." She looked at Xance to try to gauge his reaction, "If you know what these marks are and why we both have them, you have to tell me, *please*," Merryn pleaded. "I feel like I'm going mad. There have been so many weird things, and there just doesn't seem to be a feasible explanation for any of them."

"I'm sure that everything has a meaning and that you will understand soon. Explain to me what else has happened that was unusual," Xance said.

Merryn breathed in and closed her eyes briefly as she exhaled and prepared to speak.

"I had been up to the Koyt. I know that you won't believe me, but ever since I first saw it, I have had this feeling that I had seen it before. I can't think where though. I feel like it must have been a long time ago otherwise I would be able to recall it more easily. It is so weird."

His eyes were fixed on hers as he listened intently, "Go on," he encouraged, squeezing her hand gently for encouragement.

"I'd been having nightmares. I know everyone has nightmares, but I don't usually remember mine. They've been happening often, and a lot of them had involved the Koyt. I read that Porthrosen has a mysterious history, and that there are lots of myths and spooky stories based around the village; the Koyt seemed to be at the centre of most of them. So, I went up there to see if I could find some answers. I don't know what I was expecting to find, but it was all driving me mad."

"And?" Xance was now leaning even closer towards her, still clasping her hand.

"I can't tell you. You'll think that I have gone crazy. I mean, we barely know each other, and you're going to want to run a mile if I tell you the rest," Merryn could feel the stress gathering in her temples as her head began to throb.

"I promise you that I won't. Nothing that you say can shock me. I've seen a lot of stuff, believe me. When the time is right – I will tell you. But right now, it's important that *you* tell me. It's important that you say it out loud. Don't worry – it doesn't matter what you say. I'm not going anywhere," he reached out and tenderly moved a stray hair that had fallen partially over Merryn's face, stroking the side of her head as he did so. His touch reassured her.

Merryn tried to compose herself and continued, "When I got to the Koyt, I had some sort of vision. It was like the stones were glowing purple. I saw myself walking into the Koyt. I disappeared in the light," she took a breath, "it was like it was a passageway, or an entrance to somewhere. The weird thing is that it doesn't feel like it was a dream or a vision. It feels like a memory, but I don't know why. Do you believe in déjà vu, Xance? Has it ever happened to you?"

Xance smiled and asked, "What if it is *actually* a memory?"

"What? How could it be?"

"I can't say too much, Merryn. You have to realise for yourself otherwise it could have consequences. For everyone."

"Realise what? You're not making any sense again, Xance."

"I'm sorry. It's just really complicated."

Merryn was becoming agitated. The stress was

consuming her, making her whole being tremble. She began to feel nauseous.

Xance stroked the side of her hair then held her face in his hand. He leant in towards her, so that he was so close that she could feel his breath on her lips, and said almost inaudibly, "They must mean something. They're there for a reason. Think carefully, think about what you know or might know. Look deep into your mind."

He held his position; no more than a centimetre from her face. He nuzzled her nose with his nose. She closed her eyes, desperate for him to move that last final step, and close the space between them. Desperate for him to touch her lips with his.

Xance whispered, "I want to kiss you more than anything, but I can't. I want you to remember. I need you to remember …" his voiced broke off as he gently collapsed in to her and placed his cheek to hers.

At that moment, Merryn felt something click into place. The feeling in her body was indescribable; like minute electric shocks crackling across her skin. She closed her eyes as bright rays of iridescent lights filled her thoughts. A kaleidoscope of colours hurtled through her brain. Then a montage of her dreams, visions, experiences and more: the Koyt, the view out to sea from the headland, the water, the boat, the harbour, deep blue eyes, the triangle of dots, her hand grasping the phosphorescent sword, Xance holding the sword, Xance holding her hand and Xance hugging her. Faster and faster the images flickered through her mind. Over and over again. Then all of a sudden Merryn knew. She remembered. A loud gasp left her lips, and she pushed backwards slightly away from

Xance. She surveyed his face as if she needed to notice every tiny detail. She studied him carefully; her lips apart, a look of disbelief on her face.

"It's you. You're the key to all this!" she exclaimed; an excited relief now visible in her whole being. Her chest rose and fell noticeably as her breaths grew deeper. She ran her hands through her hair, and mouthed something silently. "I was here before! With you! We … we … we were together. It was a long time ago. *Hundreds* of years. I saw us! Not the same as now, our clothes were different, but it was us! I've been here before! On Earth. In Cornwall. In Porthrosen. With you!" Merryn was shaking, and her eyes were transfixed on Xance's face. She was in total disbelief. *How could this be possible?*

"It's ok," Xance reassured her, reaching out his hand to touch her arm. "I know." The relief on his face was unmistakeable.

"You … you know?" Merryn, asked in disbelief, "Are we reincarnated?"

"No … It's not quite the same. We have lived before though. We are Nyss or Sefwarian Nyss. Our souls transcend time – when it is time, we leave one body and migrate to another, but our transmigration attaches our physical features, attributes and personalities to the new body. The new being resembles us and essentially *is us* – just starting over. This way we never die – not fully.

"As a baby? Re-born?" Merryn questioned as she tried to understand.

"Mostly, but it is possible for our souls to attach to an adult. To other Nyss they would appear as they always did. Our souls simply travel to somewhere new and we continue as before, with all of the knowledge of our real world tucked away inside us. Our souls are able to keep the same time-frame as our peers, therefore as you and I lived at the same point in time before, we are now living again, at similar ages, at the same point in time. As people, Nyss are drawn to be near to others of our kind. It is believed that all Nyss will move, migrate or travel to live near to each other. Usually, we will be drawn to people that we have known before, but not always."

"Why didn't you tell me?" Merryn was shocked. Her body trembled, and she began to feel quite sick.

"I wanted to from the first moment I saw you. I knew it was you when you arrived in the art lesson. I have been waiting for you for so long, but I knew you would come eventually," Xance reached out and held Merryn's hand.

"But if you knew, why didn't you say something?" she questioned.

"I couldn't. To reveal someone's hidden gestord, or hidden soul, is against the Sefwarian Nyss lore, which is controlled by magic. If I had told you, then it would have destroyed the Sefwarian Nyss world. It would have caused an apocalypse. Our ecosystems would have broken down. Also, our ability to transmigrate our gestords into new beings would be gone forever. The Magister Worlega, who ruled Nethergeard, put a hex on Nyss and all our people. Many years ago, after a lengthy war between our two worlds, he had made an agreement with the Luminary Synod of Sefwarian Nyss that we must keep our powers and gifts secret in exchange for their warriors withdrawing. This included never divulging knowledge of a hidden gestord to anyone who was unaware of their hidden reality. It was designed to make our lives more difficult, in the hope that our people would eventually never learn of their true identities, and therefore allowing the Nethergeard to have free rein over modern Earth and Sefwarian Nyss. What was never made clear to the Synod of Sefwarian Nyss, was that our part of the agreement came in the form of a spell." Xance clasped Merryn's hand. "Because of this, you had to find me and realise your true identity on your own. You had to pick up the pieces of your former life without any help. I couldn't tell you. I couldn't even kiss you because it would trigger your memories prematurely and activate the hex. Fortunately, your gestord is powerful. It would have been constantly hinting at clues about your past, plus, our bond is strong. The two things combined have made your realisation much quicker. It was only a matter of time before you remembered. Some people take almost a lifetime to find other Nyss; some never do at all."

Merryn stared at Xance in disbelief, "This is a lot to take in," she said, trying desperately to process everything that Xance had just shared with her. "So, you're telling me that there is a whole different world somewhere, and you and I are from *there*?"

"Yes. Well, there are actually several different worlds in existence, our world is just one of them," Xance explained.

"And these dots? What are they?" Merryn pointed to the tattoo on her wrist.

"They are the Nyss rune – it is a symbol for our world. It means 'safe journey'. All Sefwarian Nyss people have them. You won't necessarily know who is one of us though, as some people have their dots in places that are hidden most of the time, so you may not see them!" Xance grinned at Merryn, "Humans can't see them though," he added.

"Well, if we are from this Sefwar …" Merryn broke off as she failed to recall the name accurately.

"Sefwarian Nyss," Xance clarified the words for her.

"Right, so if we're from there … why are we here, on Earth?"

"It's complicated, but put simply, we, the Nyss Cempalli soldiers, are protecting this place from the Nethergeard. They are a ruthless race: with an unending desire to conquer worlds that do not belong to them. They have not made a move as yet, but we know they will, when they believe the time is right."

"Why Porthrosen though? It seems a bit strange – this place being such a quiet backwater," Merryn questioned.

"Porthrosen is the predominant gateway to other worlds. It contains several portals or egresses, the Koyt being one of them," Xance explained.

"I knew it was significant. I felt drawn to it, but I didn't know why. I thought I could remember it!"

"It is really important. It can take you to wherever you want to go. You just have to think of the place. It can take us back to Sefwarian Nyss."

"So, when I had the vision of stepping into it – that *actually* happened to me sometime in my past?"

"Yes – many times! As we are Nyss, we can travel to many different places on Earth and also to a variety of other worlds. There are Nyss living in a multitude of places across the Earth. Most of these places have ties to ancient lands and their people. It's complex, and I'm happy to explain, but I think you have enough to process and come to terms with right now." Xance smiled at her gently, and stroked her hand delicately as if to reassure her.

Merryn nodded in agreement, "This is really unbelievable, Xance. I thought I knew who I was. Who my family are. Where I'm from, but now I'm so confused!"

"You are still *you*. That will never change. Your family are your family for this life. You have had others in the past, and you will have others in the future."

"When I saw you and me together in my vision, it was a long time ago. We weren't dressed like this. When were we last here?"

"To the best of my knowledge, it was around the 1780s."

"That's unbelievable." Merryn's heart raced. "We were together? Boyfriend and girlfriend?" Merryn felt slightly embarrassed asking, but she needed to know. Her vision had shown them holding hands so it seemed natural to assume that she was close to Xance all those years ago.

Xance smiled, "Yes, we were together ... a couple."

"Do we look the same as we did back then?" Merryn continued her questioning, trying to make sense of the situation.

"Yes, well mostly the same. It's a bit odd how our new bodies have the same features as our previous ones, but the gestord carries these elements with it so visually and mentally we are virtually the same in our new lives as we were in our old ones."

"This is incredibly weird," Merryn rested her elbows

on her knees and covered her mouth with her hands whilst she was thinking.

"Look, it's a lot of information. Try not to worry too much. It's a lot to process. There are other things for me to share with you, but all in good time," Xance tried to reassure her again.

Merryn could not speak any more. Her head was a whirl of images and memories. She was systematically replaying them, repeatedly, trying to find some level of understanding.

Xance encouraged her to relax by lying down in the grass. He lay next to her. The sun's heat had weakened, and a stronger breeze had replaced the gentle waft of wind that accompanied the earlier part of their walk. A plethora of grey clouds had amassed overhead. Blocking out the sun's rays, and throwing the bank of the stream into a darkened state although the air remained warm. Xance did not speak to her. He seemed to know that she needed time and quiet in order to absorb and come to terms with her altered reality. Xance rolled from his back to lie on his side. He was now facing Merryn. She was aware that he was looking at her, but she continued to stare up at the ashen sky through the leaves. Gently, he stroked the back of her hand with his. Merryn liked how this felt. His touch made her feel good. She rolled over to face him. His eyes were fixed on her face as he leant up on one arm, as if to get a better look. He caressed the side of her face lightly with his fingertips. Merryn couldn't quite believe how good-looking Xance was. His eyes were the bluest of blue, and his skin was clear and smooth. She liked the way the front of his blonde hair fell slightly across his face sometimes, and how he scooped it away with his hand. She loved his strong, muscular forearms; the shape of some of his veins visible under his tanned skin. She also liked the look of a dark-leather bracelet adorned with tiny metal rings which was wound several times around his wrist. Merryn breathed in deeply. The forest had a wondrous smell of earth and trees and flowers, but her deep breath was to breathe in Xance's scent. He was so close to her and he smelled so good. He had a clean, soapy, but masculine, fragrance that excited her senses and made it difficult for her to concentrate fully on her thoughts. She was desperate to be even closer to him right now. The knowledge that they had some sort of history together was driving her attraction to him. To her, it meant that whatever she was feeling for him was real. She had been worried about developing such strong feelings for Xance in such a short space of time, but now she felt she understood a little better why this had happened. She didn't know how serious their past relationship was, but she knew there was a definite connection between her and Xance: a bond or link that bound their lives together. This was why she was so transfixed by him. This was why she trembled right now.

Just at that moment, Merryn felt a tiny drop of rain land on her cheek. She brushed it away but another replaced it; then another and another. The splashes came quickly now. The heavens had opened, without warning, and rain clattered musically through the foliage of the trees to the forest floor. Merryn squealed and laughed as Xance leapt up and took her hand, pulling her to her feet.

He laughed as he brushed back his damp hair from his face.

"Come on, I know where we can shelter," Xance said as he began to run, still clasping Merryn's hand.

Merryn ran with Xance through the trees, away from the river. The rain hammered down, soaking the two of them. They laughed as they ran. The ground was uneven and covered in tree debris. Merryn stumbled on a fallen branch, and the two of them tumbled to the sodden ground, landing in a heap together. They giggled and shrieked, rolling through the drenched leaves on the forest floor. Quickly, they recovered and ran again. More cautiously this time, but still with purpose, as the rain continued its relentless, torrential thrashing. Xance led Merryn to an old stone-built bridge that crossed a narrow dirt path. The bridge was mostly hidden by the surrounding greenery. Trees and bushes shrouded its presence, making it difficult to see for anyone who didn't already know of its location. As they approached, Merryn had an overwhelming feeling that this place was familiar to her also.

The bridge provided them with shelter from the beating rain. They breathed heavily whilst still laughing. Merryn was soaked through. Her denim shorts now appeared to be a darker blue than their original pale colour, and her white strappy top had become virtually transparent with wetness. Her long, brown hair dripped in gentle curls down her back, and her face glistened with rain. She looked up at Xance who was still holding her hand, facing her as they stood under one side of the bridge with Merryn's back against the wall. The rain was still partially making its way underneath the arch, but they were safe and sheltered where they stood.

"It was lucky that you knew this place was here," Merryn said as she wiped rainwater from her face.

"It's another egress, like the Koyt," replied Xance as he stepped slightly closer to Merryn, looking deep into her eyes and then gently removing some forest debris from her top. His closeness was making Merryn both nervous and excited at the same time. She could feel his breath on her cheeks. Her heart began to pound loudly within her chest. Her eyes moved to his forearms which seemed even more muscular and attractive with the shine of the rain on his tanned skin. Her stomach fluttered as she looked back into Xance's eyes. His face glistened with wetness and his hair hung dripping across part of his face. He brushed it back with both hands whilst never removing his gaze from Merryn's face. He then reached out his hand and leant it on the underside of the bridge next to Merryn's shoulder, his face was now millimetres from hers. She breathed deeply. Her body quivered with excitement and anticipation. Xance gently brushed her lips with his lips. A tender, perhaps over-cautious kiss that lasted for merely a second. He moved backwards slightly and looked at Merryn. It was as if he wanted reassurance from her that it was alright to kiss her. She gently smiled at him. He leant in towards her and kissed her again, a delicate, soft brush of the lips; quick but gentle. A warm feeling radiated through her whole body. Merryn was overtaken with an inexplicable emotion as he pulled away from her. Without thinking, she grasped the back of Xance's saturated hair with one hand whilst holding his cheek with her other hand. At the same time, she pressed her lips firmly to his. His lips felt smooth as he reciprocated her kiss; more passionately now with a slightly open mouth. It was a long, powerfully intense kiss – a kiss that they had waited years for. Now, he held her face in his hands as their lips moved together firmly and wantonly. Merryn's body felt as if there was a tiny electric current running through it, pulsing through from her head to her feet. In this moment, nothing else mattered. She became unaware of her surroundings: the sound of the rain above them as it battered the stone, the wind as it blew through the leaves on the overhanging, tangled trees. She squeezed his hair and moved her hands through it. He kissed her cheek. Then his lips made their way down her neck; planting tiny, gentle kisses. Merryn stroked her arms down Xance's back. His T-shirt was loose at his waist and her hands caressed his taut, bare back underneath it; revealing his firm, shapely torso which was pressed against her. His hands now held her hips and she arched her back slightly as his kisses moved to her clavicle and across her bare, damp shoulder. His hand slid up her body and hovered dangerously close to her breast before gliding around to her back. The strap of her top fell off her shoulder and down her arm. Merryn thought she might explode with emotion at the touch of his lips on her body.

"I'm sorry," Xance whispered into her ear through exhausted breaths. He nuzzled her skin with his face and then embraced her, wrapping his arms tightly around her back and pulling her even closer to his body. It was as if he didn't want to let her go. Merryn didn't want the embrace to end. She loved feeling his chest against her cheek and his body pressed against hers. They remained in this hold for several minutes as if absorbing each other's heated tension; their breathing steadied gradually. Xance stroked Merryn's hair tenderly, running his fingers through the damp waves. She wanted this feeling to last forever. She was intoxicated with Xance's kisses, and at that very moment, under the bridge in the torrential, ceaseless rain, she knew that she had unequivocally fallen in love with him.

15

Shock

Sunday evening was warm. Merryn was at a table on the terrace outside Kitto's Cave with Chloe, Amelie and Erin. They had arranged to meet up with Xance and his friends, and while the girls waited they chatted about the boys. Merryn knew that Chloe was nervous and excited about spending the evening with Carter. The girls had talked at length about how Chloe could not stop thinking about Carter after he had bought her the drink last Friday. Chloe had seen it as a sign that there was a possibility that he liked her, and had told Merryn that she was grateful for them all getting together at the cafe. Erin had confessed to the girls that she had a crush on Harry. She had liked him since they were in the same class at primary school. He had pulled her hair once to get her attention because he wanted to borrow a blue pencil and that had been it – she was smitten. Sadly though, he had never really bothered with her much after that.

Merryn was nervous too. She had spent all day lying on her bed thinking about Xance. She had reviewed everything that he had told her about her past life: The Sefwarian Nyss, the tattoo, their relationship and the conflicts between the Nyss and the Nethergeard people. It was still all immensely unbelievable; to think that she has lived before – a whole different life that she has no real memory of.

At the dining table, having Sunday lunch, with her family, Merryn had looked at them one by one, noting how much she loved them, even her younger sister, Tamsyn, who irritated her on a daily basis. She thought about her past parents and wondered what they had been like and considered whether she may have had sisters or brothers before. Merryn had smiled internally at the possibility of having a brother. The thought was strange to her as she only really knew what it was like to have a sister. Most significantly though, she had thought about the reality that she had known Xance in her past. She felt a nervous prickle of excitement when she remembered running with him in the rain yesterday afternoon, and she had closed her eyes and pictured every tiny detail of their kiss over and over again.

Xance and his friends arrived together and bought drinks for everyone from the bar before sitting down with the girls. To Merryn's relief, Xance sat in the chair next to her, pulling it up as close as possible to hers. She smiled up at him trying not to show her nervousness. Jason, Luke and Tom had pulled seats up opposite Merryn with Bryn and Harry to her right, next to Amelie and Erin. Carter appeared annoyed that there wasn't a spare seat next to Chloe, who sat to Merryn's left the other side of Xance; he grabbed a chair from another table and slid it towards Chloe.

"Is it ok if I squeeze in here next to you?" he asked her, seemingly conscious that the rest of the group were staring at him.

"Sure," responded Chloe as coolly as she could manage. The group chatted and laughed together, Merryn enjoying getting to know Xance's friends. She noticed that Harry and Bryn seemed to be close. At one point Harry leaned his arm on Bryn's chair and Bryn had tilted towards him, their heads almost touching. She wondered whether they were a couple. There certainly seemed to be a subtle connection between them. She looked across at Xance who was in the middle of re-telling the story, to the whole group, of their walk in the rain yesterday. Merryn was slightly terrified that he was going to share the details of their first kiss. She tensed as he explained about using the bridge as a shelter. However, she had nothing to worry about. His story ended there. As if he could sense her concern, Xance placed his hand on her thigh and rubbed it gently and reassuringly.

Later that evening, the girls were in the bathroom of Kitto's Cave. Merryn had always tried to avoid the clichéd scenario where all the girls go to the bathroom en masse, but for some reason this evening it appeared that her bladder was perfectly synced with that of her friends, and the situation became unavoidable. Erin was attempting to tidy her hair in the mirror whilst expressing frustration at the fact that Harry was not showing any interest in her.

"He doesn't like me at all," Erin whinged.

"I'm sure he likes you, but maybe he just likes you as a friend. He's kind to you after all." Chloe tried to reassure her, whilst Amelie nodded positively behind her.

Erin smiled, but it was obvious to Merryn that Chloe's attempt at reassurance hadn't worked. Merryn felt bad, because she thought that it was entirely possible that Harry was not into girls at all, although she had no real evidence to support this. She didn't want her friend to be let down or to feel the disappointment she would feel if this were the case; knowing she would never be Harry's girlfriend. Merryn thought about how devastated she had felt recently when she believed that Xance was not interested in her. It hurt, more than she wanted to admit, and she knew that she wouldn't want Erin to feel a similar pain.

Merryn washed her hands using the liquid soap on the sink. As she rinsed away the bubbles under the tap, she became aware of a strange sensation of tingling coupled with a gentle throbbing on her lower arm. Then she noticed something dark on her wrist. She rubbed at it under the stream of warm water, but it didn't budge. It continued to throb as she dried her hands on a paper towel. As she inspected her wrist once more, to her shock, Merryn could clearly see a tiny, new, black tattoo positioned on the underside of her left wrist. She tried not to make it obvious that she was transfixed by her wrist as her friends giggled and chatted beside her. The tattoo was shaped like a sideways 'v' and had a small round dot inside it. Merryn was confused and her face started to feel hot. She knew she needed to show it to Xance.

On returning to the table outside with her friends, Merryn was surprised to find Xance and the others preparing to leave. Taking her gently by the arm, he pulled her into the alley next to the cafe.

"I'm sorry, but I have to go. I'll try to come back later. I'd like to walk you home, but I have to do something, and I don't know how long it will take," Xance explained to her. He seemed anxious and on edge.

"Is something wrong?" Merryn was worried as Xance usually seemed so calm and together, even in stressful situations.

"No, it's nothing for you to worry about. There's just something I have to do," Xance said as he noticed the new mark on Merryn's wrist. He took her arm in his hand and pulled it closer to him. "How long has this been visible?" he asked, now with real concern in his voice.

"About five minutes, I think. I was just about to ask you what it was," replied Merryn.

Xance pulled the short sleeve of his T-shirt to one side and displayed a black mark, identical to the one on Merryn's wrist.

Merryn looked at him quizzically.

"I don't have time to explain now. I have to go. I'll tell you everything soon, I promise," Xance said as he stepped out of the alley and gestured to his friends.

They joined him as he walked quickly away into the village. Merryn went back to the table and sat down. Her friends were curious as to where Xance and the others had gone in such a rush. Merryn explained as best she could. She noticed that Chloe seemed disappointed, and looked over her shoulder several times as the boys disappeared from view.

Merryn sat for a moment and pondered the situation. She had a real feeling that something was wrong. A feeling in the very depths of her stomach, which made nervous flutters within her chest. She attempted to involve herself in the conversation her friends were having about music, but she couldn't focus. All she could think about was where Xance had gone. On impulse, she apologised to Chloe, Amelie and Erin, explaining that she was worried about Xance, and left the cafe too. She half-ran down the narrow streets of the village. Her eyes searched from left to right as she crossed over the tiny lanes. Whatever it was that had made them leave so suddenly couldn't be good, she thought. She looked at the new tattoo on her wrist. Had this got something to do with it? After all, it seemed more than a coincidence that the tattoo had appeared just as Xance decided he needed to be somewhere else urgently. She continued on, looking for Xance down each of the side streets. As she turned the corner into a narrow, cobbled lane with a mixture of old, stone and painted buildings on either side, she noticed Xance's group ahead of her. They were stood all together at the far end, a short distance from a T-junction with another road. A row of different coloured shops and houses lay before them in the next street. Merryn stepped up into a small alcove outside one of the shops, which gave her a place to watch without being seen. Her heart was thudding in her chest and her hands shook. She was worried about what was going on, but in addition to this, she was nervous in case Xance saw her. What on earth would he think of her if he caught her following him and spying on his group of friends? It didn't exactly shout out "I trust you", she thought.

As if from nowhere, several male figures turned the corner of the road ahead. They were all dressed in dark trousers with double-breasted, black, fitted tunics buttoning in a military-style to the front. It was obviously some sort of uniform, but Merryn had never seen anything like it before. They appeared to be holding large stick-like weapons with a glinting point on one end. They huddled together and moved as if they were one entity: dark, fluid and viscous.

Merryn watched from her hidden position in the alcove as the new arrivals moved closer to Xance, Carter and the others. The two groups of boys were now face to face. Xance's group had spread themselves out slightly across the street. Merryn was struggling to see what was happening, but it appeared that the boys were deep in discussion, and that their body language alluded to tension between the two groups.

She leant against the wall of the building, placing just one eye proud of the brickwork in order to observe inconspicuously. Just then, Harry lifted his arm high. A bright gleam of shining deep purple light emanated from the hilt in his hand. The short arc of light tracing a subtle curve through the air. Merryn gasped aloud, shocked by the sight before her. This was the weapon she had seen in her vision! She saw Xance gesture to Harry with his arm outstretched. He appeared to be indicating to him to wait or stop. She noticed the rest of Xance's group tense –

their arms held strongly at their sides. Each of them holding something small and solid in their hand. Harry lowered his sword, but it still glowed majestically at his side. Xance took a step forward. He was now just a few steps away from the white-haired warrior at the front and centre of the other group, who was flanked by a power-fully-built, dark-haired male whose eyes appeared cemented on Xance. The three enemies exchanged more words. Merryn was annoyed that she couldn't hear what was being said.

Then it began. In a flash, Xance's weapon blazed a deep green. Within seconds, his friends all activated their swords too; a dazzling spectacle of purple, pale-blue, red, green, white, yellow and blue. Merryn watched in horror and disbelief as the boys fought. Streaks of iridescent colours seemed to fly through the air leaving arcs of glowing light in their wake that gradually dissipated and disappeared before re-appearing again. Harry was thrown to the cobbled road by the force of one of the enemy's stakes. Merryn heard him let out a shout of anger or pain as his head met the stone with a thud. He quickly and deftly rolled to his side and sprang back to his feet, narrowly avoiding the silver-speared end of a stake which had been brought down swiftly by its owner towards his body. She watched as Xance fought two of them at once; kicking one in the chest, causing him to fall unceremoni-ously onto his back, and striking the other one down his arm with his blade. The two were clearly injured and seemed to back off slightly, still brandishing their weapons in a show of defiance. Xance then turned his attention to assisting Carter, whose head was locked under someone's arm, whilst one of the others beat the back of his legs with their stake. Xance waded in, kicking the stake out of his opponent's hand and knocking him to the ground with the back of his arm. He wielded his blade menacingly in the face of his next foe. His anger appeared to have reached boiling point; he sliced at the dark-haired fighter's arm, expertly avoiding Carter's head. The blow was enough to force the release of his friend, who fell to the ground clutching his throat and gasping for air. Whilst Xance had been occupied with releasing Carter from the grip in which he was held, his other friends had found themselves virtually surrounded by the rest of the enemy gang, their stakes held aloft aggressively.

Merryn felt helpless as she watched from afar. She didn't want any of them to get hurt, but she was desperate for Xance to escape unharmed. At that moment, when all seemed futile for Xance's friends, someone ran into the lane from behind them. Merryn could see a glow of bright orange as a blade was swung in the direction of the enemy. The arrival of the additional warrior had taken everyone by surprise. Merryn watched as the new arrival confidently began to fight. Long, dark-auburn hair fell into the warrior's face as they moved aggressively, slicing the knife at each of the enemies in turn, knocking two to the ground and kicking a third in the torso. Merryn watched as the victim fell onto his backside and rolled over before standing up and beginning to retreat. This new addition to Xance's side had given him and his friends the chance that they needed; Harry, Bryn, Luke, Tom and Jason now turned to tackle the lead fighter who did not seem keen on giving up easily. Merryn had concluded that he was the leader, as it was he who had been doing all the talking at the beginning. He had white-blond hair and a pale complexion. He had a slender physique that made him appear perhaps taller than he was. Merryn was worried as she watched, but as the five boys raised their blades in unison, the fair-haired adversary stepped backwards, gesturing defeat by lifting his hands with his palms facing outwards. He grabbed one of his dark-haired allies by the arm, stopping him from wading in to continue the fight. The pair continued to retreat backwards as they joined their group, and then they all turned and left the same way that they had arrived.

Xance patted his friends on their backs as they all huddled together in comradeship, obviously relieved that the conflict was over. The latecomer swept her thick hair back away from her face. Merryn was intrigued to note that the unknown fighter was a girl. It was clear that she was an expert fighter, and had managed to arrive just at the right time to help Xance and his friends. Merryn felt that she looked vaguely familiar, but she couldn't place where she had seen her before.

From her hiding place, Merryn took several deep breaths – in and out – trying to calm her heart rate and steady her nerves. She had never seen anything like the spectacle that she had just witnessed. She leant against the wall and closed her eyes, but the stress seemed to overwhelm her, and she slid slowly down the wall as her legs began to feel weak. She sat on the step with her head on the brickwork of the building. After a few moments, she felt a little calmer and opened her eyes.

She thought about what she was going to say to Xance, having followed him without his knowledge, and having witnessed the fight. As she glanced up the cobbled street once more, Merryn was panicked to find that Xance and his friends had walked down the lane and were now almost opposite the alcove where Merryn sat. She was unsure of what she should do. Her first thought was to attempt to remain hidden, however, if she tried to stay hidden and he saw her, she would be embarrassed. She felt awful because she had followed Xance, and was concerned that he would be angry, and think that she didn't trust him. She knew that there really wasn't a perfect solution to this awkward situation that she had created, and so she made the decision to be honest with Xance, regardless of the consequences. After all, she had only pursued Xance because she was worried about him. She hoped that he would find this reason an acceptable excuse and not be too angry with her.

However, all her worry drained from her as she stood up and stepped out into the street to stand in front of them. She was no longer thinking about what she would say to Xance, as she was shocked to see why the female warrior had seemed so familiar to her; standing before Merryn was her friend Chloe!

16

Another World

Merryn, Xance and the others had walked back to the harbour, and were now sat in various spots either along the harbour wall or on the walkway. Merryn was relieved as Xance had kindly reassured her that he completely understood her actions when she followed them. He told her that it was natural for her to be curious about what was going on, especially when she was still coming to terms with who she was and where she was from. Carter and Chloe sat on the path leaning against the wall, whilst Harry and Bryn sat above them, to the left, on top of the wall. Luke, Jason and Tom were strewn in different spots on the concrete. Merryn, who sat cross-legged next to Xance, was still in shock from what she had witnessed.

"Chloe, are you Nyss too?" she questioned with a hint of disbelief in her voice.

"Yeah. I'm sorry. I couldn't say anything until I was certain that you knew who you were." Chloe smiled apologetically.

Merryn was struggling with all of the new information. It had been difficult enough over the past few days, having to come to terms with the knowledge of exactly who she was and the details of her past. Yet now there was all the added confusion of her best friend being from Sefwarian Nyss also, and being a particularly skilled warrior as well!

Xance explained to Merryn that his tattoo had appeared at the same time as hers, "It's the Elkalind rune – it means protection or shield, and it appears when Nyss are in danger," he explained.

Merryn looked down at her wrist and noticed that the rune had faded and was almost gone.

"It's how we knew that the Banas Mihtig were here again," Xance continued.

"Who are the Banas Mihtig, and what do you mean 'here again'?" Merryn questioned.

"They are the army of the Nethergeard people. Many years ago, when the accord was made between them and the Nyss people, part of the agreement was that there would be peace between our two worlds. Winnans are banned between us ..."

"That's a fight in this world," interjected Carter.

Xance smiled and continued, "For some reason, after all these years, they have chosen to break the pact. Today was their third visit, and our most serious conflict. That Maddox – he's a nasty piece of work. He gave me the excuse that they were 'just visiting' as it had been 'a while'. He's a smarmy, lying git. There must be a reason why they keep coming here. It must be something important, if they are willing to start a war. They are capable of using the Koyt egress as a passage from Nethergeard to here, but the accord stated that they were forbidden from entering either Sefwarian Nyss or Earth."

"Well, they're definitely going to start a war if they keep coming here," Harry said, rubbing the back of his head where it had hit the ground during the fight. "We're not going to put up with them breaking the accord. We've kept our side of the agreement."

"What could they possibly want?" Merryn questioned.

"No idea, but we need to find out," Carter said. "Whatever it is, it's obviously something they are prepared to go to war over, so it must be valuable in some way."

"Either way, they are clearly after something that is not theirs to have. We need to stop them, otherwise their actions will only cause harm to the people of Earth and Sefwarian Nyss. That's something we can be certain about," Xance added, trying hard to sound calm and disguise his anger. "I need to go to Sefwarian Nyss tomorrow to report the Banas Mihtig to the First Luminary."

Merryn stood up and brushed the dust from the back of her jeans, "Well, I'd better get going. I'll see you all tomorrow," she said.

"Shall I walk you back?" Xance offered.

"Yeah, that would be good, thanks."

Xance had walked Merryn home. At the gate to Harbour View cottage, Xance held Merryn's hand as he turned to face her. "You should come with me to Nyss. The First Luminary has been waiting to meet you."

"Come with you? How?" Merryn asked feeling nervous.

"I'll take you with me through the Koyt egress. I'll look after you, you'll be safe, I promise." he stroked the side of her hair gently as his deep blue eyes looked into hers.

"Why has the First Luminary been waiting to meet me? How does he know about me?"

"He's always known that you were here on Earth, he's just been waiting for you to realise who you were. We've both been waiting." He smiled at her gently.

"Ok, I'll go, if you think I should go."

"We'll go tomorrow straight after school," Xance said as he leant in and placed a delicate kiss on Merryn's lips.

Merryn went through the gate and walked up the path to the house. She wondered what tomorrow would bring. As she watched Xance walk away down the hill, her stomach fluttered with nervousness at the thought of visiting Sefwarian Nyss.

* * *

MERRYN WAS EXHAUSTED. She couldn't sleep. Her bedroom was hot, and the desk fan which she had positioned on the bedside cabinet was merely circulating the warm air. She rolled over in bed and kicked the covers off her legs. She closed her eyes and pictured Xance smiling at her. She heard him re-telling her that the First Luminary had been waiting for her. It was strange to think that someone who had never actually met her or who didn't even know her name had been waiting to meet her for almost seventeen years. She opened her eyes and looked at the clock beside her. It read a quarter past two. She lay on her side for a few minutes just staring at the face of the clock, watching the two dots in the centre of the numbers flash to the beat of the seconds ticking by. Just then, Merryn sensed that someone or something was standing at the end of the bed. The feeling made her whole body jump in shock. Like the realisation that someone else is in a room with you when you thought you were alone. She flicked her head quickly to look, but there was no one there. At least there was no one that she could *see*, but the feeling that someone or something was present in the room was still with her.

She sat up slowly, without removing her gaze from the end of the bed. However, she now felt that the presence had moved, and was now much closer to her. She had an overwhelming feeling that something was standing to her right. Was she imagining it or could she feel cool breath on her face? Merryn's heart thudded. She tried desperately to calm it by slowing her breaths in and out, but it wasn't working. Her whole body began to sweat and shake, despite the fact that she now felt certain that whatever it was that she could sense had brought with it an icy chill to the room. All of a sudden, the voile curtains at her window began to move. At first it was simply a gentle swish from side to side, but as the moments passed, the movements became larger.

Merryn grabbed her quilt and pulled it up to her chest. She tried to make herself as small as possible, curling her knees up tightly within the secure grasp of her arms. Even though she was petrified, she resisted the urge to bury her head underneath the cover. She wanted to know what was causing this strange phenomenon. She *needed* to understand it. The curtain was blowing into the room violently now, like a wild beast thrashing within a net. She felt the cool breaths on her cheek again, and sensed that the entity was inches from her face. Surrendering to her fear, Merryn pulled the quilt above her head, and curled herself up into a tight ball below it. She lay there for a few moments, trembling and shaking; listening to the curtain flapping uncontrollably.

After what seemed like forever, but in reality was probably only a few moments, the curtain stilled and settled. Merryn slowly emerged from beneath the quilt to find that her room appeared as if nothing had happened. The feeling of the presence had gone; she felt alone in the room once more. She sat for a few minutes trying to get some control over her erratic breathing. When she had steadied her nerves enough, she climbed out of bed and crossed the room to the window. She had no idea how she had mustered the courage to leave the security of her bed, but for some reason it seemed the right thing to do. It was almost as if she was being pulled or called to the window; as if she had a curiosity that was not within her control. It was a curiosity that coupled with fearlessness.

She pulled the curtain open and noticed that the window was merely ajar. There was no way that it was windy enough outside to have caused the curtain to behave the way it had done. She pushed the window wide open and leant on the window sill, breathing in the fresh, warm air. Still feeling nervous, she took several glances behind her, but felt that she was definitely alone.

She looked out of the window into the blackness of the night. As she looked across towards the harbour, she could see the silhouetted shape of the headland reaching out into the sea in the distance. She couldn't see the boats in the harbour, but she imagined them bobbing gently, as if in a relaxed sleep, on the calm harbour water. Just then, her focus was drawn back to the darkness of the headland. A yellowy light flickered for a moment. Then it was gone. Then it appeared again. It flickered and danced. Then another light appeared just behind the first. The two lights twinkled and remained equidistant from each other as they moved across the headland in the blackness. Merryn watched as the lights moved further inland, their golden glow clearly visible, gleaming and quivering against their dark background. They seemed to be moving towards the abandoned white house that she knew was up on the hilltop. Just then, as if Merryn's thoughts had flicked on the light switch themselves, a static light appeared in the vicinity of the old house on the hill. Its glow was white and clean compared to the two moving lights. The two amber lights had now disappeared, but the light in the house remained on for some time. Merryn observed from her window, wondering who on earth would be out wandering on the headland at this time of night, and who had turned on the light in the white house if no one lived there. Eventually, the light was gone once more and the blackness of night prevailed.

Merryn partly closed the window and went back to her bed. She laid down and noticed that the clock now read five to three. As she finally drifted off to sleep, Merryn's mind pictured the mysterious yellow lights dancing through the darkness.

1 7

Sefwarian Nyss

Merryn was in the school library looking through some local history books. It was lunchtime, and her friends had gone off to sit outside on the grass in the sun. Merryn had made an excuse about needing some research for her art homework from the library, and had agreed to meet up with them later. The library was large and had many, huge, wooden bookshelves situated in various formations, which provided some secluded areas tucked away from the main space.

Merryn had seated herself at a table in the far corner: somewhere quiet where she could read. Her plan was to attempt to find information about the white house on the headland. Her inquisitiveness had been fuelled by the mysterious lights that she had seen last night, and she now wanted to know who owned the house and why it was abandoned. She knew about the rumours of ghosts within the property and wanted to find out more. For some strange reason, she felt that whatever the presence in her bedroom was, it had been trying to tell her something. There must be a reason why she was drawn to the window last night. She knew that she had been scared of the feeling that something was in the room with her, and the coldness that she felt on her face was definitely real, therefore why would she decide to go over to the window just after the curtain had stopped blowing? It didn't make any sense unless something, or someone, was trying to show her something. Merryn knew that ordinarily she would have been too scared to rise from her bed until the morning light brought with it the reassurance that all was well, and therefore she felt that she was being influenced by a mysterious force.

She wasn't having much luck. There was nothing in any of the books about who had lived in the house in recent times, but she did manage to find out that the property was once the vicarage and family home to the local reverend, his wife and their two daughters. The house had a name: Perfect Haven. It was within close proximity to the village church, which occupied an enviable position next to the beach, Church Cove, right on the water's edge just around the headland from the harbour. This information all seemed to link to the research that Merryn had completed before when she had been curious about the Koyt. She remembered that there was definitely something to do with a vicar and tales of smuggling which centred around the church.

Merryn was so engrossed in her reading that she

didn't notice Tyler pull out a chair and sit down next to her. He sat for a few moments, silently watching her read, waiting for her to notice his presence. Eventually, as she turned a page in the large reference book, her elbow brushed Tyler's arm, and she glanced up to apologise.

"Sorry... oh! Tyler, hi. I didn't see you there!" she gasped. "You made me jump!" She smiled as she slowly closed the book, trying not to draw Tyler's attention to her chosen reading material. Merryn felt slightly embarrassed that she was researching about the house on the cliff, and she didn't want him to think that she was boring. It wasn't the most interesting of pastimes for a sixteen-year-old. In addition, she really didn't want to answer any questions about why she was so interested in the house.

"It's ok," Tyler smiled, "I didn't mean to sneak up on you! I just wanted to say hello quickly. I've got to get going now, I've got to be somewhere, are you ok?"

"Yes, great, thanks, are you?" Merryn replied, leaning her arm on the book to hide its front cover from Tyler.

"Yes, I'm good, thanks. I'll see you soon," Tyler said as he stood up and pushed his chair back under the table, throwing his bag over his shoulder as he walked away.

Merryn smiled after him before continuing her reading. She sat for several more minutes absorbing as much historical information as she could before realising that it was time for the start of her afternoon lesson. She closed the book, and swiftly returned it to its correct place on the shelf, telling herself she needed more time to research. She was intrigued about what she had learned, and was able to make links with the information that she had read on the internet previously, but she knew that she had to find out more. For some reason, Merryn had a feeling that whatever those lights were, up on the headland, they were linked to the stories that she had read. Something was going on up there and she needed to know what it was. She was sensible enough to know that people could write anything on the internet, and just because these stories and myths existed didn't make them true, but she also knew that what she had seen was unusual and that there must be an element of truth or reasoning behind some of the stories. In addition, she had to find out what the apparent entity in her bedroom was trying to show her, and why it needed her to know.

STANDING before the Koyt in the gentle sunlight, Merryn felt nervous. She had worried about this moment ever since Xance had suggested that she go with him to Sefwarian Nyss. He had told her that the First Luminary had been waiting to meet her. This, in itself, seemed strange to her, but she was even more intrigued that someone she had no prior knowledge of could know who she was. Why did he want to meet her? His title was one of importance. He was in charge of the Sefwarian Synod, a Council that ruled and made the laws for Sefwarian Nyss. He was a decision maker and an authoritative figure for the Nyss people. He was responsible for knowing and tracing where all his people were living, and as whom. He had been instrumental in helping create the peace pact between Sefwarian Nyss and the Netherworld. What

could he possibly want with her? Surely, she was insignif-
icant compared to the many other pressing tasks he had
to fill his day.

"How does this work, Xance? How do we get there?"

"The cemp's magic enables us to travel through the
gateway." Xance took her hand in his and squeezed it
reassuringly. "Are you ready?" he smiled.

"Promise me you'll look after me?" Merryn asked
tentatively, looking nervously into Xance's blue,
mesmerising eyes.

"I promise. You don't have to worry. It'll be fine. I'll be
with you." Xance tried to make her feel more confident.

Clasping his hand a little too tightly, Merryn stepped
forward towards the Koyt with Xance. As they grew
nearer, a gentle purple hue could be seen emanating from
the bottom of the huge rock. They stood for a few
seconds and watched as the mauve glow became brighter,
and expanded to cover the stone, almost in its entirety.
The light then began to pulse brighter then darker;
brighter then darker, like a heartbeat. Xance stepped into
the purple glow taking Merryn with him.

They became engulfed in the haze. Merryn's pulse
began to race. She tried to control her nervousness by
concentrating on her breathing. A deep breath in for
three counts followed by a slow breath out for three
counts. It wasn't really working, and she could feel herself
starting to shake. She noticed that Xance had tightened
his grip on her hand as the light intensified. Her vision
was now completely filled with the purple light; she could
see nothing else. Within a second or two, the light
vanished immediately, plunging them into total darkness.

Then, as if someone had flicked a switch, her world was filled with light once more. Merryn found herself under an archway with cobbled stones beneath her feet. Golden sunshine streaked into her eyes and she squinted slightly before her adjusting her eyes to its warmth. Xance still clasped her hand as she stood motionless and surveyed what lay before her. It was difficult for her to absorb everything. The expanse of buildings which surrounded her was more than impressive. A huge, white-washed stone structure in a similar style to Georgian architecture stood majestically around the edge of a huge rectangular area of grass. Merryn noticed that the archway in which she stood was one of several on the inside perimeter of the building. Each archway marked the halfway point along a covered terrace which continued around the entire building on all four sides, and was supported by beautiful white stone pillars. A series of white, stone steps appeared periodically along the terrace and all led out onto a path which enclosed the perfectly manicured grass in the centre. Everything was immaculately tidy and clean – not a leaf nor any litter marred the pristine picture.

Merryn noticed the people that walked along the terrace and through the courtyard. She was surprised to see that they were all dressed in a business-like manner: suits, jackets, ties; some carrying work bags or briefcases. A woman wearing a skirt-suit with black patent, heeled shoes and carrying a stack of files in her arms crossed the terrace in front of them. Nothing looked unusual. In fact, this place had a peculiar familiarity to it. She could be in London or any large city for that matter.

Merryn turned to face Xance, "It's just like home," she said to him.

Xance laughed, "Well, what were you expecting?"

"I'm not sure really. Just not this! I didn't really have any expectations, I just thought it would be different to home, I guess," Merryn explained.

"This *is* actually your home. You have been here many times before remember."

"I didn't think of that. I don't really remember, yet it doesn't feel *new* either, if that makes sense?"

"Perhaps that's why it doesn't seem so strange to you – because you have memories of it in your subconscious."

"Maybe. It all appears so normal – the clothes and everything," Merryn smiled at Xance. She felt a bit silly making such simple observations, but was struggling to understand and express her feelings concerning this place.

"Sefwarian Nyss exists in parallel time to home. People live here in a similar way to those who live on Earth. Some Nyss are chosen to live again on Earth, whilst others live and work here. It's an honour and a privilege to be chosen to migrate your soul, but all Nyss strive to live lives that have a positive impact on those around them regardless of where they live," Xance explained.

Merryn walked with Xance to their right, following the terrace round until they arrived at a large, black, wooden door bearing an ornate brass doorknob which had been meticulously polished. Xance knocked twice on the door, but just as he did it swung open. A tall, slightly built man carrying a box appeared in the doorway. He smiled and held the door open with his hip in order to allow them access. Xance took Merryn's hand and they entered the building, thanking the man for his courteousness. Inside, a rather glamorous woman, with her hair pinned loosely on her head smiled gently and ushered them to take a seat on some leather chairs before taking a seat at a large desk by the window. The walls of the reception room were panelled in a dark wood. A large cheese plant, which resided in the corner of the room, along with a couple of flowering pot plants on the shelf beside them, gave the space a slightly homely feel.

Merryn and Xance sat in complete silence listening to the clicking of the receptionist's keyboard. After several minutes had passed, the heavy, panelled door to their right swung open and an immaculately dressed man appeared. He looked around thirty years old. He wore a navy-blue suit with a white shirt and pale-blue silk tie embellished with a delicate diamond pattern. His dark hair was short and as neatly presented as the rest of him. He smiled and gestured with his arms for them to come forwards towards him. "Xance, it's been a while, how are you?" he said, as he clasped Xance's hand and arm in a firm handshake before pulling him in for a quick hug and several pats on his back.

"I'm good, sir … erm … Anthony, thank you." Xance grinned. "You're looking well – it's good to see you."

"And who is this?"

Xance placed his arm reassuringly on Merryn's back, "This is Merryn Devereaux, sir."

The First Luminary stepped forward and took Merryn's hand in his, placing his other hand over the top of hers. He looked directly at her as if he was studying her face and features carefully.

"It's a pleasure to meet you, Merryn, at last," he smiled. I am Anthony, the First Luminary of the Sefwarian Nyss Synod."

"Hello, sir, it's nice to meet you," Merryn replied smiling nervously.

"Anthony ... you must call me Anthony, please." He smiled. He continued to look at her face for a few more seconds before releasing her hand and telling them both to make themselves comfortable on the chairs opposite his desk. Xance and Merryn did as requested, Xance carefully moving his seat slightly closer to Merryn's before sitting down.

"Well, Xance, what brings you to Nyss? I understand that you have brought Merryn to meet with me, but your request for a meeting alluded to something else," the First Luminary said as he seated himself at his desk.

Xance began his explanation; detailing how the Banas Mihtig had been visiting Porthrosen, and picking fights with the Nyss Cempalli warriors. He expressed concern that Maddox was a loose cannon, and was not to be trusted. "This is the third time in recent weeks that Maddox has started a conflict with us in Porthrosen. He appears power-hungry and ruthless. There has to be a reason why they are causing problems and looking for trouble after all these years. We just need to find out what it is."

"I am concerned, as you are, that there must be a reason why they are causing conflict. Continue as you have been doing, and keep me updated if they show themselves again. I will set a team on investigating the cause of their defiance," the First Luminary spoke calmly and authoritatively. He continued, "When I agreed to the pact with the Magister Worlega, I always doubted that he would keep his word. I cannot imagine that his soldiers are acting without his knowledge. If he has broken the agreement, we will not take it lightly. They will not get away with this behaviour when we have stuck by our promises." He paused, looking pensive, and then continued: "Now, let's deal with why you have brought Merryn here today." He stood up and walked over to a tall metal filing cabinet. On opening the top drawer, he began to work his way through the files towards the centre of the drawer. Merryn felt a wave of nervousness take over her body. She glanced anxiously at Xance who smiled back at her reassuringly.

"It's ok," he mouthed quietly to her as he tapped her hand gently.

After a few moments, the First Luminary closed the filing cabinet drawer, placed a small, ornate key on the desk, and walked away towards a door at the back of the room. He opened the door and disappeared through it. The office was now completely quiet. Neither Xance nor Merryn spoke. Xance took Merryn's hand and held it. He squeezed it gently. Merryn's heart was beating quickly within her chest as her nervousness grew. What was he doing? Where had he gone? She glanced across at Xance, who seemed completely calm and was looking back at her smiling reassuringly. Merryn released her hand from Xance's comforting hold, and wrung her hands together in an attempt to alleviate the anxiety. Xance reached over and re-took her hand in his.

"You have nothing to worry about, I promise. I wouldn't have brought you here if there was anything for you to be scared of," Xance whispered as he leant in closer to her.

Merryn managed a slightly forced smiled. She knew that he was trying to make her feel better.

At that moment, the First Luminary came back into the room. He was carrying a metal, rectangular-shaped box of approximately thirty centimetres in length. It did not appear heavy, as he carried it with ease. He placed the metal container on the desk in front of Merryn, and sat back down in his chair.

"I've been waiting a long time to give this back to you," he said, looking at Merryn and smiling.

Merryn eyed the box nervously. It was grey in colour and appeared to be made of metal. Its surface was adorned with decorative scroll-type etchings. The top of the box bore the inscription, Kerenza, in the most beautiful lettering that Merryn had ever seen. The First Luminary picked up the key which he had earlier placed on the desk. He leant across and positioned it on top of the metal box.

"Open it." He smiled.

Merryn's eyes widened as she looked at Xance briefly. She tried to smile in order to hide her true feelings. Inside, she was nervous. Her head was swimming with countless questions. *Where has this box come from? What's inside it? Is it important?* They continued to swirl within her head. Faster and faster. Merryn's anxiousness grew. She began to feel hot and could sense her cheeks turning a warm pink colour. She looked up at the First Luminary who had now leant back in his seat, and was exuding a calm, almost relaxed demeanour.

"The box is yours. I've kept it safely for your return. Go on ... take a look. Open it." He smiled encouragingly. Merryn picked up the key, and placed it in the lock at the front of the box. She breathed out loudly as she lifted the lid and looked inside.

She could see what looked like a metal rectangle about the size of a small phone. Lifting it out, she was able to inspect it more carefully: its surface was covered in delicate, intricate engraved patterns, and she could clearly see a large calligraphic 'K' in the centre. Merryn brought the object closer so that she could observe the detail. She turned it over in her hands to look at the other side, which was also decorated with the same delicate pattern as appeared on the front. From the moment that she had picked up this object, Merryn began to experience feelings which she could not explain. The object felt familiar to her, but she could not place where she had seen it before. As she held the metal shape in her hands, she encountered a feeling of calmness – like she was "home" and this was meant to be. She somehow felt safe. She realised that her heart had slowed to a normal rate, and she no longer felt nervous or anxious.

"It belongs to you," the First Luminary said, breaking the silence and quiet tension.

"What is it?"

"It's a cemp – it is powerful."

"A cemp?" This was not a word Merryn was familiar with.

"As well as its powers, it also transforms into a cempedge. A weapon or sword. Do you have any memory of it at all?"

"No, well ... not really." Merryn recalled the fight that she had witnessed between Xance, his friends and the Banas Mihtig. She remembered the arced glow of their weapons. Each one a different colour. Then she remembered her previous vision: "I think I have seen them before, and also I had a vision that I couldn't explain. I saw my hand holding this. It had a blue-green arc," Merryn explained.

The First Luminary responded "That vision is from a memory that you hold. This is your cemp. The engraved 'K' is for Kerenza – the name you bore as your previous gestord. As you can see it is written on the box. Kerenza means 'love', I believe." He smiled.

18

Intrigued

Erin slumped down on the grass next to her friends, using her bag as cushion to lean on. Her lips were down-turned, indicating a disgruntled unhappiness.

"Are you ok, Erin?" Chloe asked with concern in her voice.

"Yes … well no, not really," Erin responded whilst scrunching up her face for effect, "Harry hates me."

"What's happened?" Merryn and Amelie asked simultaneously.

"Nothing really. I just saw him in the hallway and he said hello."

Chloe patted Erin comfortingly on the arm, "That's good, isn't it?"

"I suppose. It's just that if he was really interested, he

would have done something about it by now. He clearly doesn't like me," Erin whined.

Merryn and the others quickly disputed Erin's comment, trying to reassure her that Harry was perhaps just shy or nervous. Merryn felt slightly awkward with this approach, but couldn't really see another way to deal with the situation at present. She had no idea how Harry really felt about Erin, but she suspected he may be interested in someone else. Merryn cared about Erin, as she did all her friends, and she would never want her to be hurt or upset. Since moving to Porthrosen, she had been surprised at how quickly she had become friends with this group of girls. They had entirely embraced her arrival, and unquestioningly, had welcomed her into their friendship group. Although Merryn still missed her old friends back in Leicestershire, and still spoke to them occasionally, she felt blessed to have made such amazing new friends in Porthrosen.

"Oh, no!" Erin whined, "I forgot that I need to go to the library!" She jumped up, grabbing her bag as she did so. "I'll see you later?" She smiled.

"Definitely," Merryn said.

"Hang on, I'll come with you," Amelie got up from the grass to join Erin.

"Meet at the harbour at seven thirty?" Chloe called after the two of them as they walked back towards the school building.

Erin half turned around, giving a thumbs-up gesture.

Merryn lay back on the grass and stared at the sky. It had felt like a long week. She had completed various subject assignments, and on top of that she had met several times in the evenings with Chloe for coaching. Chloe had been teaching her how to use her cemp, and in particular how to handle it in a fight. Merryn recalled how she had held the cemp-edge with its glowing arc of blue-green, and practised moving it in a rhythmical pattern from side to side and forwards and backwards. She practised slicing and stabbing actions: turning and twisting as her friend imitated being an enemy warrior – darting in front of her and moving swiftly in response to Merryn's attack.

Chloe had explained to Merryn that the more she practised using the cemp, the more she would remember, and the more powerful the cemp would become in her hands. The sessions had been quite gruelling, both mentally and physically, and Merryn felt exhausted. She was still trying to come to terms with all that had happened in recent weeks. Her life now was unrecognisable to what it was when she first arrived in Porthrosen. She could have never imagined the events that had taken place since then. She was still struggling with the reality of who she was, and that she had a past that she could barely remember. A significant past that included Xance and a whole other world.

"Merryn?" Chloe's voice broke into Merryn's thoughts. "Hello?" Chloe teased.

"Sorry, I was thinking," Merryn said as she sat up.

"Well, I could see that! Daydreaming about Xance I'm guessing," Chloe teased some more.

"Erm … no!" Merryn pretended to swipe at Chloe's arm in a gesture of fake anger.

"Seriously though, you're lucky to have him, you

know?" Chloe said, "He's good and honest, and it is obvious how much he cares about you. My last boyfriend turned out to be a lying snake."

"Oh, that's not good. What happened?" Merryn showed genuine concern in her voice.

"We'd been together for a while and I thought he cared for me, but he proved himself to be a cheat. Worse than that though, he was found to sympathise with the Banas Mihtig, and turned out to be untrustworthy with keeping the secrets of the Sefwarian Nyss. It appeared that he had something to do with rumours of certain stories about dubious activities based around Porthrosen dating back to the late 1700s. I don't really know much more than that. The Luminary Synod were forced to take away his ability to migrate his gestord. He has to stay in Sefwarian Nyss." Chloe picked at the grass by her side. Her sadness at this recollection of the past was evident.

"I'm so sorry, Chloe. That must have been awful for you," Merryn said.

"It's ok. I have had to learn that life goes on. I know that, logically, I shouldn't care – not after what he did, but it doesn't always work like that. When you care about someone it's not easy just to switch your feelings off when things don't turn out the way you wanted."

"No, I guess it isn't. Matters of the heart are never straightforward." Merryn paused for a second then tentatively asked, "Did he not care for you at all?"

"He said he did. He asked me to choose to stay with him, rather than coming to Earth. It was a hard decision to leave him." Chloe managed a smile.

Merryn squeezed Chloe's hand gently to show her that

she understood. At that moment, the bell rang for afternoon school, and the two girls grabbed their belongings and headed to their lessons in thoughtful silence.

* * *

As it was Friday, the girls had agreed to meet at the harbour and go to Kitto's Cave. Merryn was looking forward to relaxing after a stressful, busy week. She was mostly looking forward to seeing Xance. They had not really seen each other properly since their journey to Sefwarian Nyss on Monday. She knew Xance had been preoccupied with the Banas Mihtig and was awaiting instructions from the First Luminary. He would be meeting her tonight though, and a smile crept onto her face as she thought about seeing him.

Merryn had left home a little earlier than needed, and so she was walking at a gentle pace along the cobbled streets towards the harbour. She took in the scenery as she walked. The boats in the harbour, all at rest now after their working week. The lush green of the headland reaching out to meet the brilliant blue sea. The white crests of the sea crashing spectacularly against the array of rocks just off the land. It really was beautiful here she thought to herself. She turned a corner into a particularly narrow lane that was lined on one side with a row of pretty terraced houses, and had a stone wall running the length of the other side.

All at once, Merryn felt her arm being grabbed, and she was pulled into narrow alley to the side of one of the properties. Her head hit the wall of the house as her back was slammed against it, sending a searing pain through her skull. A tall, powerfully-built male stood in front of her. His medium-length, dark, slightly wavy hair and olive-toned skin, coupled with his black, military-style clothing was immediately recognisable to her. He was one of the warriors from the fight that she had witnessed: a Banas Mihtig!

Merryn moved quickly, attempting to run back into the street. He pulled her back and pushed her up against the wall, this time stepping closer to her. He kept one hand on her arm as he stared into her face. Merryn struggled and writhed, attempting to pull her arm away. He tightened his grip, and moved even closer so that she could feel his breath on her skin. His eyes scanned her face, seemingly absorbing every detail. His gaze lingered on her eyes. He stared deeply into them and Merryn, although uncomfortable with his demeanour, felt compelled to look back. She stared, trying not to show how scared she was. He had angular cheekbones and a clear, if not slightly rugged, complexion. He was stunning and powerful to look at, and for a few fleeting moments Merryn was lost in his gaze, her eyes now fixed on his deep-brown, intense eyes. She knew that she should look away, but something was giving her the courage to hold her stare for just a few seconds.

"Kerenza," he said, as he brushed her hair away from her eyes with his free hand, "I knew it was you." His voice was calm and controlled. He moved in closer to her face with his own, and breathed in the scent from her skin.

Merryn squirmed and tried to move away, but the wall behind her prevented any backwards movement. She turned her face away from his so that her ear now faced him and she closed her eyes briefly. His hand grasped her face and pulled it toward him, forcing her to look at him. He leant in even further and hovered his lips above Merryn's mouth. He had a fresh, clean scent: a freshly-showered, almost powdery fragrance. Her chest pounded thunderously as she tried to control her breathing. She was determined to not show her true feelings: to not show how scared and out of control she felt.

"You are so beautiful," he whispered. He released his grip on her face, and stroked the side of her cheek gently. As he did so, his eyes moved down her neck to her chest which was rising and falling with her rapid breaths. He lingered for a few seconds, before leaning in and kissing her delicately on the cheek. He then stepped back away from her, but continued to fix his stare on her face. As he turned to walk away, Merryn thought she noticed him half smile.

She did not move for several minutes. It was as if she was cemented to the spot. She reached her hand to the back of her head, and let out a slight "ouch" as she felt the part of her skull that had hit the wall. Her body was shaking and her breathing was heavy. She scraped her hair away from her face with both hands and concentrated on her breaths for a few seconds to calm herself down.

What just happened? Who was he? Why had he called her Kerenza? She stood for a few moments and replayed what had happened again in her mind. Merryn's emotions were mostly indicative of someone who had just been scared out of their wits. However, she was confused: she was intrigued and possibly beguiled by this boy. He was strikingly beautiful, but it wasn't just that. There was something else. Because of this intuition, Merryn knew that there was a small part of her nervous reaction that was strangely due to excitement ... not fear.

As Merryn approached Kitto's Cave, she could hear the thudding of up-tempo music filling the air. She had waited a few minutes before plucking up the courage to leave the alleyway and head for the music cafe where she hoped her friends had arrived and were waiting for her. Her walking pace seemed to grow quicker and quicker as she nervously continued her journey. She had given a few glances backwards: nervous that he would be following her. Her eyes had searched out any alley or possible hiding place that he might use in order to take her by surprise again. Fortunately, there was no sign of him, and she made it to Kitto's Cave safely.

Her group of friends were seated at a large table on the cobbled patio area outside. It was one of the best places to sit as it had comfy seats, and the patio was decorated with an array of multicoloured fairy lights overhead, which gave the area a cosy, relaxed feel.

"Here she is!" Carter announced loudly as Merryn turned the corner to the harbour.

The group turned to look at Merryn as she approached. Xance stood up to pull Merryn's chair out from the table, and slid it closer to his own seat. Before she could sit down, Xance spoke with a concerned tone to his voice,

"Are you ok? You don't look too well." He gently took her arm and led her to the seat that he had saved for her next to him. They sat down. Merryn's eyes were slightly glazed over, and she was not really seeing everything clearly. She was, however, completely aware that the whole group had stopped their conversations and were all now looking at her. Xance rubbed her arm affectionately as he questioned her again: "Did something happen?"

"Yes," Merryn responded, realising that she was causing a fuss, and beginning to feel slightly embarrassed.

Xance leant in a little closer. "It's ok, I'm here. Would you like to go for a walk?"

"No, thanks, don't worry, I'm ok. Someone just grabbed me in the street." Merryn blurted out the information without really thinking it through.

Now as everyone at the table gasped in horror, and almost simultaneously questioned if she was alright, she became acutely aware that some of the friendship group were not Nyss, and she had to be careful with what she said. She continued to tell the group what had happened, leaving out the part where she thought she recognised her assailant.

Xance stood up whilst giving her a reassuring rub on the arm. "Which way did he go? He's not going to get away with this!" he growled in obvious anger. His fists were clenched tightly at his side, and Merryn could see the veins in his arms beginning to rise up underneath the tanned skin of his forearms.

"I'm not sure where he went. I didn't see. Don't worry,

leave it. I'm ok." Merryn stroked Xance's arm in a bid to calm his anger.

"You're not ok. He had no right!" Xance almost shouted.

Merryn could see that some of the other customers on the patio were now taking a keen interest in what was happening at her table. The last thing she wanted was the whole school knowing. Xance left the table and walked around the corner from where Merryn had arrived. Carter and the rest of his male friends followed quickly behind. Merryn left the table too and followed Xance, telling Chloe and the others that she would be back. She turned the corner swiftly, but could barely see Xance and his friends who had made a fast exit into the village and were just visible at the end of the street. Panicking, she yelled, "Xance!" as she began to run towards him.

Xance stopped and turned around. Seeing Merryn, he ran back to meet her.

"Xance, I have to tell you!" Merryn gasped. "I couldn't say in front of the others …"

"Say what?" he questioned anxiously.

Xance was quite clearly agitated and Merryn didn't want to fuel his emotions further, but she also knew that she had to share what she thought she knew with him.

"He was one of *them*," she said quietly.

"Them? Who?" Xance looked puzzled.

"One of those Banas Mihtig. He was at the fight. The dark-haired one," she explained.

"Nix," Xance said through gritted teeth.

"Who?"

"Phoenix Branok … are you certain?" Xance's eyes squinted slightly as his temper began to rise once more.

"I'm sure it was him," Merryn said tentatively, "The dark-haired one that stood at the front," she repeated.

"Ok. Go back to the cafe. Stay with the others. I'll see you there later."

"Xance, please don't do anything stupid. I'm ok, really." Merryn was anxious. She didn't want Xance to get hurt because of her.

"I'll be fine, I promise," Xance turned to run back to his friends.

"Wait! Xance! I forgot to say, he called me Kerenza!" Merryn yelled after him. However, she could not see Xance's eyes narrow with uncontrollable rage, when he heard what she said, as he ran up the street to meet his friends.

19

Waterfall

Xance took Merryn's hand as they ascended the six stone steps leading to the small wooden bridge which straddled a gentle flowing stream. They had walked for around a mile so far, having left the village behind and walked for a while along the coastal path before heading slightly inland to a woodland area. The vegetation was dark-green and lush. Moss and ferns grew up the side of huge rocky inclines and their dampness caused them to sparkle in the sunshine which streaked through the circle of treeless sky above. They walked a little further, Merryn carrying a tote bag in which she had packed towels, snacks and drinks for them both, and Xance with a blanket tucked under one of his arms. She had no idea where they were going as Xance had told her that it was a surprise. She knew that he wanted to spend some time with her after the events of last night. She thought it was sweet how he appeared to care about her. Xance had returned to Kitto's Cave, with his friends, having had no luck finding Nix. He had reassured Merryn that Nix wouldn't get away with what he had done.

As they walked out of the shade of some trees and into the warmth of the sunshine, Merryn could see a small pool of water ahead of them. The trees had given way to bright blue sky allowing the sun to glisten spectacularly on the water's surface. A rocky backdrop rose up from one side of the pool, and the most magnificent waterfall cascaded down, majestically, through the green foliage that clung to the rocks. The sound was both relaxing and uplifting as the water poured rhythmically down the stone and crashed into the clear pool below. Merryn stood with her mouth open and simply stared at the wondrous place.

"What do you think?" Xance questioned, smiling smugly.

"It's just beautiful! I had no idea this place existed," Merryn replied, still unable to remove her gaze from the stunning waterfall.

"Yes, it's tucked away a bit, so only locals tend to come here. It's usually quite quiet, but we're especially lucky to have the place all to ourselves today," Xance said as he placed the blanket on a flat piece of grass just in front of a large cluster of rocks not far from the water's edge.

They sat together and chatted for around an hour, discussing school, assignments and Sefwarian Nyss. Merryn felt relaxed and comfortable in Xance's company; they had a strong connection and she felt completely at ease with him. Merryn rolled onto her stomach so that she could watch the waterfall cascade into the pool. It was at this point that Xance reached into the pocket of his black shorts and took out a small dark-coloured, velvet drawstring bag.

"Merryn, I want you to have this," Xance said nervously as he held out the bag for Merryn to take.

Merryn sat up and turned to face him. "What is it?" She smiled.

"Have a look," Xance said as he put the velvet pouch in her hand.

Merryn looked deep into Xance's eyes as if searching for the answer to her question. He looked back at her anxiously. She slowly untied the knot in the cord at the top of the bag and gently pulled at the cuff to tease it open. As she tipped up the bag, a silver object landed in her palm. It was a ring. Merryn picked up the ring with her other hand and examined it more closely. It was simple in design, having a large, oval blue stone with flecks of gold inside.

"It's beautiful!" Merryn gushed, her cheeks blushing pink, I can't take it though … it looks really expensive," she said as she held the ring out towards Xance. Merryn did not want to appear ungrateful, but she was quite over-whelmed by Xance's generous gesture.

Xance shook his head. "I'm not taking it back, silly," he said smiling, "I want you to have it. You must have it. I really care about you, and I want you to know how special you are to me. I'd like to give it to you as an early birthday present, if that's ok. I know it's not for a few weeks, but I really want you to have this now."

"It's really lovely, Xance, but are you sure? It must have cost you so much money."

"I'm certain. It didn't cost me anything – not really … it was my mum's. My Sefwarian Nyss mum."

"Oh, Xance, no, I definitely can't take it. If it was your mum's, it's so special."

Xance looked directly at Merryn; his crystal blue eyes fixed upon her green eyes. He had always had the ability to look deeply into her, and make her feel that he could see into the depths of her thoughts.

"I know what you're thinking," he said, "but you *are* special."

"No, Xance, I can't."

"Yes, you can. I need you to have it. The stone is a lapis lazuli. Many Nyss women wear them because the stones have the ability to heal naturally, but this ring has additional properties. It's a haelan lind – a shield. It has special powers. Like my bracelet, which does the same thing," Xance explained.

"What kind of special powers?" Merryn was intrigued. She moved the ring between her fingers, eyeing its beauty.

"It can heal illnesses and injuries, and it can slow the ageing process quite considerably. However, its main attribute is the magic within. It has the power to keep you safe and protect you. If you are in danger, you only have to think single-mindedly of the ring, and it will produce a hex to protect you. It also serves as a blocker so that people from Earth do not witness Nyss events or any supernatural happenings. It is an ancient Sefwarian Nyss ring, which belonged to my mum, and her mum before that, I believe. If you wear it, I'll feel more confident that you are safe ... please."

"But it was your mum's – it must be something you treasure."

Xance took hold of Merryn's right hand and delicately placed the ring onto her ring finger, "Yes, I do treasure it – and I treasure you too. Which is why I gave this to you before, many years ago. I had the First Luminary keep it safe for me until I knew I was ready to give it to you once more. It was another reason for my trip to Sefwarian Nyss with you."

"I didn't notice the First Luminary give you anything though," Merryn said, with a slightly confused look on her face.

"Well, that doesn't surprise me at all. You were quite preoccupied and there was a lot to take in." Xance smiled.

Merryn looked down at the ring on her finger, "It really is beautiful, Xance, thank you. I'll look after it, I promise." Merryn reached out with both her arms and embraced Xance.

Xance held her hands and rubbed his thumbs across her skin tenderly. "After what happened with Nix, I don't want to take any chances. If you wear the ring, it will protect you. Promise me that you will wear it, always?" Xance seemed insistent.

"Ok, I will." Merryn smiled. "I did have a thought about what happened though. You know, when I was walking to the cafe before it happened?"

"Yes," Xance was listening intently.

"My Elkalind rune didn't appear. I never felt it and I checked afterwards and it wasn't visible. I thought that you said that it would appear if the Banas Mihtig or anyone from Nethergeard was nearby. You said it was a warning, didn't you?"

"That is how it's supposed to work. Maybe he has a way of blocking it, I ... look, don't worry about that for now. All that matters is that you know to be vigilant and to keep away from Nix, ok?"

"Yes. I understand that, but who is he? You seem to know him. He seemed to know me – he called me Kerenza." Merryn was desperately trying to make sense of what happened.

"Yes, I know him. All you need to know is that he's evil. Let's not use up any more of our time talking about him. Not now. I want to enjoy being with you." Xance smiled.

Merryn smiled back and nodded, but she was unconvinced. Maybe she was mistaken, but she felt that she knew Xance well enough to sense when he was uncomfortable. He definitely appeared to be uneasy about discussing Nix. But why?

Xance stood up and removed his T-shirt, revealing an impressively toned torso that looked as if his muscles had been artistically carved on to his stomach. Merryn tried not to gasp as she observed his strength and beauty. Seemingly unaware of her awe, Xance playfully threw his T-shirt at Merryn. She giggled and squealed, "Oi!"

"Come on, let's go in," said Xance, as he began to remove his shorts to reveal a slightly shorter, thinner pair of swim shorts and his Nyss rune tattoo just above the crease at the bottom of his torso.

"Really?" Merryn was unsure whether Xance was serious.

"Yes, come on! I need to cool down." Xance walked forwards and stepped into the pool of clear water.

"Is it cold?" Merryn asked as she removed her outer clothing. As Xance had told her that they may be swimming, she had put on her black bikini underneath her shorts and sun top.

"It's ok once you're in," he replied whilst gently splashing and flicking water up at Merryn playfully. She entered the water slowly to give herself time to adjust to the cooler temperature, moving carefully and pausing after each step. When she felt more comfortable, she lowered herself into the pool. She gasped and laughed as the cool water lapped over her shoulders. The two of them alternated between swimming calmly, and splashing water over each other playfully. They laughed, swam and splashed until they were exhausted.

Xance swam towards Merryn, took her gently by the waist and pulled her close to him. She felt a flutter in her body as the skin of his torso met hers. He moved the pair of them towards the waterfall and Merryn had to catch her breath as the water plunged down onto their heads, soaking her hair and face. As they recovered and moved out of the stream of water, she brushed her wet hair away from her face.

Xance kept one hand on Merryn's waist whilst he flicked his hair away from his face with one hand. The water was now falling just behind them, a torrent of foaming white against the green and grey of the foliage and rocks. Xance pulled Merryn to him. He looked deep into her with his piercing blue eyes. He stroked her soaked hair and drew her face nearer to his. They kissed. His lips were strong on Merryn's mouth, but there was a gentle tenderness that made her feel that he really cared for her. She wanted to be close to him. She loved this feeling. Her hands reached down to the small of his back and she massaged his skin as she pulled him in closer to her body. Xance moved his lips away from hers, and traced a pathway of gentle, but firm, kisses across her cheek, past her ear and then down her neck. Merryn responded by leaning her head backwards allowing him to reach her clavicle and shoulders. She moaned quietly as his tongue flicked and moved lower across the top of her chest. It felt warm in contrast to the cool water that now ran down her skin. She moved her hands round to Xance's chest and caressed the firmness of his torso. She allowed her fingers to follow the centre line of his body down towards the top of his swim shorts. Lifting her head forwards again, she nuzzled Xance's neck and cheek until her lips found his again, and they kissed passionately once more. Xance moved his hands to Merryn's cheeks and he held her face affectionately as they continued the kiss. Merryn then leant away from Xance, arching her back and allowing him to plant an array of kisses down her neck and through the centre of her breasts to her torso. His kisses were more powerful now, and his arms wrapped around her as if he did not want to let her go. Merryn's head was being lightly splashed by the tumbling of the water off the rocks, but she didn't seem to care. She stroked and teased at the crease of muscle where his Nyss rune lay, just below his waistband. She was now aware, and could physically feel, that Xance was all consumed and immersed in this moment of uncontrollable passion as he pressed himself against her. Merryn too was engulfed with a desperate need to be closer to Xance. He made her feel so special. The touch of his body against hers, and his tongue and lips on her skin made her tremble. More than this, now, though, her whole being seemed to have been taken over by an uncontrollable force.

There was no sensible reasoning – she was in the moment. Merryn wanted Xance fully. Right now. She felt that nothing would ever feel better than this. She kissed him intensely on the lips whilst running her hands through his wet hair. He appeared to reciprocate her ardour; responding with stronger, deeper movements with his tongue and lips. Merryn was out of control now, and was being carried entirely by her emotions. Underneath the water, she could feel his pelvis pressed hard against her, and she knew this physical reaction to their embrace alluded to his undeniable excitement and desire for her.

Just then, as if something had flicked a switch in Xance's head he moved slightly away from Merryn and looked into her eyes.

"Merryn, I want to be with you, but we shouldn't just yet," he gently stroked her skin.

She could see his chest rising and falling as he tried to gain control of his breathing and emotions.

"I'm sorry, I … you make me feel …" Merryn started to speak, but she suddenly became overwhelming aware of what had just happened, and was completely embarrassed that she had allowed herself to become so carried away in the moment when Xance's feelings obviously didn't echo hers.

She now had a crushing feeling in the pit of her stomach. She looked into Xance's eyes, desperately trying to see if they would give away his true feelings. "You don't feel the same way … I'm so sorry, Xance," Merryn managed to say, bowing her face towards the water awkwardly.

"Of course I feel the same way!" Xance took her face gently in his hands and looked at her affectionately, "I want you more than anything, but I just think we should wait a while. I need you to be sure. I would feel so bad if you had any regrets. I don't want you to be confused by your previous feelings for me. It's very easy for our emotions to be obscured by the things we experienced in our past. I want you to be clear that what you are feeling is *real.* You need to be sure that your affection is for me *right now*, in the present, does that make sense?"

"I guess," Merryn said sheepishly.

"We have lots of time." Xance smiled at her reassuringly.

Merryn nodded.

Xance reached out and embraced her reassuringly. "I love you, Merryn. I've always loved you."

He hadn't said that to her before, but Merryn liked hearing it. Her heart fluttered at the sound of the words. She knew that she felt the same way, and her response was entirely natural, "I love you, too," she said, blinking away a single tear as she placed her head on Xance's chest.

2 0

She watched from across the harbour as the tiny, amber lights dotted and danced through the blackness. After several minutes, the lights seem to accumulate at the large white house high up on the tor. She watched as they seem to move from room to room: remaining still for a few moments before moving once more into another space in the house. Then all she could see was black before the sound of violent thrashing water filled her ears.

NOW SHE WAS STANDING in a small cave: surrounded by dark rock on all sides. She could see the rock reaching up in an uneven arch above the water; one side had a rather acute slant, rising almost completely vertically from the ground, then curving widely and magnificently at the roof of the cave and down to a small stone path on the other side. Ice-cold sea water lashed and snarled at her legs and feet. It landed in white foams, gushing, waving and slapping at the hard, rocky surface beneath her. Squinting her eyes, she could just see the form of what appeared to be a person below her, in the water. As she thudded her knees down onto the hard, wet ground, she felt an intense pain shoot through her legs. She leant forwards into the darkness and out across the water, trying to steady herself with one hand on the rock below. The skin on her knees tore and ripped as she thrashed her arm from side to side, attempting to make contact with the form in the water.

SOMETHING BEAT against her hand in a downwards motion. She clenched her fingers together in a bid to grab whoever it was, but a wave of freezing water hit her fully in the face, causing her to lose purchase on the ground below as her hand slipped in the wet. She tumbled forwards, smashing her body into the ground, and her face, now centimetres from the surface of the water, was again engulfed for a few seconds by the sea. Sliding herself backwards to safety, she tried once more to reach out her arm and grab the flailing body, but suddenly, there was silence. Total, eerie quietness. The water stilled and the only sound was her heavy breathing as she lay on her stomach on the drenched rocks.

Now, before her sat a large, brown chest-like box. It had metal hinges and a key-hole at the front. One side of the box had visible damage; a large crack ran from one corner to the other. She lifted the lid, and instantly her face lit up with the reflective glow of the impressive contents of the box. It was full of gleaming gold and silver objects: coins, rings, necklaces adorned *with brightly coloured gem stones. She grabbed at the haul. Picking up a handful, she allowed the precious objects to slide from her hand and cascade back into the box.*

2 1

Spirit

Merryn woke abruptly. She stared up at the ceiling of her bedroom and blinked her eyes several times at the darkness. Her dreams had become more and more frequent of late, and she was becoming increasingly disturbed by their clarity. They appeared so real and each time she slept, they became more and more vivid.

She reached across to her lamp and clicked the switch. A warm, hazy, glow emanated from beneath the light-shade, and Merryn squinted slightly as her eyes adjusted to the light. She was hot. It was a particularly warm night for the time of year anyway, but the stress of her dream had definitely added to her rising temperature. She slid out of bed and over to her desk where she pressed the button on the fan. The blades began to spin quickly, and a gentle whir could be heard as the cool breeze migrated across the room. She stood for a moment and allowed the draught from the fan to cool her. She bent down nearer to it, and blasted her face with the air for a few seconds.

Merryn walked over to the window and opened it wide. The air outside was warm, still and calm, and she soon realised the act of opening the window was entirely futile. She leant onto the window sill and looked out. It was the early hours of the morning, and the village was silent and peaceful. She could see the small vessels in the harbour, which were being illuminated by the brightness of the moonlight, sleeping quietly on the surface of the water, and an owl could be heard somewhere off in the distance. She allowed the scene from her window to distract her from her dreams for a while; enjoying the soothing calm of the quiet of the night.

Her mind drifted back to Xance and their time at the waterfall. It had become commonplace for Merryn's thoughts to be dominated by Xance in recent weeks. He was virtually all she could think about in the moments when her time was not taken up with studying, and even then she would find herself daydreaming about him; her mind wandering off to picture Xance's smile, his blonde hair or his muscular forearms. Sometimes, whilst staring at her books she could almost smell his clean, fresh scent. Her eyes would close for a few seconds and she could imagine him there with her. Her preoccupation with him was, at times, overwhelming. She knew that she had known him just a short while, but it didn't feel that way. She felt as if he had been with her forever – she could barely remember what her life had been like before Xance.

Of course, there was all their history together before; something that Merryn was wholly aware of. But accepting all the information about her past had been challenging for Merryn. The details that Xance had shared with her, of Sefwarian Nyss and Nethergeard, of magic and powers and migrating gestords was fantastical. These were not stories that Merryn would usually allow herself to be taken in by, yet she had witnessed events and experienced visions that she knew could have no logical explanation in the world in which she had grown up.

In the pool, at the waterfall, she had become so consumed by Xance; desperate for his touch, which she received with delightful rapture. She had been entranced by him, and her want of him had transitioned into a *need*. She had found herself craving a closeness with him that would have taken their relationship to a place of no return. Merryn knew that her actions and behaviour in that moment were unusual for her. She was not usually impetuous. She was the one who would always be cautious, sometimes a little too much. Everything had to be thought through and considered carefully. There was no room for error or mistakes; she wouldn't be able to live with the regret of the result of foolish choices.

Xance had quite rightly questioned whether her heightened emotions could have been a result of their previous time together. Merryn knew, as her actions were so incredibly out of character for her, that Xance was probably correct, and that there had undoubtedly been a blurring of her emotions. However, she was also aware that she knew her own mind. She was resolute that she was fully in control of her feelings, and that she knew how she felt about Xance. Maybe her emotions from past to present had become interwoven, but she didn't care. *She knew how she felt about Xance.* She was, however, increasingly plagued by the notion that Xance had an ulterior motive for bringing the possibility of her confused sentiment to her attention, and that he may not wish to reciprocate her depth of commitment.

Several minutes had passed when Merryn, once again, had on overwhelming feeling that she was not alone in her room. She had no idea where this sense had come from, but she could feel the presence of something or someone behind her. A feeling of eyes on her back; watching. Her heart began to quicken. It thudded in her chest and pounded through her ears. Her face became instantly hot. She turned around slowly.

As she did so, she could see a person seated at the bottom end of her bed. She knew that it was a person because of its general shape, however, the figure was far from clear. It appeared hazy and fuzzy as if she was looking at it through a very dirty or wet window. Merryn was petrified. She was unable to move from her position by the window sill, her eyes fixated on the blurred form before her. The thundering in her ears, as her heart beat faster and faster, was all that she could hear.

As she stared, the image began to focus and Merryn could now see that the figure was female and wearing a pale-coloured long dress. The neckline of the garment was scooped low, and a row of small buttons rose up vertically from the waist area. Also, it was now possible to see that she had long, brown hair which was styled in a loose, single plait to the side of her head. Merryn blinked. *This cannot be real.*

She blinked again in the hope that when her eyes re-opened the vision would have gone. It was at this moment, that Merryn noticed the entity move. It appeared to turn towards her, shifting itself on her bed. Merryn could now see clearly the face of a young girl staring at her. She looked to be possibly late teens or early twenties at the most, but it was difficult to tell as her clothing didn't seem to be from the present era. Merryn's heart was racing now. She was still unable to move; fear was gripping her, and all she was able to do was stare in disbelief. The girl moved again. Merryn watched, motionless, as she appeared to place her hands to the centre of her breastbone, laying them flat and slightly overlapping her fingers. She bowed her head as if looking at her hands then looked up at Merryn once more.

All of a sudden, Merryn began to see vivid images in her mind. As had happened before, the images played like a series of short film excerpts, jolting abruptly from one to another in quick succession: The white house up on the tor; Porthrosen church at Church Cove next to the beach; yellow lights blinking in the blackness of the headland; a covered pathway, dark and winding; a cave with water. The images cycled repeatedly in Merryn's vision. Then they were gone. She blinked and strained her eyes slightly, attempting to regain clear focus on the dimly-lit room. The girl was now standing at the side of the bed. She smiled at Merryn; a kind, delicate, gentle smile as her shape began to blur once more. Within seconds, her form had become an indistinct haze. Merryn observed as it began to fade and then eventually had disappeared completely.

She let out a large, loud breath, and slumped to the floor in a crumpled, distraught heap. She breathed loudly, in and out, her chest rising high as she seemed to gasp for more air. She had not noticed that she had been holding her breath almost the entire time that the spirit had been present.

Having sat for a while and allowed herself to calm down, Merryn started to consider what had happened. This person that she had seen had to be a ghost or spirit of some kind. There was no other explanation. She had always had an open mind to whether ghosts actually existed or not, and had occasionally had debates with her parents about the subject. She thought that it was strange that the presence seemed to be in her room around the time that she had been dreaming. She racked her brains trying to remember if she had felt the presence previously around the same time that she had dreamt about the cave and the water and the drowning person. She concluded that she had, and that the two events were inextricably linked. What Merryn needed to know now was *how*.

22

First Winnan

The school library was unusually busy for a Monday lunchtime. This level of activity would often be seen only on a Friday, when most assignments were due to be handed in. There was a gentle hum of quietened chatter, coupled with the occasional laughter from a group of year nine girls who were positioned behind a bookshelf in the far corner. Merryn was trying desperately to complete her maths work, but was finding it difficult to concentrate. She would have loved to have apportioned blame on the hive of movement and sound around her, but she knew that her inability to concentrate was in part due to lack of sleep and partly due to her, almost incessant, reverie of Xance. She watched as the librarian strode over to the noisy girls and gave them a hushed, but firm warning before swiftly tidying a stack of books and then gliding back to her desk, where a queue of students had formed awaiting her attention.

Merryn flicked back and forth through her textbook searching for the solution to a maths problem that was giving her particular trouble.

The sound of a stack of books thudding onto the table in front of her broke her from her apparent fruitless search. Merryn jumped at the unexpected noise and looked up to see Emily Harper staring at her menacingly. She was accompanied by her constant companions, Orla, Anna and Isla, who stood in a supportive semi-circle behind her; like a bastion of strength.

"I suppose you think you're better than me, don't you?" Emily snarled at Merryn through partly gritted teeth.

"Excuse me?" Was the only response that Merryn could think of, as Emily's comment took her by surprise.

"You think, you've got one over on me," Emily added, as her friends smirked in encouragement.

"I don't know what you mean," Merryn said quietly.

"He won't stay with you. He and I have had a bond since we were small. You're just a phase. An amusement. It won't last."

"Oh! Xance," Merryn said, realising that Xance had clearly informed Emily that they were seeing each other. She smiled inwardly. Not because she wanted to be smug or hurt Emily (even though she probably deserved it), but because it was the confirmation that she needed that Xance was serious about her. She now felt that all her doubting and questioning of his true feelings had been superfluous, as his apparent conversation with Emily had confirmed what she had been hoping for.

She deliberated for a few seconds; searching for a suitable retort, whilst Emily glared at her through narrowed eyes. Merryn did not wish to get into an argument with Emily. She was conscious that her dad had been ill, and although she had been told that he had now made a good recovery, it did not sit right with her to fall out and argue with someone who had recently experienced such a trauma. In addition, as it was clear that Xance had obviously made his feelings clear to Emily, feuding with her seemed childish.

"Look, Emily, I really don't want to argue with you, and I'm trying to work," Merryn said as forcefully as she could without trying to sound aggressive or antagonistic. She pretended to go back to looking through her textbook, flicking through the pages erratically.

Emily leant forward intimidatingly across the table. She glowered at Merryn and hissed, "I'm serious – back off!"

"You back off!" a male voice barked at Emily.

Merryn looked to her right to see Tyler standing there, his bag slung over his shoulder, and a stack of books in his arms. He did not look at her; his eyes were fixed upon Emily. He pursed his lips as he continued to eye her disdainfully. Merryn was shocked to watch Emily fling her hair over her shoulder and, without uttering another word, strut off with her friends in dutiful tow behind her.

Merryn let out a large breath of air and smiled at Tyler, "Wow – you are going to have to let me know your secret," she laughed.

"There's no secret, you've just got to be firm with bullies. It's the only language they understand." Tyler grinned. He sat down next to Merryn placing his books on the table.

"Yes, I know you're right. She's obviously reeling from learning that Xance and I are together." Merryn instantly regretted her sentence. She looked down at her textbook and picked at the corner of a page to avoid making eye contact with Tyler. She felt awkward sharing this information with him as she was still unclear about whether his interest in her was purely friendship or whether he wanted it to be something more.

She realised, from Tyler's response that she needn't have worried. "That's great that you two have got together. Emily will just have to get used to it, won't she? Just ignore her – and if you have any more problems from her, let me know."

"Thanks, Tyler – I will." Merryn smiled.

"Look, I'm disturbing you, I'll let you get on with your work," Tyler said as he stood up and gathered up his pile of books.

"No, it's ok, you're not. I wasn't really getting much done anyway – I can't concentrate. You look like you are going to be busy," Merryn said, eyeing the selection of books in Tyler's arms.

"Yes. I've got a shared project to do with … erm … Amelie," he said smiling sheepishly.

"Amelie? I didn't know you even knew her that well." Merryn beamed at him.

"Yeah, we go way back, and we've been getting closer recently, but it's early days, you know?"

Merryn smiled and nodded.

"I'd better get going, see you later – and don't forget what I said, if Emily gives you any more trouble, you know where I am."

Merryn watched as he walked away towards the exit. She smiled to herself. Perhaps that's why Amelie had kept dashing off to the library all those times, so that she could meet up with Tyler. Now she thought about it, it made perfect sense. It was a mystery to Merryn why Amelie had been so secretive about her blossoming romance with Tyler, but then if it was early days, why would she say anything? Plus, Merryn knew, if she was honest with herself, that she had been more than preoccupied with the events of her own life, and that maybe she just hadn't made Amelie feel that she could share this with her just yet.

MERRYN HAD TOLD Xance about the episode with Emily in the library as they alighted the bus on the way home from school. She could sense that he was not happy about this incident, but she had a feeling from observing the expression on his face, that he was as equally annoyed with Emily as he was with Tyler for intervening and helping her resolve the conflict. She was aware that Xance seemed to be very protective of her, perhaps she was making too much of it, but it appeared that he wasn't too keen on her friendship with Tyler. She was looking forward to spending some time with Xance alone, and was hoping to be able to lift his mood. They had arranged to meet at the harbour after dinner.

The evening was warm and the sky was a cloudless blue. Xance held her hand as they chatted and walked up to the Koyt. This was one of Merryn's favourite places. It was usually peaceful, apart from the occasional dog walker, but the main reason that Merryn liked this spot was because this was where she had first spoken to Xance. This was a place that pointed to their history. She hadn't known it at the time, but it had been a significant location from her past, and for this reason she was drawn to the headland, and the Koyt in particular.

They picked a spot on the grass just in front of the Koyt, choosing to sit in the sun. Xance, removed his T-shirt and used it as a pillow underneath his head as he laid down next to Merryn and basked in the warm sunshine. She sat and looked out to sea, observing a huge tanker sailing way off on the horizon, and trying not to be distracted by Xance's bare torso. The sun glinted beauti-fully on the surface of the water, and waves crashed gently, white and frothy, against the isolated rocks which rose proud from the sea just off the point of the headland.

After a few tranquil moments, Merryn spoke: "I have something to tell you. I dreamt again and then ..." she started, but faltered because she feared what she was about to say would sound ridiculous.

"What did you dream this time?" Xance sat up and faced Merryn, clearly interested in what she had to share.

Merryn described the events of the previous evening in her bedroom. She explained the dream, recalling every detail to Xance. She then told him of the girl who had appeared to her, and of how she had experienced the visions. Xance listened intently and didn't interrupt.

"Xance, I think the visions are like the ones that I had before. I think that they are linked to reality; they're my memories from the past."

"Yes, that sounds feasible. It's also most likely that the girl spirit you saw is someone from our past. It's quite common for Nyss to enter the spirit world after death, and to be able to communicate from there. It is possible that you are connected to her in some way, and that she is prompting your visions."

"Do you mean, she's trying to tell me something?" Merryn's voice echoed her confusion.

"Possibly. She certainly seems to be linked to your dreams. As you have already highlighted, your visions are most probably linked to a memory that you have hidden within your gestord. You just need to work out what all the information means." Xance leant forwards and kissed her lightly on the lips. He looked deep into her eyes, "We'll work it out, don't worry," he added as he tenderly moved a strand of her hair away from her face with his hand.

It was then that Merryn noticed the Elkalind rune on Xance's arm. She stroked it with her fingers, "Xance, your Elkalind rune ..."

He twisted the top of his arm round slightly so that he could see the rune, "I thought I could feel it tingling," he said.

Merryn held up her own wrist as it started to prickle and throb; her rune was clearly visible now too. Shocked, they looked at each other; both of them knowing what this meant.

Suddenly, they saw a light-purple glow beginning to radiate from the Koyt. Merryn knew that this glow heralded a transition through the Koyt's egress. As there was no one else standing before it, this could only mean one thing. Someone was about to enter Porthrosen via the Koyt!

Without speaking, they both scrambled up. Xance grabbed Merryn's arm and pulled her towards a large clump of bushes to the right of the coastal path. He hurriedly put his T-shirt back on and they ducked down just far enough to cover their presence, but allowing them to peer over the top and observe. Merryn's heart raced as she watched the glow of the Koyt become darker and brighter. The three large stones now appeared to be completely enveloped in the purple light.

Suddenly, from out of the glow stepped a Banas Mihtig soldier. He was swiftly followed by another then another, until eventually six of them stood in a cluster. They were quite a spectacle when standing en masse. Their black, military, double-breasted jackets creating a powerful, uniform presence. Each one of them held a spear-like weapon in their hands; a black, metal stick with a wide, arrow-like, silver point at one end. On their feet, were heavy, black boots with sturdy soles.

"Maddox, Nix," Xance whispered under his breath, "What are they doing here again? They obviously want trouble."

The soldiers moved off, walking in unison and staying in close proximity to each other. It was strange to watch them, their movement like one entity: fluid and effortless. They turned and headed straight for where Merryn was hidden with Xance. She felt him grab her hand as he pulled her lower behind the shrubs they were using as a screen. She found herself holding her breath; her heart pulsing rapidly. She listened to the Banas Mihtig soldiers make their way past their hideout in the shrubbery, and head off down the coastal path towards the village.

Once they were alone again, Xance took out his phone and messaged Carter.

"Come on. I've told him to meet us in the village with the others." He reached into his shorts pocket and took out his cemp. Merryn did the same, clutching hers tightly in her right hand.

She stayed close to Xance, and, keeping a safe distance, they followed the unwelcome visitors down the path and towards the village.

Once there, the pursuit became tricky as they had to remain far enough away to not be seen by the Banas Mihtig, but this made it difficult to keep them in sight as they navigated the many twists and turns of the tiny streets. They hid behind a collection of waste bins whilst waiting to be able to continue their pursuit. When enough time had passed, they moved off down the cobbled street staying as close to the buildings as possible. However, on turning the next corner, they realised that they had lost the Banas Mihtig. There was no sign of them. Xance ran the few metres to the far end of the road. Merryn could see him up ahead as he turned in all directions desperately trying to catch sight of them. As he began to walk back towards her, she knew that the soldiers had gone.

"We've lost them," he said, clearly exasperated.

Merryn heard Xance's phone buzz. She watched as he read the message and then sent a quick reply.

"The others are at the harbour, I said we'd meet them," he explained.

Having met up with Carter and the others, a plan was made to split up and search for the Nethergeard soldiers. They went off in pairs, scouring every corner of the village, to no avail.

After around an hour or so, it was decided that they should gather up at the Koyt to discuss what to do next, concluding that the Banas Mihtig had left. Darkness was closing in as they all sat down on the grass, exhausted and hot.

"I want to know what they're doing here again," Carter said. "Xance, did you hear anything from the First Luminary yet? Do they have any idea what's going on?"

"I haven't heard from him. I'll contact him again tomorrow," Xance replied. "I'll let him know that we've seen them again."

Harry spoke. "There has to be a reason why they keep coming here."

"It makes me think that they are here for a specific reason, and it doesn't appear to involve us," Luke added.

"Why do you think that?" Xance questioned.

"Because they've been here several times now, and they haven't gone out of their way to seek us out. It's like they don't want us to know that they're here," Luke explained.

"You've got a point," Xance agreed. "They have definitely been elusive during their visits to Porthrosen. If they were looking for trouble with us, you'd think that they would be more antagonistic – more obvious, but they've been sneaking around and hiding. There's absolutely more to this. Something's not right."

The group all nodded and gestured in agreement with Xance.

"We need to get some more information, Xance," Carter said.

Xance nodded, "I'll sort it tomorrow."

The group gradually stood up one after the other and began to disperse onto the path heading back towards the harbour. All of a sudden, Carter, who was at the front of them all, turned around and began to run back up the coastal path. In the growing darkness, it was difficult to see, but as he ran, he gestured with his arms for the others to retreat too. They did so, and gathered together by the Koyt, each one of them poised in nervous anticipation: their cemps clutched ready in their hands.

Merryn's nerves were fuelling her adrenaline. She was finding it difficult to keep her body from shaking; the arm in which she held her cemp was beating rhythmically against her thigh. She knew that there was about to be a conflict, a "winnan" as the Nyss called it. Her Elkalind rune, clearly visible on her wrist, signalled that the Banas Mihtig were in close proximity. Merryn had studied and practised using her cemp-edge. She had worked tirelessly with Chloe on many occasions to hone her weaponry skills and channel her previous knowledge of wielding the cemp-edge. This was it. She was going to be expected to fight! All she could hope for was that her hidden gestord would allow her to remember what she knew about combat, otherwise she feared that this was going to end badly.

In reality, only seconds had passed before the Banas Mihtig soldiers came into view, however, to Merryn, as she stood apprehensively awaiting their imminent arrival, it felt more like minutes. Xance was standing at the front of their group alongside Carter. Merryn noticed him glance backwards and give her a reassuring look, but he didn't smile. She knew that he was entirely focussed on the impending and inevitable winnan. Maddox and Nix walked ahead of the rest of the Nethergeard soldiers. They didn't seem fazed by the sight of the Nyss group, who stood steadfast.

Xance spoke first. His voice forceful and authoritative, "You've got no right to be here, Maddox. None of you have. You've been warned before that you are breaking the pact that was made between Nethergeard and Sefwarian Nyss."

Maddox hissed back at him, "Yeah, well, that pact was made a long time ago. Maybe I've got a short memory."

"You need to leave. Now! We're not negotiating. You and the rest of the Banas Mihtig know how this works," Xance said, angrily as he cast his eyes across the assemblage of soldiers.

Unwavering in his stance, he continued, "The pact was made for a reason – to keep peace between our worlds. If you won't leave peacefully, and stay away, we will have no choice but to use force." Xance took a step forward towards Maddox.

"I told you before, we're just visiting. There's no need

to be so defensive. We won't bother you," Maddox sneered at Xance.

"Well now, you see, that's not acceptable, is it, Carter?" Xance glanced to his side as his friend stepped forwards to stand next to him.

"Not at all," Carter added. "You see, we've kept our side of the bargain. You've had no trouble from us for years. Let's be honest, we all know that you are here for a reason, and whatever it is, it's not going to be good. You're trouble. Always have been. Now go home and don't come back!"

Merryn's heart was in her mouth. The thumping of her blood was almost deafening in her ears, and she was straining to hear the details of the conversation playing out before her. She was conscious that Xance's patience was being tested and the winnan was now assured.

"What if we don't want to?" Maddox smiled nastily, having first looked briefly over his shoulder at his comrades.

As he spoke, the four of them moved slightly forwards to show their support of his defiance.

"Then I'm afraid, we're going to have to make you leave," Xance responded angrily as his arm tensed, and a sudden light of deep green appeared explosively from his cemp.

All at once, the rest of his friends activated their cempedges too, and an array of arced colours was now visible throughout the group. Merryn's weapon glowed an iridescent blue-green at her side; her hand clinging so tightly to her cemp that her knuckles had turned white, and the veins in the back of her hand strained through her skin.

Then it began. Carter struck the first blow directly at Maddox. The two of them engaged in an aggressive exchange of strikes. Xance was second to join in, focussing his efforts towards Nix. His battering of him was relentless as he rained down strike after strike in Nix's direction. Nix was at first forced backwards by the attack, but as Xance paused, Nix managed to gather himself and pressed forwards towards his opponent, thrusting his spear aggressively. At one moment, Xance lost his footing and stumbled to the ground, causing him to land on his back on the grass. His attacker's spear plunged towards his chest and he beat it away with his hand. It thrust towards him once more, this time it narrowly missed his bicep. Xance's response to this near-miss was to kick Nix fully in his chest using both his feet. Nix flew backwards and landed in an awkward heap at the base of a large bush.

Chloe had stayed with Merryn. The two of them worked in tandem to thrash one of the soldiers, who had wasted no time in running at them, his spear held aloft. He had swung first at Merryn who, fortunately, was agile enough to duck quickly and miss the strike. This appeared to throw the soldier off balance, and as he crashed to the floor, unceremoniously landing on his face, Chloe used this to her advantage and struck at his back with her weapon. As the orange glow of her cemp-edge made contact, he let out a roar of pain. He quickly recovered, rolling onto his back and somehow flipping himself instantly back up onto his feet. He steadied himself and leant forwards menacingly. Chloe and Merryn stood side by side, their swords thrust out in front of them defensively. Merryn was aware that there was a fury of movement all around her, and she was finding it difficult not to think about whether Xance had been hurt or not. She forced herself to focus as she lunged forwards at her opponent.

As the fight had developed, Merryn felt more confident in her movement and weaponry skills. It had appeared that the very act of combat had released within her the memories that she had of her gestord and former self. To any onlooker, she appeared to be a fierce warrior. In fact, as Merryn was now learning, her practical warfare skills were exemplary, and she was proving to be a formidable adversary for any of the Banas Mihtig soldiers. She glanced around quickly and observed three of the enemy soldiers had been put out of action, at least temporarily, as they lay in a crumpled heap on the floor. Carter and most of the others were now encircling an opponent in a forbidding manner. Xance was still engaged in his lengthy combat with Nix: a relentless battle of, apparently, equally skilled warriors; neither of them displaying any weakness.

Without her knowledge, Maddox had circled round behind the Koyt, and was now looming behind Merryn. Without warning, he grabbed her from behind, throwing his left arm around her throat and pulling her in to his body. The move took her completely by surprise and she let out a loud yell in shock. She thrust her bottom backwards, bending herself forwards, in an attempt to release herself from Maddox's grip. Her shout stopped Xance and the others dead in their tracks. They all swung round in unison to see Maddox holding a spear dangerously close to her body. Nix saw his chance, and in the seconds that followed, as he appeared to realise that they had the upper hand, he ran to join Maddox; the rest of his comrades not far behind him. Merryn struggled and writhed under the pressure of Maddox's arm.

"I wouldn't," Maddox warned her, "I've put down bigger than you."

He pressed the spear's point against her ribs and she yelled out as it ripped her skin. She could feel the blood beginning to ooze from the small wound and knew that she should stay still, if she wanted to survive.

Xance and the others had moved in closer to Merryn. She could see the stress in all their faces as they approached, and this added to her anxiety; confirming her fears that she was in real trouble.

"Let her go, Maddox!" Xance demanded.

Maddox tightened his grip on her throat, and Merryn was now battling to breathe under the pressure. Both her hands were gripping Maddox's arm, but she did not want to give the impression of resistance for fear of him driving the blade of his spear into her again.

"Back off, Xance," Maddox hissed, "I'll kill her. You know I will!" He nuzzled his nose intimidatingly into the side of her face, and Merryn squinted her eyes and cheeks up in disgust as she felt his skin touch hers and his white-blond hair rest against her forehead. His hand tightened a little more on her throat and her battle for air intensified.

Merryn could see that Carter was aware of Xance's intense anxiety. She watched as he ushered Xance backwards slightly into the fold of the group. Perhaps he thought Xance may act too impulsively under the circumstances, she thought.

"Let her go, Maddox," Carter said calmly but assertively as he stepped towards him. "Just you and me, come on," he gestured with his hands encouraging Maddox to step forwards to fight.

Merryn looked directly at Xance who seemed to be mouthing something to her. She was in real difficulty now. The constant pressure on her throat was starting to cause her vision to fade in and out. She could see that Xance was trying to tell her something, but it was difficult to focus long enough to grasp the words. She blinked slowly, trying desperately to see Xance's lips clearly. The dizziness in her head indicating that she was about to lose consciousness. Digging deep, she closed her eyes once more, knowing that this may be her last chance to see the word that Xance was desperately trying to communicate to her. She opened her eyes and fixed them on Xance. *Ring.* Ring? Ring! Was he saying "ring"?

Merryn directed all her thoughts to the lapis lazuli ring which she was wearing on her right hand. For a second, her vision went black and she lost consciousness, but on opening her eyes once more, she tried to re-focus on her ring. Within a fleeting moment, a tiny cracking sound was heard and a light resembling a small spark flashed near Merryn's hand. Maddox winced with obvious discomfort and Merryn found herself free for a split second or two. Her freedom was short-lived however, as Nix grabbed her by the arm and pulled her to him, stepping backwards away from Maddox as he did so.

Merryn was too weak to fight him, and she allowed herself to be enveloped in his strong arms. She could feel his breath on her neck and face as he held onto her. Xance made a move forward, heading for Merryn, but he stopped abruptly when Nix moved one of his hands to grip Merryn's throat and dramatically shook his head in Xance's direction.

"I've got you now," Nix spoke quietly into Merryn's ear, "Don't struggle."

Meanwhile, Carter had advanced on Maddox, who had initially fallen to the floor after receiving the shock from Merryn's ring, and the two were now engaged in battle once more. Carter's red cemp-edge blazing brightly against Maddox's black and silver spear. The two fighters were evenly matched and it was due only to the fact that Maddox was disarmed, as he tripped on an uneven piece of earth, that it came to such an abrupt and fairly swift end. Merryn watched as Xance grabbed Maddox and pulled him to his feet by the throat, whilst Carter wielded his cemp-edge as a warning.

"You and your mates will leave here now and you won't return," Xance said forcefully, his face just inches away from Maddox's face. He turned to address the other soldiers, "Leave, now!"

None of the Banas Mihtig moved. They stared at Maddox as if waiting for instruction. Xance shook Maddox, still holding him by the neck as Carter raised his cemp-edge threateningly.

"Leave! Go! Now!" Maddox yelled.

The soldiers did as they were instructed and walked quickly to the Koyt. Within seconds, the purple glow of the egress emanated from the large stones. One by one, the Banas Mihtig disappeared into the Koyt, leaving behind Maddox and Nix. Merryn found herself pushed forward towards Xance as Nix stepped towards the purple haze. Once she was safely in the company of her friends, she watched Xance walk Maddox to the Koyt and thrust him towards the stones. The purple glow consumed both Nix and Maddox, and they disappeared into the safety of the purple mist.

Phoenix

Merryn leant back against the front door of her home, having closed it quietly behind her. She was exhausted. It was past eleven thirty and she was aware that the rest of her family had gone to bed. The house was in darkness apart from the warm glow of the lamp in the lounge, which oozed its light through into the hallway where she stood. She had managed to message her mum that she would be late home and that she was safe with Xance, yet she still didn't want the drama that would ensue if she woke up everyone on her return.

As she stood still for a moment, she recalled how neither of them had spoken much as Xance walked her back, but she had felt that he was holding her hand just a little tighter than usual, which indicated to her that he was still fired-up from the fight. He'd reassured her that her ring would heal the wound that she had sustained from Maddox, and that she should wear it overnight to give it time to work. Then he'd kissed her gently and pulled her in to hug her and stroked her hair, before walking off down the path towards the harbour.

Merryn heard a quiet tap on the door behind her. Then another two. Quiet but quick. Thinking that Xance had forgotten something, she quietly unlocked the door. Looking out into the darkness of the night, she had expected to find Xance standing before her, yet he was not there.

As she leant out, past the door frame glancing right and then left, she found herself being pulled out of the house by her arm. She let out a quiet squeal in shock as she was dragged in to the night by a dark figure. A warm hand covered her mouth preventing her from making any more sounds. Within a few seconds, she found herself in the side garden of the cottage. The soft cream hue from the street light on the nearby public path provided enough illumination for Merryn now see who this person was as he released his hold on her and uncovered her mouth.

"Don't scream, I'm not going to hurt you," Nix said quickly.

Merryn backed away shaking her head in disbelief. "What the hell are you doing here?" she whispered.

Her heart was thumping rapidly within her chest and she was trying desperately to control her breathing. She wondered how far away Xance was, but soon realised that he would be long gone by now. Her hand reached into her pocket and seized her cemp. She noticed Nix's eyes flick towards her pocket.

"You won't be needing that. Don't worry," he said.

"No? Well, I needed it earlier, didn't I? So, what's different now?" she replied as forcefully as she could muster, trying to disguise the shaky voice betraying her inner, hidden terror.

"It's just you and me now," Nix said.

"Is that supposed to reassure me?"

"Of course. I told you, I'm not here to hurt you," Nix said, stepping towards Merryn.

"If that's true, why are you here then?"

"I wanted to see you."

Merryn was convinced that his voice had softened, and this both confused her and put her on edge all at once. Her hand squeezed at the cemp in her pocket nervously. "What for?"

"I needed to, I guess."

She was convinced that she saw him half smile.

"Why?" she said, more forcefully now.

"Look, let's sit down," he gestured with his arm towards the garden sofa.

Merryn was unsure whether this was a request or a command. She considered the possibility of running. In her mind, she imagined making it through the gate and only part-way down the path, in pursuit of Xance, before Nix apprehended her once more. She couldn't go back into the house – her family were in there and she would never forgive herself if something happened to them because of her stupidity. She edged forwards towards the large, comfy garden sofa then changed her mind and retreated again.

Nix sat down in the centre of the sofa and patted the cushion to his right, "Sit with me."

Merryn could feel the heat rising in her body as her blood pumped wildly through her arteries.

"Come on," he patted the cushion once more and adjusted his seating position; bending one leg up slightly so that he could twist and face towards the empty seat.

Merryn thought that she had no choice but to do what he said. Keeping her hand inside her pocket and firmly attached to her cemp, she sat down next to him on the sofa. She stared straight ahead, not daring to look at him, "You're not supposed to be here," she said boldly, "You're breaking the pact."

"Yeah?" he responded, sounding nonchalant, "I don't care about a stupid pact. I'll do what I want. The problem with the Nyss is they are all so self-righteous. They think they are untouchable. They think that they never do wrong, and therefore think that they can hold judgement on other people, when in reality, nothing could be further from the truth." His voice was tinged with anger.

Merryn took a big breath before speaking: "They just want peace."

"No, they don't. They want control."

The conversation paused.

Merryn could feel Nix's eyes on her. His stare was so powerful it was as if it heated the skin on her face. She plucked up the courage to look at him; her heart beginning to thud more powerfully once more. Not brave enough to look at his face, she stared at his torso. It was then that she noticed that Nix was not dressed in his Banas Mihtig uniform. Instead, he was wearing dark casual trousers and a black shirt. Her eyes travelled up to his chest, then his neck, where she saw that he wore a short, dark-leather necklace adorned with one single, silver bead. His shirt was unbuttoned slightly and she could see the toned skin of his smooth chest underneath which burst forwards through the material indicating that his body was muscular and powerful. Merryn's nerves fluttered; the thudding of her heart had calmed and she was now conscious that her state of fear and uncertainty had subsided slightly. With renewed courage, she allowed herself to look up at his face. His eyes were still fixed on her. He did not speak, but simply stared. As before, during her first encounter with Nix, Merryn studied his face. The light in the garden was limited to that which the nearby street light provided, with the addition of the soft glow from the moon. In this illumination, she could see his features clearly. His complexion was clear, but had a gentle ruggedness. His cheekbones were angular, giving his face a shapely, masculine outline, and his mid-length hair was raven-black. She noticed it had a natural wave to it and its texture was smooth, thick and shiny. It flicked out slightly in places and was higher on the top, flopping to one side in a slightly unpredictable and erratic shape.

He leant closer to Merryn and stroked her hair away from her face, tucking part of it behind her ear. She flinched at his touch.

Suddenly he spoke: "You don't need to be afraid of me."

He exuded a delicate, familiar, powdery scent. Clean

and manly. His hands were powerful and strong; their surface texture alluding to a life of working physically or in the outside elements. The skin on his palms appeared smooth, but there were ridges and several notable scars or marks on the back of his hands that Merryn noticed as he placed one hand back on his thigh as the other continued to rest on the back cushion of the sofa. Merryn moved her hair back in front of her ear. She felt uncomfortable with his touch, yet was also not repulsed by it either. This realisation concerned her greatly. She knew that she should find his touch repugnant. This was a Nethergeard soldier whom, earlier that evening, had been part of a fierce winnan and had held his hands around her throat. This was the man who had grabbed her and pushed her up against a wall as she made her way to see her friends. The Nethergeard were evil, she knew that. Xance had told her.

"You have a bad opinion of Nethergeard people, don't you?" he questioned.

"I usually judge people on their actions and how they treat me, not where they are from," Merryn replied. "You haven't exactly given me a great impression of yourself, have you?" she added.

Nix looked directly at her, "No, I guess you're right. I never meant to hurt you. I would never hurt you."

"No? Your actions say otherwise," Merryn said tentatively. She knew that she should be careful with her comments. She didn't wish to make Nix angry as she was frightened of what he may do.

"I am truly sorry for that. Sometimes my emotions fuel my actions. It's not an excuse. My intention was not to cause you harm. I can't really explain right now."

"Why not?" Merryn pressed Nix for more information. Strangely, Nix didn't answer.

"I'm guessing it's a Nethergeard thing? What's it like there?"

"That's a strange question. Why are you interested?"

"I just wondered whether you liked it there, as you and your friends seem to be spending a lot of time *here* recently that's all." Merryn instantly regretted her comment, fearing that she was antagonising Nix.

He didn't seem to be fazed though, and continued, "I'm not sure that you could argue that we've been here *a lot.*"

"You're here again now."

"I told you before, I came to see you," he said, shifting slightly in his seat.

For a brief second, his knee touched Merryn's thigh. She jolted her leg at the contact and her shoulders recoiled slightly. She realised that she was still desperately scared of what Nix may be about to do. Breathing deeply, she tried to steady her nerves.

He reached out and caressed the top of her arm with a tenderness that took Merryn completely by surprise. Instinctively, she pulled her arm away and rubbed the skin where he had touched her.

"I see Xance has given you the lapis lazuli haelan lind," Nix said, eyeing the ring on her finger.

Merryn was taken aback.

"Your ring. It's a haelan lind – a shield," Nix said smiling.

"Oh, I know, but how do *you* know that?" Merryn said, looking down at the ring.

Nix chuckled slightly and replied, "I know lots of things."

Merryn stared at the ring for a few moments, unsure of what to say.

"You have no idea who I am, do you?" Nix asked, his eyes fixed upon hers.

"No, should I?" Merryn replied.

Nix shook his head. "It's not that easy, unfortunately."

Merryn thought she sensed a waver in his voice, but she couldn't be certain. She looked at him, trying to read his face. His eyes were a deep, dark brown. She stared into them for far too long … mesmerised and fascinated by their depth of colour. Her gaze was fixed on them and she was finding it difficult to look away as Nix pinned his eyes upon hers. It was as if he was staring into her soul. Merryn was suddenly conscious that there was something familiar about this feeling. A butterfly sensation in her stomach signalled that her nerves had been triggered once more. She looked away; aware that there was an undeniable tension between the two of them. Her cheeks flushed pink, as her embarrassment revealed itself.

"You are so beautiful, Kerenza," he spoke gently.

Merryn's chest fluttered as her nervousness increased. Then it dawned on her. He knew her! So she must know him!

"You know me? From … before?" she managed to stutter.

"Do you know me?" Nix leant closer and she breathed in his heady scent.

"No. I … I don't know. I'm not sure," Merryn replied in a confused voice. She couldn't control her feelings now.

She was perplexed and bewildered by her conflicting emotions. The notion that there was a familiarity between her and Nix, but she couldn't remember why, was making her feel frustrated and vulnerable. She suddenly had an overwhelming sensation that she was going to vomit. Her head began to spin, and her stomach turned over. She breathed slowly and steadily, trying to control the nausea that had enveloped her.

"Are you ok?" he asked.

She was no longer able to exercise caution with her thoughts or speech – she was too preoccupied with trying not to vomit. "Of course I'm not ok!" she yelled at him, oblivious to the fact that her voice was far too loud and that she risked waking her family. "Why would I be ok? You turn up late at night – uninvited … and unwelcome, I might add. You accost me and drag me in to the garden, scaring me half to death. Then you expect me to sit and make small talk with you! You're pretending to be nice when we both know that you are not!" she ranted barely pausing for breath.

Nix sat up upright, clearly riled by her outburst. "Who told you I wasn't nice? Xance, I suppose." his voice was gravelly and sharp.

"I can make my own mind up – I don't need someone to tell me what you are!" Merryn responded. For some reason, she no longer cared that her comments and tone were being provocative.

"And what am I? Tell me Kerenza, if you know me, tell me what I am." Nix stood up and now seemed to be looming over her.

Merryn looked up at him. "You're not supposed to be here, so leave!"

"I have every right to be here!" Nix raised his voice.

"You're breaking the agreement."

"I told you before … I don't care about the pact."

"Yes, but Xance and the others do."

"You should stay away from him, he's trouble," Nix growled, his growing anger now evident.

Merryn's comment had obviously aggravated him. The tone of his voice had changed and something inside told her to ease up. She steadied her breathing as the sickness in her stomach subsided slightly.

"Funny, he says the same about you," she said, speaking more softly.

"Yeah?" Nix responded to her softer voice and appeared to calm slightly, "He'll hurt you, you know. He's dangerous," he added.

"Xance would never hurt me."

"Well, I guess we'll just have to wait and see, won't we?" Nix spoke softly.

Then without warning, he turned and walked out of the garden gate and away into the darkness.

Rage

Merryn had spent the morning at school in a semi-daze. It was partly due to extreme tiredness, and partly because her head was full of yesterday. To all intents and purposes, attending any of her classes had turned out to be a complete waste of time. She may as well have stayed in bed. But that wasn't Merryn. She'd dragged herself out of bed, and made her way to school trying to pretend all was well with the world. In reality, nothing could be further from the truth. The fight had proved itself more than enough for her to contend with, however, the thing that was really bothering her was her encounter with Nix.

She was struggling to deal with the conglomeration of opposing feelings that she was experiencing. In the early light of the morning sun which streamed through the gap in her bedroom curtains, she had laid in bed attempting to fathom whether it had all been part of one of her strange dreams. She concluded, however, that it hadn't. The meeting with Nix had most definitely taken place. Surreal as it was – it had happened.

Merryn had sat up on her bed as she recalled the touch of Nix's hand on her arm. She remembered his dark, brown eyes boring into her; the tanned, smooth skin on his chest; the scent of a masculine fragrance as he moved closer to her. What concerned Merryn mostly about all that had occurred last night, was how she was feeling about it now. She knew that the unexpected meeting with her uninvited guest should have fuelled an anger within her, yet it did not. Instead, Merryn was feeling confused. There was something weirdly familiar about Nix; she couldn't get past that. The things that he had said to her had stirred emotions within her that she could not explain. She had at first thought that the nausea she had endured had been due to extreme stress, but what if it was something else? What if it was, as she feared, caused by feelings of guilt?

Merryn knew that it was a preposterous thing to consider, but deep down she had a gut-wrenching aware-ness that she had some sort of connection to Nix, and that even though she didn't know what the link was, or why her emotions were so confused, she felt that she was betraying Xance in some way.

"So, who's looking forward to Luke's party on Friday night?" Chloe asked as she seated herself at the canteen table with her friends, "It's his birthday, he's the first of us to turn seventeen, quickly followed by Merryn in a couple of weeks' time," she added smiling.

Everyone answered affirmatively in unison.

"I can't wait!" Erin said excitedly, "I know Harry will be there and fingers crossed he'll at least talk to me!" she held up her hands with both her middle and index fingers crossed.

"I'm sure he will, Erin. You said he's been chattier recently so this will be your perfect opportunity to pounce!" Chloe said jokingly.

"Hey! I'm not going to pounce. I'm going to look absolutely gorgeous and be aloof, and he won't be able to resist," Erin smiled, then added, "Who am I kidding? I'll probably spend all evening sat alone in a corner being miserable and watching everyone else have a good time."

"Wow, Erin! That's incredibly pessimistic. Come on, stay positive. We'll have a great time – all of us," Amelie commented.

Merryn decided now was as good a time as any to broach the delicate subject of Amelie's love life. "Will you have your eye on anyone special, Amelie?" she said tentatively.

The other girls paused and listened for a response.

"Stop teasing, Merryn. Tyler told me that he let you in on our secret. Well, it's not actually a secret, it's just we hadn't got round to sharing it with anyone yet." She grinned, and it was acutely apparent that she was excited about her new relationship.

Chloe squealed, "You and Tyler Reynolds?"

Amelie nodded.

"That's fantastic!" added Chloe.

Merryn noticed that Erin remained quiet. She couldn't help wondering if Erin was feeling a little sad. After all, at this point in time, she was the only one of the group without a boyfriend. Merryn knew that having a boyfriend was not the most important thing in the world, however, if you were the only one out of all your friends who was single then this might not make you feel so great. She rubbed Erin's arm reassuringly and said, "Friday night will be great, don't worry."

Erin forced a smile.

A while later, having eaten their lunch, the four girls made their way outside to sit on the grass in the sunshine. It was warmer than Merryn had expected so she suggested that they settle under the large silver birch tree to take advantage of the shade it provided. She leant up against the tree with her legs outstretched, her head resting on the white, mottled trunk. In the distance, she caught sight of Xance and Emily. He was sat on the short wall that ran in front of the school building and Emily was standing in front of him. Merryn watched carefully, intrigued but nervous. It was never a good thing when Emily was near Xance. Merryn had believed Xance when he had reassured her, so many times that he was not at all interested in Emily. That was not the issue. The problem was Emily. Merryn found her to be an irritant. She was certainly proving to be persistent where her attentions to Xance were concerned. Xance appeared to be annoyed with Emily. Merryn noticed from his body language and the manner in which he used his hands that he appeared to be gesturing for her to go away. Merryn held her breath as Emily stepped towards Xance and attempted to wrap her arms around him, but she needn't have worried. Xance took Emily gently by the arms and averted the intended hug. Merryn smiled to herself, concluding that Xance must be speaking to Emily about the episode in the library when she had threatened Merryn. She didn't like that fact that he was speaking to her, but it was a comfort to see that he appeared to be supporting their relationship and putting Emily in her place.

After school, Merryn had arranged to meet Xance at the harbour. She had to speak to him about last night, and she hadn't had chance to during the day. There were always too many people around and she needed to have this conversation when they were alone. As she turned the corner into the harbour, and made her way past Kitto's Cave, her stomach started to flutter. She began to feel sick as her nerves kicked in. She had tried to rehearse in her head what she was going to say, but the words just kept coming out wrong, and each time she tried a different version, her speech became more and more ridiculous. She wasn't even sure why she thought Xance would be upset. She just had a feeling. Perhaps in her subconscious mind she knew that all was not as it seemed, and this was what was fuelling the ominous feeling within her.

Xance was waiting for her. He was seated on a bench facing out to sea. She approached quietly, and gently placed her hands over his eyes playfully. Xance laughed as he removed her hands. This was a good attempt to alleviate some of her stress, but unfortunately it hadn't worked, and she was shaking inside as she joined Xance on the seat.

"Are you ok?" he asked. "You look worried."

Merryn let out a huge puff of air from her lungs as she scrunched up her nose and shook her head. "Not really," she said, looking at Xance nervously.

Xance instantly sat up and moved towards her, "What's wrong?"

"I'm ok, sorry. I just have something to tell you and I'm worried about how you are going to react," she explained.

"Oh, no, this is about Emily, isn't it?" Xance looked concerned, "If you saw me with her at school, it was only because I was giving her a talking to. I've told her to back off, and to leave you alone. I made it really clear that I'm not going to tolerate her crap anymore."

Merryn could see that Xance was anxious. She held his hand to reassure him, "No, don't worry, I did see you with her, but I trust you to do the right thing – it's not a problem."

"Then what is it? I can see that you're upset," Xance said apprehensively.

"I am upset, but it's only because I don't want you to be upset."

"This sounds bad," said Xance as he appeared to prepare himself for whatever it was Merryn was about to say.

Merryn explained what had happened the previous night. She tried to recall the conversation and events chronologically so that she didn't miss out any details. She was finding it difficult to look at Xance during the re-telling, and so was staring out at the water blankly. Her eyes did not register the boats entering and leaving the harbour. She saw nothing but blue. When she had finished speaking, she breathed out audibly once more. She felt a small amount of relief that Xance now had all the information.

"I can't believe that he would do something like that. Are you ok?" Xance grabbed her and pulled her into his chest. "I should have been there. I'm so sorry."

"Xance, I'm ok," she reassured him. "It's not your fault. You didn't know that he was going to be there." She could see that Xance was racked with guilt.

"I can't bear the thought of him hurting you though. He's not going to get away with this. He's gone too far," Xance said, as he pulled her away from him so that he could look at her face.

She looked back directly into his brilliant blue eyes, "Xance, it's ok. He didn't hurt me."

"Good. I'm glad, but if he wasn't there to hurt you, why was he there? What's he up to?"

Merryn could sense that Xance was becoming more and more agitated so she answered tentatively: "I'm not sure. We just talked."

"Talked?"

"Yes, for a while."

"You talked to him for *a while*? What about? What did he say?"

Merryn could hear by the tone of Xance's voice that he was growing more and more angry. Initially, he had seemed concerned for her welfare, but now he just sounded infuriated. She tried to calm him by stroking his forearm, but he recoiled from her touch as if her hand was burning his skin, "He seemed to know me ... my past gestord. He called me Kerenza again," she said nervously not wishing to add fuel to the flames of Xance emotions. "Does he know me? Do I know him?"

Xance didn't answer her question. "You shouldn't have spoken to him, Merryn!" he almost shouted, "What were you thinking?"

"Don't put this on me, Xance! I never asked him to turn up in my garden," Merryn responded with growing frustration.

"No, you didn't, but you still shouldn't have spoken to him. He's bad news. Dangerous. He had his hands at you throat during the winnan for heaven's sake, and you choose to sit in the garden with him having a cosy chat!"

Merryn's eyes filled with tears. She choked them backwards, forcing herself to speak. "I can assure you that I didn't feel I had a choice. What would you suggest I should have done?"

"Well, not speak to him for a start!"

Merryn was conscious that they were now half-yelling at each other. This was not how she had anticipated this conversation playing out. She knew Xance was going to be upset, but this reaction was far worse than she was expecting. "Why are you behaving like this? What is it that you are so concerned about? Is it that he spoke to me or that he might have hurt me?" she questioned. The tone of her voice was full of hurt and confusion.

"Of course, I wouldn't want him to harm you, but you shouldn't be talking to him. He's pure evil. You don't know how dangerous he is!"

Merryn's tempered flared now. She couldn't escape the feeling that Xance was withholding something vital. "Of course, I don't know how dangerous he is! Why would I? You won't tell me anything about him!" she yelled.

"You know everything you need to know, for now," Xance retaliated.

"So, it's your decision; what I'm told and what I'm kept in the dark about?"

"I didn't mean it like that!"

"There's something you're not telling me, Xance."

"Merryn, I *can't* tell you!"

"Really?"

"You have to believe me … I can't tell you!"

"Then I'll have to ask Nix again, won't I?"

"He can't tell you either!"

"You are being ridiculous, I think he will, if I ask him," Merryn was feeling exasperated now.

"That's it … I'm going to deal with him once and for all. I told him not to come near you. I warned him!" Xance stood up and began walking towards the cliff path. Merryn could see his rage in his tightly clasped hands.

"Where are you going, Xance? What are you going to do?" she called after him.

"To do what I should have done a long time ago!" Xance hastened his walk.

Merryn followed behind. As he turned onto the path that led him away from the harbour, Merryn tried once more. "Xance, please!"

He did not respond. She had never seen this side of Xance, and it frightened her. Merryn feared that he was going to do something stupid. She knew that she had to think quickly. As she started to run back towards the village, she caught sight of Emily standing next to the pasty shop. Emily smiled at her. A closed-mouth, sarcastic, nasty smile. *Was she watching us?* Merryn thought to herself as she continued running. If so, she had most likely witnessed the argument, but Merryn couldn't worry about that right now. She had to get help.

Fortunately, Carter was at his home when she arrived there. He lived in a painted-white terrace cottage in the main part of the village so Merryn hadn't had to run too far. His mum had answered the door, wiping her hands on a tea towel. She was short in height with a slightly plump body and blonde hair. In contrast to her son, who was tall, slender and dark-haired. She greeted Merryn with a gentle 'hello' and a friendly smile then she turned around and bellowed for Carter to come to the door. Carter arrived at the door looking nonchalant, but this changed to instant surprise when he saw Merryn standing there. She explained hurriedly what had happened between herself and Xance whilst Carter leant on the door frame, listening intently. When she had finished, Carter's face displayed a look of grave concern.

"He's going to Nethergeard," he said knowingly.

"He's going to do something stupid; I know he is!" Merryn's voice was starting to squeak now as her hysteria grew.

"Don't worry, I'll get the others and we'll go after him." He tried to smile reassuringly, but Merryn could tell that he was worried.

"I want to come with you," Merryn said as Carter stepped out of the house and closed the front door behind him.

"No!" Carter said forcefully.

Merryn looked hurt at his response.

"Sorry, Merryn, but it's just too dangerous. Nethergeard is not a place that welcomes strangers, and we will be breaking the pact as soon as we enter. You should stay here. I'll bring him back," he said.

"What about Chloe?" Merryn asked.

"I'll ask her to stay here just in case things don't work out the way we want. She'll know what to do."

"You said it would be ok!" Merryn's stress was showing in her voice.

"It will be – trust me. Look, I need to go." Carter squeezed the tops of Merryn's arms reassuringly. He then turned and ran off into the village with his phone pressed to his ear.

Nethergeard

Rain and mist dominate the landscape in Nethergeard. The spring and autumn seasons are the worst for rainfall (with summer being only marginally better having the advantage of dashes of intermittent sunshine). Sometimes, whole weeks pass with no ease from the torrential downpours that burden the ground heavy with mud and giant murky pools of water. Occasionally, the deluge causes the land to flood, leaving the small roads impassable and fields resembling great lakes. The rain is accompanied by a multitude of dark-grey and black clouds, filling the sky with intense anger.

The nimbostratus often lies low and heavy over the vista, blocking out the sunlight and making the daylight hours indistinct from the evening. Nethergeardian's are seen hurrying home from work, either on foot, underneath large umbrellas, or in their small electric cars with the windscreen wipers whipping frantically to and fro. In the waterlogged and dense woodland areas, eerie mists often creep in, creating a shroud of opaque white that lingers and hangs low to the ground between the skeletal, lifeless trees.

Winter in Nethergeard is bleak. The temperature plummets and rarely rises above freezing for much of the season. Emulating arctic conditions with prowess, dense snow and biting ice govern the landscape. Trees and buildings become camouflaged under the deep, white snow. Roads and pathways are rendered invisible as if they never existed save only in the imagination. The towns and villages are quiet and deserted; devoid of busy adults or playful children.

Nobody ever travels far. There is no need. Most of them live and work within the same small town. The Magister Worlega, leader of the Nethergeard world, has vetoed any plans to create or establish large companies and businesses. His official mandate is to keep the towns and villages discrete from each other, and to maintain control through disallowing any new building or development.

It's all about retaining power. Everything is small. Everything is controlled. The small communities support and rely upon each other. They are the kind of places where everyone knows everybody else. Couples are married within their own communities or parishes; usually to someone who they lived near to and attended school with. Most have settled down by the time they reach their early twenties. There is no reason not to. Any ambition to better oneself is futile and unnecessary. Life is simple and that is the way the Magister Worlega wants it to continue.

The Magister Worlega heads an army of elite Banas Mihtig soldiers. They are mighty warriors, whose role is to uphold the laws of Nethergeard and keep order. These men are selected by the Magister Worlega himself, and trained to fight, using the Banas spear. They spend hours and hours honing their skills and learning to work as one strong, powerful unit. Autonomy is not encouraged. They are employed not to think but to fight. Simple. Some of the Banas Mihtig have been recruited because their fathers had been soldiers before them. Some are recruited due to their useful skills or attributes. Being exceptional with technical computer skills will automatically put you on the Magister Worlega's list for recruitment, as will being good at combat or espionage.

There are also the Worlega Mathikoy; a special minority contingent of Banas Mihtig soldiers, who are bestowed with the gift of magical ability. Although they share the common capability to produce incantations and perform various magical acts, some of their powers are diverse and individual to each other. Their powers are closely monitored by the Magister; no magic is permitted without his express permission or instruction. This is not because he wanted it used for good purposes only, for he is an evil man and capable of wreaking much terror and torment on anyone who dares to provoke or disobey him, but due only to his unending mission to retain omnipotent control.

The people of Nethergeard are led by their long-practised and revered traditions. They freely believe in the supernatural, particularly in dark magic – however, that is not to say that these notions are an overt part of daily life, far from it. Witchcraft, wizardry and indeed any form of occultism or the supernatural is never spoken about by the ordinary folk of Nethergeard; their fear of its possible existence and capabilities keep it swathed in mystery. Those who do practice in sorcery, and who follow paths of the paranormal, keep their participation a hidden secret.

The existence of Galdray Estate, the Magister Worlega's home and the base for his Banas Mihtig soldiers, is portended by a huge, moss-strewn, stone archway which spans the entrance to the driveway. At either side, the brickwork extends upwards to create a square-shaped turret with a pointed top. Tiny slit-like windows within the brickwork on all sides provide an occupant with a clear view of any approaching or exiting visitors. On entering the estate, guests follow the long, twisting, stone driveway that cuts through the dense, dark forest. Gnarled, contorted branches overhang the road in places, looming down and creating ominous shadows. During the summer months, the deep-green, heavy foliage renders the path in virtual darkness even in daylight. During the wetter months, the journey up to the main house becomes fraught with difficulties. Gigantic muddy puddles form in certain places, having been pushed onto the driveway from the forest floor by the torrential, almost ceaseless rainfall. The stone surface becomes perilously slippery in areas, and it is necessary to navigate with care the low, sweeping, knotted tree boughs in the shadowy darkness.

Galdray House stands, majestic, in a clearing at the end of the driveway, surrounded by forest on all sides. Its grandeur and opulence creating a spectacle for anyone to behold. One of its most noticeable features is its pure expanse and size. Having a frontage width of approximately ten standard properties and a depth to match, with three clear storeys, the house is both impressive and striking. The creamy-yellow facade is highlighted against the dark greens and browns of the surrounding woodland. There are an imposing number of huge windows, each decorated with a five petal-shaped arch at the top point. Being grouped into threes or fours, the windows cover a large proportion of the front of the property. The largest bay-type window is positioned at one end, just to the left of the arched entrance porch. At certain parts of the house, tall, round towers in a Gothic style with pointed roofs rise impressively towards the sky. One tower in particular, stands taller than the rest with a much smaller square base and a thin pointed turret. It is situated just off the centre of the roof and appears to house a bell. The main entrance consists of two giant, wooden, arched doors; masterpieces of craftsmanship made from quality, dark wood, with ornate carvings and a wrought iron, hooped knocker.

Detracting from the splendour of the mansion are its surrounding grounds. Bushes and shrubs in various shades of green and brown tangle and weave their way across the ground. Growing as high as they are spread, they strangle the walls of the great house and devour its staggering beauty. The enormous grey, stone water feature that resides in the centre of the circular driveway is green with moss and algae and trickles a pathetic stream of murky liquid, rather than an impressive fountain of clear, sparking water.

26

Xance

Xance's anger burned within him as he strode purposefully under the entrance archway of Galdray Estate. He was conscious that his Elkalind rune had appeared on his arm and was now mildly irritating him; an obvious sign that he was approaching Nethergeard inhabitants. This did not faze him, for this was his sole purpose. He was here for one thing only; to confront Nix and put a stop to him, permanently. Under different circumstances, Xance would have talked himself out of this brazen act of stupidity. If Carter, or one of the other Cempalli soldiers had embarked on this risky deed, Xance knew he would have stepped in to point out the perils and pitfalls of such a foolish act. However, he was not thinking sensibly right now. The red mist had swept over his emotions, hijacking his body, and rendering him no longer able to consider the reality of the consequences of his actions. He knew that he would do anything to protect Merryn, and that meant that he had to deal with Nix. Nix was more than an irritant, he was dangerous. Evil and corrupt – just like the rest of the Banas Mihtig soldiers. He had proven himself to be untrustworthy on many occasions in the past, and Xance was not about to give him the upper hand this time. His decision to travel to Nethergeard using the Koyt egress, and seek out Nix was fraught with danger, but he didn't care.

Xance continued his steady pace along the stone driveway. At certain points he had to duck down to avoid the many tree branches that hung over the road like a protective cloak. His hands made intermittent fists as he thought about what he would do when he eventually found Nix. He had been walking for around ten minutes or so when he caught a glimpse of the yellow-cream stone of the estate house's facade. His heart thumped even faster in his chest as the adrenalin carried him forwards. Moving stealthily, his eyes scanning the scene skilfully, searching for any movement.

Xance moved to hide behind one shrub after another until he had managed to reach the left side of the huge building. He paused for a moment, crouching behind a large bush. He attempted to steady his breathing and focus his mind on the next stage of his mission. He had just wiped a pool of sweat from his brow with the back of his hand when he heard a distinct rustle coming from behind him. He glanced backwards, first over one shoulder then the other. Nothing. His eyes flicked and darted, searching for the cause of the noise, yet he could see nothing. Perhaps he had imagined it in his heightened state of stress.

Xance thought he could see a side door to the property situated through an archway to his left within a small courtyard. He glanced around, and seeing no immediate danger, made a move towards the entrance. He hadn't taken more than a few steps forwards when he sensed something or someone behind him. Quickly, he swung around, his cemp clutched tightly in his right hand. A Nethergeard soldier stood before him. It was Maddox. His white-blond, neatly-groomed hair made him instantly recognisable. He smirked at Xance, who was taken completely by surprise and took a step backwards.

Maddox moved towards him intimidatingly. "You seem to be breaking the pact, Xance," he said shaking his head mockingly, "you know that you're not allowed in Nethergeard."

"Really?" Xance replied sarcastically. "Well, I'm just visiting. What I'm here for won't take long, but it's not you I've come to see so you don't need to involve yourself." Xance knew that he was treading on delicate ground. There was no way that Maddox was going to just let him go. He would know that Xance was here to cause trouble. Besides, Maddox was one of Nethergeard's more ruthless soldiers. He had been part of the Banas Mihtig since the mid-1800s. He had been blessed with the Libanal; a magical gift bestowed on Nethergeard's who prove themselves faithful to the Magister Worlega, and on those who lead productive, trouble-free lives. The gift allows its recipients to live for centuries, free from illness and ageing. Maddox had proven his loyalty to

Nethergeard and the Magister Worlega many times over. He was a killer. He was a young, merciless, cruel and savage man, who had no understanding of remorse or repentance.

Maddox gripped his spear in preparation and advanced towards Xance, "Well now, you see, I can't allow that. You're here uninvited. I would suggest that you leave. However, I quite fancy a fight – it's always eventful with a Nyss Cempalli – you guys are trained well," he sneered.

"Maddox, I don't want to fight you," Xance said forcefully. Adrenalin was pulsing around his body now and his anger had grown, if that was at all possible.

"Well, you're obviously here to cause trouble, why else would you be in Nethergeard? And where are your mates? Surely, you haven't been foolish enough to have come here on your own?" he said looking around tentatively for other Nyss. "This is going to be more fun than I thought." He smiled maniacally.

Without further deliberation, Xance activated his cemp-edge and held it out in front of him as it blazoned a bright, deep-green colour. He created a wide stance with his feet and prepared himself for the ensuing and inevitable fight. Maddox made the first move. He lunged at Xance thrusting his spear forwards. It narrowly missed, and Xance was able to shunt his body sideways to miss the blade. He swung around and swiped at Maddox with his cemp-edge. The glowing, green blade nipped Maddox's forearm as it skimmed the surface of his skin. He recoiled his arm for a second as the pain ripped through his body. Xance could see that he had hurt

Maddox, and this drove him on in his pursuit of a win. He knew that he had to be ruthless as Maddox would not give in easily.

Xance thrust forwards towards Maddox's head, swinging his cemp-edge high through the air, but Maddox was too quick and he managed to dodge the weapon, despite stumbling. They now found themselves next to a small water feature that had a low, square, stone wall surrounding it. Maddox regained control of his balance. He executed a swift roundhouse kick, catching Xance off guard. Xance grimaced as the lower leg of his rival made contact with his side, and he found himself falling backwards onto the stone wall of the water feature. Maddox did not waste any time. He dived forwards, dropping his spear to his side, grabbing Xance's throat with both his hands. Maddox's face was exuding a look of sheer determination. His mouth and nose scrunched up as his eyes squinted. Xance was aware that Maddox was using all of his force now to pin him in position; the hands on his neck were squeezing tighter and tighter as Xance was pushed slowly back towards the water.

In his despair, Xance's thoughts now turned to Merryn: *If he beats me, I have failed her.* Gathering all of his remaining strength and using his strong, stomach muscles, Xance was able to lift one of his legs and jab his knee into Maddox's ribs. Maddox loosened his grip on Xance's throat slightly as the blow winded him briefly. This allowed Xance to inhale a huge gasp of air fleetingly before, unfortunately for Xance, Maddox was able to dig his elbow into Xance's torso and regain his strong position. He squeezed at Xance's throat once more as he raised one knee and placed it onto Xance's chest. Xance could now feel the splashes of fountain water hitting the top of his head as he was pushed nearer to the small pool of water. He knew that he was in real difficulty now and was struggling to breathe. He kept seeing intermittent black, and knew that he was close to losing consciousness. His cemp-edge slipped from his hand and clattered to the ground. Maddox gave one large shove of Xance's throat, and Xance felt the icy-cold of the water envelop his face as his head was now completely submerged in the pool. He tried to lift his knee once more in an attempt to dislodge Maddox, and although he was able to strike him in the torso, he was unable to muster enough power to displace his opponent and free himself. Although Xance's Cempalli soldier training had taught him to be resourceful and determined, at this point in the fight, he knew that his situation was hopeless, and he felt himself steadily drift away into blackness.

XANCE OPENED his eyes and tried desperately to focus them. He blinked several times slowly to clear his vision. An array of four or five pairs of black-booted feet lined up before him. He was aware that he was lying on his side on a dark, wooden floor. His neck ached and throbbed and his back was bruised. Suddenly, a pair of black boots appeared in front of his face and he was pulled up on to his knees abruptly. The soldier returned to the fold of his fellow comrades and Xance was left isolated in the centre of the room. He glanced around him. The circular room was large and encompassed by huge dark, wooden book-cases that stretched to the ceiling. Forwards of Xance's position was a small wooden balcony, raised above the room impressively, being reached by a spiral staircase which led up from the main floor below. Xance noticed that the room was dark as there were only a few small windows that were positioned around the top of the walls. Dim, yellow-toned lights hung on wires from the ceiling in intermittent places. Xance was struggling to remain upright on his knees. His head felt heavy and nausea was creeping into his stomach. His body was clearly reacting to his losing consciousness earlier. He still felt angry, and despite his current, dire predicament, he did not regret journeying to Nethergeard.

Just then, a muscular, powerfully-built man, dressed in a black shirt and trousers, appeared up on the balcony. He had shoulder-length, poker-straight, brown hair and a long, slightly angular nose. Xance knew that this man was the Magister and leader of the Banas Mihtig, as he had encountered him on several occasions prior to this. The Magister Worlega had entered the room through a small door at the back of the upper gallery, and was now leaning on the ornate, wooden balustrade eyeing the scene below him. He paused for a few seconds before speaking in a low, gravelly voice, "I see that the Sefwarian Nyss are no longer wanting to adhere to the pact I made with your Luminary Synod to bring peace between our two worlds."

Even though Xance mustered as much energy as he could, his voice was barely audible and came out in a raspy whisper, "My intention was not to break the pact."

The Magister Worlega responded, "Then what indeed *was* your intention? Under the terms of the agreement, you know that you are not permitted to enter Nethergeard, yet here you are, in my house; uninvited." He spoke with a steady, calm tone, tinged with menace.

"I came here to … deal with Nix," Xance managed to say hoarsely.

"That is no excuse! You dare to come here to attack one of my soldiers. Do you really think that I am going to allow that?"

Xance eyed the Banas Mihtig soldiers before him and braced himself for the beating that he was convinced was imminent. He was sure that this would be the end for him as he could not perceive how he could gather enough energy to survive this next onslaught, having not been able to fully recover from the first fight with Maddox. However, what happened next was a complete shock to him. The Magister Worlega straightened up his body, as if breathing in deeply. In a split second, he lifted both his arms forwards and flicked his hands towards Xance. A flash of bright, white light, reminiscent of lightning, fired from his hands. The thin, jagged beams of light hit Xance in the torso, forcing his back to arch and throwing his face upwards to the ceiling. He yelled out, a deep, thunderous roar as the searing, burning pain ripped through his body. The light then stopped briefly before the Magister Worlega, with a look of smugness on his face, flicked his hands once more and the ray of luminescent light carried through the space and locked on Xance again. Xance's ordeal continued for several minutes leaving him writhing and bellowing in pain.

He lay prostrate on the hard, wooden floor. His mid-section lifted and dropped as the electric-like light battered him. Xance had forfeited all ability to think anything. His very being was so wrecked that he had lost the function to feel either pain or emotion. He was numb and his consciousness was waning once more. The room became a blur and he could see very little as his responsiveness dwindled.

Suddenly, the heavy, double doors at the back of the room swung open aggressively, and a blaze of multi-coloured lights entered the room. Carter, Bryn, Harry, Tom, Luke and Jason entered the room with their cemp-edge swords ready for battle. Xance could see the coloured lights in his peripheral vision as he lay face down on the floor. Somewhere in the depths of his subconscious, Xance knew Carter and the others were present in the room.

"How did *you* get in?" The Magister Worlega bawled from his position up on the balcony. The Banas Mihtig soldiers instantly prepared for conflict; their spears ready in their hands.

Carter responded with pure aggression in his voice, "Well, it seems that none of you were paying attention, were you? You seem to be preoccupied with torturing my best mate here." He gestured towards the ground where Xance lay motionless.

The other Cempalli soldiers moved to create a semi-circle around Xance, fronted by Carter. They stared directly, revealing no emotion, at the Banas Mihtig soldiers, who stared back, unwavering in their determined stance.

Carter spoke again, "Your actions here today will start a war with Sefwarian Nyss – you know this, Worlega."

"We did not ask for your friend to enter Nethergeard. He broke the pact by arriving uninvited. He came here looking for trouble. What did you expect me to do?" The Magister Worlega responded belligerently.

"You should have acted more responsibly. You know the consequences of your actions. Our First Luminary will not take this lightly." Carter stepped forwards, in a show of defiance and anger.

At this point, Nix and Maddox absented themselves from the group of soldiers and made their way up the stairs to the balcony. Carter watched, intrigued, as Nix appeared to be reasoning calmly with his leader, whilst Maddox displayed a demeanour of exasperation. After several minutes of whispered conversation, whilst the rest of the room remained on guard and poised for conflict, the Magister Worlega spoke to Carter:

"I do not wish to start a war with Sefwarian Nyss because of your friend's personal grievance with Phoenix Branok. The agreement was made many years ago and we have had a long period of peace. It would be foolish of me to continue down this path over what is a personal issue between Xance and Phoenix. You shall leave, and we will not pursue this any further." He gestured to his soldiers to stand down.

"Tell me what the Banas Mihtig have been doing in Porthrosen, on Earth. I demand to know!" Carter said forcefully.

"I'm not sure that you are in a position to make such demands, besides, I have no idea what you are talking about. Now, I think that I am being lenient enough, under the circumstances, so please leave. Now!" The Magister Worlega said angrily.

Carter and Luke immediately grabbed Xance and pulled him to his feet. They walked between him, supporting his weight and resting his arms across their shoulders. The others followed behind, walking backwards and wielding their swords, to ensure their safe exit from the house.

Xance's strength was greatly depleted and he strained and struggled to take each step, but he was determined to walk out of Nethergeard with his friends – he couldn't let them down now. He knew that they had risked their lives to rescue him. It was his fault that they were there. He had put them in danger because he was unable to control his emotions and anger towards Nix. This was personal; the Magister Worlega was correct. Xance also knew that, despite them all leaving Nethergeard now, this was far from over.

2 7

No Way Back

It was Friday. The last three days had been fairly quiet. Xance had stayed home from school for the last two days, and Merryn had neither seen him nor spoken to him since they quarrelled. She felt dreadful about their argument, and was desperate for things to be right between them. The thought of this being the end of her relationship with Xance was too much to bear. She had tried to catch him at lunchtime, but he had been elusive, and she was convinced that he was avoiding her and that he wanted it to be over between them. Eventually, she managed to find him as they left school at the end of the day. He was standing, alone, underneath the large silver birch tree at the front of the school. She tentatively approached and stood motionless before him, barely daring to breathe as she waited to see what his reaction to her would be. She soon realised that she needn't have worried because he looked deep in to her eyes and smiled sheepishly. He then gave her a hug, reassuring her that things were alright between them.

"I'm so sorry, Merryn," Xance said breathily in to her ear. She could sense the emotion in his voice and knew that he was being genuine.

Merryn eventually plucked up the courage to speak to him about the events in Nethergeard.

"Xance, Chloe told me about what happened. You could have been killed."

"I was alright. I was wearing my haelan lind bracelet. They could inflict pain and hurt me, but they would have found it difficult to kill me," Xance said as he took her hand reassuringly.

"Yes, but it was stupid of you to go there, especially alone. Even with your haelan lind, they would have been able to kill you, don't pretend that they couldn't – I know it's possible," Merryn replied.

Xance lowered his head towards the floor, looking slightly abashed.

"Xance, I was so worried about you. I don't know what I would have done, if you hadn't come back," Merryn felt close to tears.

"I'm sorry that I made you worry. I was so angry at Nix, and I acted irrationally. You're right. I should have thought it through, but I just know that he's not going to give up. He's not going to leave you alone," Xance explained.

"What do you mean? Why is he never going to leave me alone?"

"Nothing, don't worry. It's my problem. I'll just have to find a way to deal with him."

Merryn wasn't satisfied with Xance's response, but she didn't want to push things any further at the moment. She hadn't spoken to him all week, and she didn't want to risk another argument so soon. She had a feeling that there was much more to the situation, and that Xance was obviously not telling her something. She could only hope that he would feel able to explain and make things clearer soon.

Merryn and Xance walked from the school bus together back into Porthrosen. Once they reached the path where Xance would need to head off in a different direction to Merryn, they stopped and sat down on the kerb to chat.

"Are we still going to Luke's party together tonight?" Merryn asked.

"Yeah, of course, but I'm going to have to meet you there a bit later, if that's alright with you?" Xance said hesitantly looking deep into Merryn's eyes.

She couldn't help being disappointed by what he said. After all, it was the first party that they had had the chance to go to with each other, and she was really excited, but she concealed her feelings as she didn't want to cause an issue right now. "Oh, ok, that's fine. I'll meet you there, but why?"

"I'm really sorry, but Anthony, the First Luminary, has requested a meeting with me tonight. It's important and I can't get out of it," Xance explained.

Merryn watched as Xance scuffed the front of his trainer slightly as he kicked at a stone that lay in the road.

She could see that he was not happy about having to go to the meeting so she reassured him. "It'll be ok. I'll be fine until you get there. The others will make sure I'm alright. Are you worried about what the First Luminary will say to you?" She rubbed at his arm briefly to show him that she cared.

"No, not really. He's asked to speak to me because he has some crucial information to share. He had tasked a team of Nyss to gather intelligence on the Nethergeards. They've been investigating why the Banas Mihtig have been visiting Porthrosen. I'm guessing he will also speak to me about what happened in Nethergeard."

"How does he know about it? Did you tell him?" Merryn questioned.

"Of course. I had to. I can't keep information like that to myself. As a Cempalli soldier, I work for the Luminary Council. It would be foolish to keep it a secret, as they would find out somehow, and then I'd be in trouble for not informing them myself."

Xance smiled, but Merryn knew it was tinged with nervousness. Feeling helpless, she gently rubbed his arm once more to comfort him.

"You will make it to the party though, won't you?" Merryn asked, as they stood up.

"I wouldn't miss it!" Xance grinned at her. "The meeting won't take long. I'll be there, I promise."

* * *

MERRYN WAS JUST APPLYING the finishing touches to her make-up, in preparation for Luke's party, when she was overwhelmed by the familiar feeling that she was being watched. She slowly placed the blusher brush down on her desk and stood up. Although she had experienced this feeling several times before, it was not something that she was used to. Her arms began to tremble and a shiver made its way down her spine. Taking a deep breath and closing her eyes for a few seconds, Merryn focussed her thoughts and turned slowly to view her bedroom. She wasn't surprised to see the spirit girl was standing by the window facing into the room. She looked just as she had done previously, yet this time she appeared to have a look of concern or angst upon her face. Merryn breathed in and out slowly, trying to control her nerves.

The ghostly figure stepped forwards and seemed to be gesturing for Merryn to walk towards her. She then looked to be patting the bed and ushering Merryn to sit down. Almost without thinking, Merryn did as she was directed. Her limbs still trembled and her heart thudded in her chest as she sat down on her bed. She did not allow herself to remove her gaze from the girl; wanting to know where she was at all times.

Merryn had been sat motionless for a few seconds when the figure appeared to close her eyes briefly. When she opened them, she looked into Merryn's eyes with a forced, unblinking stare. She then moved forwards and carefully took Merryn's hands in her own. All of a sudden, Merryn was experiencing a vision, just as she had done before, however this time she felt differently. This time Merryn sensed that these images were familiar to her, even the parts that she had not seen before. She somehow knew that they were part of her memory, held deep within her gestord. It was as if someone had placed a portable, film screen floating in mid-air before her. Again, the pictures were sliced together like the rushes from various movies; all joined in to one film clip that made no sense as a whole. The images flicked from one to another in quick succession. Merryn was transfixed and unable to move. She watched intently and could see clearly: Perfect Haven – the white house on the headland, the beautiful old church at Church Cove close to the beach, a group of Banas Mihtig soldiers carrying yellow-lit lanterns, a dark, narrow passageway, arms thrashing wildly in frothy, white water, an impressive array of jewels and coins in a wooden box, shining and colourful under the water, and a small cave.

The images replayed several times before they began to gradually fade until they had disappeared from her view completely. Merryn blinked a few times to see if they had really gone. She then noticed that the ghostly figure had stepped away from her and placed her hands over her chest in the place where her heart would have been, before clasping them together before her. She bowed her head slightly then looked directly at Merryn. She then smiled with her lips remaining pressed together as her image faded and she slowly vanished from Merryn's view.

MERRYN WAS REALLY pleased that Luke had decided to hold a birthday party. It meant that she could spend some much-needed quality time with her friends and in particular with Xance. The past few weeks had been a whirl-wind of events and happenings and Merryn was still trying to come to terms with her new life and the fantastical direction that it had taken. She would be seventeen herself the following week, and so was secretly celebrating ahead of time as she had no plans to throw her own party. She had made the decision that she should wait until her eighteenth to have a big celebration, and that she would much rather spend this birthday quietly with Xance and her family.

She had spent more than an hour choosing what to wear. After several texts to Chloe, Amelie and Erin to ascertain what they would be wearing, she had decided on a plain black dress. It was simple yet elegant, featuring a low, square neckline with short sleeves and a fitted mini skirt. Merryn was concerned that it was slightly too short. She had stood before the full-length mirror, in her bedroom, for several minutes pulling at the hem in a fruitless attempt to make the dress longer. She liked how she looked, but was concerned that she was going to spend the evening constantly worrying that she was showing a little too much of her thighs. After deliberating for far too long, she managed to convince herself that she should wear what she wanted to as she was going to a party not to school. She was also safe in the knowledge that these were the exact words that Chloe had messaged her earlier via text.

Merryn took a deep breath as she walked into Luke's house alone. This was a brave move for her, but she had arranged to meet Xance there later, after his meeting. Her friends had offered to wait for her at the harbour, but she had decided that if she could participate in a fight against Nethergeard soldiers, she was fully capable of entering a house party unaccompanied.

The lights in the main room were pulsating rhythmically in time with the thudding music, and Merryn stood for a few seconds surveying the scene. Nervously looking for her friends, she twisted her curled, long brown hair between her fingers. After few seconds, she spotted Chloe and Carter on a large sofa on the far side of the lounge. Chloe was sitting sideways across Carter's lap and they were laughing and drinking from plastic beakers. Merryn made her way over. Chloe leapt up when she saw Merryn and squealed loudly as she hugged her friend excitedly.

"Yay! You made it! Come with me, we'll get you a drink, I need to get me and Carter a refill."

Merryn mouthed "Hi" at Carter as she was led off into the kitchen by Chloe, who was half-dancing and half-walking to the beat of the music. The worktop in the kitchen displayed an array of beverages ranging from cider to fruit juices to mixers and alcoholic spirits. Everyone had been asked to bring something to drink with them. Chloe reached for a bottle of vodka and poured two slightly over-generous shots before adding coke to top them up.

"What drink have you brought?" Chloe asked Merryn, grinning.

Merryn lifted up a bottle of white rum that had been partly covered by the jacket that she was carrying, and pulled a funny face. Chloe grabbed her a cup from the stack on the side, took the bottle from Merryn, and began to pour freehand.

"Whoa! That's great, thanks," laughed Merryn, gesturing with her hand for Chloe to stop pouring. Merryn added some diet cola, filling the cup as near to the brim as she dare to try to counteract the amount of spirit Chloe had added. Merryn was not really a big drinker. She liked the occasional cider and sometimes had a white rum and cola or a glass of wine at home with her parents, but she was not at all keen on the idea of getting drunk and making a complete idiot of herself as she had witnessed so many of her peers doing at previous parties over the last couple of years. Yes, she wanted to have fun, but she did not want to wake up tomorrow morning and not be able to remember what an arse she had made of herself, whilst everyone else sniggered and giggled behind her back.

The girls walked back into the lounge and sat on the sofa with Carter, who had been chatting to Luke. It was clear that he had already indulged slightly too much in drink as he was beginning to slur his words and kept repeating that he was having an amazing birthday every few minutes, which the others found highly amusing.

After Carter and Chloe had downed their drinks swiftly, they decided to take to the dance floor – Carter was definitely not a dancer, and Merryn giggled at his dreadful attempts to twirl Chloe around romantically to an upbeat music track. After a few minutes, she decided to go for a wander to see what else was happening. She noticed that Emily and her group of friends were over on the window seat. As usual, they had their heads together, resembling a witches' coven, and were talking and watching the activity in the room. *Probably bitching about everyone*, Merryn thought to herself. As she walked to the far side of the room, she spotted Tyler and Amelie, and his other friends that she had been bowling with all huddled together in a large group. She stopped for a quick chat. Tyler had his arms scooped around Amelie's waist as she stood in front of him. Merryn thought that they looked great together.

"Where's Xance?" Tyler enquired. "You're not on your own, are you?" he added showing genuine concern.

"I am at the minute. He'll be here later. He has somewhere important to be first. He shouldn't be too long, hopefully," Merryn half-shouted over the music.

She smiled and told them she would catch up with them later as she moved off to see what else was happening. She made her way into the dining room where she could see that Bryn, Tom and Jason were playing some sort of drinking game with a bunch of other people from school. She watched for a moment as Bryn shouted and cursed when the game didn't seem to be going his way. At one point, he kicked out at a chair, clearly annoyed. Merryn approached him and tapped him on the shoulder to get his attention.

"Are you alright, Bryn?" she asked.

He swung round on his chair, and faced her. She noticed that he had added a thinly shaved line into the side of his slightly top-heavy afro hairstyle and she thought it looked great.

"Yes, everything's just great," he answered sarcastically.

"Did something happen to upset you?" Merryn continued.

"No. I'm fine, honestly. Don't worry about it. I'm just having a good time with my friends," he slurred angrily.

"Where's Harry?" she glanced around not seeing him anywhere.

Bryn shrugged his shoulders and scrunched his nose up childishly before turning back to join the game.

Merryn looked across at Tom, who smiled at her and mouthed, "He'll be ok."

Merryn moved on. She really hoped that Xance got there soon. She desperately wanted to be with him, and she was worried about what the meeting would entail for him. She was conscious that she could have lost him this week, and it had played on her mind more than she had revealed to those around her. She just wanted to be in his company for a while and have some fun.

Realising that her cup was empty, she made a brief stop off at the kitchen to refill her drink, taking care not to over-do the rum. A boy called Adam, who she only recognised vaguely from school, was leaning over the sink splashing cold water onto his face. Merryn noticed that he was not doing a great job as most of the water was hitting the front of his T-shirt. She laughed to herself as she made her way out into the back garden to get some air. The evening was warm and despite the fact that the doors and windows of the house were all open, the heat in the house was quite stifling.

On a small wall that surrounded a neat patio area in the back garden, sat Erin and Harry. Merryn had spotted them, but they appeared not to have seen her. She observed for a few moments as they seemed deep in conversation with each other, and Erin's head was leaning delicately on Harry's shoulder. As Merryn took a sip of her drink, she was shocked to see Harry lean in and kiss Erin. Not a brief peck, but a full-on meaningful, lingering kiss. *Maybe that was what Bryn was so upset about*, Merryn thought to herself as she made a hasty exit from their view and walked deeper into the garden.

Full of established trees and shrubs, the back garden of Luke's house was beautiful. Someone had gone to enormous expense stringing thousands of multicoloured fairy lights up through every available branch and bush. It gave the garden an ethereal, almost magical feel, and Merryn loved it. She wandered further along towards the bottom of the grounds. The space was divided up into smaller sections by pieces of tall trellis. At the end of the garden, Merryn found a space that was almost entirely screened off from the rest by a dark-green, thick hedge. Behind this, was a circular, stoned patio complete with garden sofa decorated with a selection of brightly coloured cushions. A painted, blue summer house sat in the corner, and several blue plant pots filled with different coloured flowers were positioned neatly in strategic places. Merryn sat down on the sofa and held a cushion to her stomach. She drank her drink, and listened to the distant thumping of the music from inside the house.

She hadn't sat there alone for long when she heard a slight rustle from behind the hedge. Looking up, she saw Xance appear through the gap carrying two drinks, one in each hand. He was wearing dark jeans and a black T-shirt as usual, and Merryn smiled as she thought how utterly gorgeous he looked. He sat down next to her and handed her one of the cups.

"Hi," he smiled.

"Hi, thanks," Merryn said before finishing the drink she was already holding and placing the cup down on the floor at the side of the sofa.

"How did it go?" she asked, turning to angle herself towards Xance so that she could look at him.

"Sorry?" Xance said.

"The meeting, with the First Luminary, how did it go?" she tapped him playfully on the arm.

"Oh, it was ok. Let's not talk about that now. It's a party. I want to be with you!" he smiled and nudged her with his shoulder. They sat and chatted whilst drinking. Merryn filled Xance in on all the stuff he'd missed earlier on and he listened intently, barely moving his eyes from her face.

She shared with him how concerned she was about Bryn and how he seemed to be acting erratically, but then how she had witnessed Harry kissing Erin. She discussed whether perhaps Harry was confused about his feelings towards Bryn as the two of them had always seemed really close, and how strange it was that he now appeared to have feelings for Erin, concluding that she wanted to support both her friends, but it wasn't really her business to get involved. Once she had reached the end of her recount, Merryn suddenly became aware that she had rattled on for several minutes without barely taking a breath.

"Sorry," she said, looking up at Xance.

"For what?" he said, entwining pieces of her hair affectionately through his fingers.

"For talking too much. I think I was nervous for you,

and nervous about being here without you and when my anxiety is released, I talk too much." She smiled at him nervously.

"It's fine," Xance reassured her taking her hand and squeezing it gently. "Come for a walk with me?" He stood up still holding her hand.

"Alright, but what about the party?" Merryn replied, standing up too.

"We can come back later, I just want it to be just you and me for a while, is that ok?"

Merryn nodded and smiled, and the two of them made their way through the house and out the front door into the street.

Luke's house was high up the hill on the side of the village that overlooked the headland. Merryn walked with Xance up onto the grassy tor and they made their way across the headland towards the Koyt. The harbour below them had a pretty display of lights coming from various buildings and some of the small vessels on the water. They could just about see the people dotted outside Kitto's Cave, which seemed quiet as most of its usual customers were at Luke's party. It was getting dark and Merryn had to watch her feet as she walked through some of the longer grass, to make sure she didn't fall. She was now feeling slightly cold and had put on her jacket. The weather had begun to take a turn for the worse; dark clouds were gathering over the water, and were slowly creeping their way inland. The breeze from the sea carried a slight chill across the headland.

On reaching the Koyt, they both stood and leant backwards against it so that they could look out to sea. One or two lights from small boats could be seen in the distance, and the sound of the waves crashing with vigour against the rocks below could be heard along with the loud whooshing of the increasing wind. The darkening sky met the deep, blue-black of the sea and created a dramatic backdrop for the Koyt stones, which were highlighted intermittently as the moon peeked from behind a blackened shroud of clouds. Xance stepped in front of Merryn and straddled her feet with his. He placed one of his hands at the back of Merryn's head and held her gently. Her body reacted to his touch and a wave of prickles moved down her spine.

"I've missed you so much," Xance whispered as he leant in and kissed Merryn gently on the lips.

She kissed him back. She had missed him too. She hadn't realised how desperate she had been to feel him kiss her again, until it happened. He caressed her hair and she arched backwards slightly, leaning on the rocks of the Koyt. She gasped as Xance moved his lips down one side of her neck, planting a succession of kisses in a line before moving back up to meet her lips once more. This time his kiss was stronger, more powerful. He grabbed at her hair and pulled it gently in his fist as his tongue flicked and moved across her lips before he kissed her deeply once more. Merryn's body shuddered and trembled at the feeling of his mouth on hers. She could feel his strong torso pushed hard against her and she wrapped both her arms around his waist and tried to pull him even closer. He felt so good in her arms. He pulled at her hair once more, this time with more energy and Merryn moaned quietly under his touch. Xance slipped her jacket from her shoulders and let it drop to the floor at their feet. His lips travelled down her neck again, but this time they continued further, gliding across her shoulder before moving back up to her mouth. Xance pressed harder and Merryn thought she could sense a feeling of desperation or angst in his kisses. There was something so familiar about the emotion that she was experiencing, but Merryn knew that Xance had never been this passionate or intense with her before. He had constantly made her feel so special, so wanted, but there was always a sense of reserve; a feeling that he didn't want to lose control. Merryn could sense that at this very moment he was different. This was him on the edge. She truly felt that this was him – lost of all composure and totally hers. She was hot with his passion and the feeling of his body against hers. Dizziness filled her head and she was no longer fully aware of her surroundings. Now Xance's pelvic area was pushed up hard against hers and he grabbed and pulled at her hair and skin with increasing urgency as his lips found their way to her chest. He jabbed and stroked hard with his tongue at the bare skin just above the low neck-line of her dress and Merryn cried out pleasurably at the intensity and ardour of his passion. Again, he lifted his head and kissed her hard on the mouth, his parted lips moving eagerly on hers. Merryn reciprocated his passion. She pushed up with her pelvis so she could feel Xance's firm body against her and she kissed him open-mouthed and fervently. She stroked his back and gently tugged at his blonde hair.

Xance whispered into her ear again, pulling her so close, "I want you Merryn. I've always wanted you."

"I want you too, Xance," Merryn breathed back huskily.

"I've always loved you. It's always a struggle to control myself when I'm with you. You do something to me," Xance continued as he nuzzled her ear affectionately.

"I feel the same. I know now that I have always loved you." Merryn leant in and kissed Xance's neck.

He stroked her side, cupping his hand to her breast as he kissed her desperately and wildly on her mouth. Merryn arched backwards at his touch. She opened her eyes and looked up at the grey clouds and blackness.

"Beautiful Kerenza, I want you so much," he spoke softly.

In that second, Merryn froze. She blinked her eyes as she looked up at the sky. Unable to move, her limbs went rigid and she held her breath momentarily. *This can't be*, she thought to herself. *It's not possible.*

Without warning, she pushed him away from her and began screaming uncontrollably, "No! No! How could you?"

"Merryn, I …"

"Don't speak to me! Leave me alone!" she screamed again. Merryn dropped down, bending her knees and leaning her back against the Koyt. She placed her head in her hands and shook it from side to side then covered her face with her arms and sobbed uncontrollably. He said nothing. After several seconds, she wiped her face and looked up. Before her stood Nix: solemn-faced and lifeless, his raven-black hair hanging partly in his face and glistening in the shards of light from the moon.

"You are so cruel, what did I do to deserve this?" she

asked in a weary, exasperated voice. She could not believe that this was possible. Nix had somehow made himself appear to be Xance! *It must be an act of magic or sorcery,* she thought. There was no other explanation.

"Kerenza, I'm so sorry. I never meant to upset you. I meant what I said," Nix stepped forwards and knelt down before Merryn so that he could look directly at her.

She looked into his eyes, "Who *are* you, Nix?"

"I wish I could just tell you, but it's not that simple. You'll remember, I promise. You just have to give it time," Nix said gently as he stretched out his hand and placed it on Merryn's arm.

She jerked her arm away. She didn't want him near her. Merryn's mind was racing with thoughts. How could she know someone from Nethergeard? She had no memories that she could recall of the place. She was a Sefwarian Nyss. The Nethergeard people were their enemies. Her heart was thudding within her chest and she felt nauseous. Wiping away another tear she cried, "Please, please, just leave me alone."

"I won't leave you like this," Nix said.

Merryn stood up and looked down at him speaking through gritted teeth, "Don't pretend to be nice. You have done a terrible thing."

Then Merryn ran. She didn't look back. She headed right, away from the harbour, and across towards the far side of the headland where the cliff had a sheer drop to the sea before graduating down in a steady slope towards the beach at Church Cove, leaving Nix on his knees and alone.

28

Mathikoy

The sea swirled menacingly below, the white foam crashing angrily against the rocks, sending the sea spray high above the circling water. In the distance, Porthrosen church was barely visible as it stood cloaked in the thick, grey mist that had crawled across the tiny beach and enveloped everything in its path.

Watching through tear-streaked, blurry eyes, Merryn stared down through the ever-thickening mist at the crests of white, frothy waves that smashed and slapped at the dark-grey rock that rose out of the water. She breathed heavily as she sobbed uncontrollably; tears soaking her face and stinging her eyes. Her cheeks were hot and inflamed, the skirt of her black dress flapped wildly at her thighs and her hair raged angrily against her face as the inevitable storm gathered power. She didn't feel the cold. Instead, she felt almost numb. Merryn knew that she should feel anger or hatred, but she couldn't seem to muster the emotion. If she was feeling anything, it was confusion. She couldn't comprehend fully what had happened. How could one person appear to be someone else? It just didn't make any sense. How did she not notice? She racked her brains, reliving every second of the evening at the party and the time after they had left. She had tried to find a moment when she should have realised that it wasn't Xance she was with. She knew that she had recognised certain nuances in his behaviour that pointed to him losing his usual restraint where their physical relationship was concerned, but she'd still thought that it was him. Why would she think anything else? She felt so stupid. Surely, she should have been able to tell that it wasn't Xance?

Then it hit her. She was feeling guilty. She should have known! How was Xance ever going to forgive her? Would she be able to forgive him, if the tables were turned? She swayed dangerously close to the edge of the cliff. For a split second, she thought about falling, but she knew that was just a foolish reaction to her stress. She would never do something so awful, so final. There would be a solution to all of this … she just couldn't see it right now. Feeling helpless, Merryn slumped to the grass and gave in to her tears once more.

In the darkness, as the howling wind raged around her, Merryn thought she saw a person walking out of the mist along the cliff edge. She wiped at her eyes and blinked. The figure was standing before her, ghostly and pale, with its white, long dress thrashing at the ankles.

Merryn instantly knew that it was the spirit girl that she had seen several times in her bedroom. She knelt down before Merryn and sat on the grass facing her. Reaching out her hands, she clasped them over Merryn's and smiled gently. Merryn instantly felt calmer. As soon as her hands were covered, she began to see the visions again; animated in the air in front of her. This time though, they seemed clearer; more vivid than they had ever been before. She could see a girl that she thought was herself. She was wearing a long dark-coloured dress, and her hair was plaited centrally down her back. Merryn recognised this girl as herself, as she looked to be the same girl that she had seen when she saw her past-self with Xance on the day that he had taken her to the river. However, this image was not quite the same. What she was seeing now was a version of herself in 1800s dress, as before, but she was standing on the headland overlooking the sea and was embracing *Nix*. Merryn continued to watch the image, and saw her past-self kiss Nix and run her fingers through his raven-black hair. She also saw the montage of images that she had seen previously; Porthrosen church, the dark, narrow passageway, Perfect Haven house, the flailing arms in the water, a cave, the dotted lights on the headland, herself embracing Xance, and finally the collection of jewels.

Once the images had ceased, the girl nodded her head at Merryn. She then stood up and walked calmly away, disappearing into the thick mist. Merryn sat motionless for several minutes. She was no longer frightened by the appearance of the apparition – in fact, she felt almost comforted by the ghost's visit. Merryn felt sure that this girl was linked to her past, and that she was trying to impart information. Xance had said that spirits from the Sefwarian Nyss world could sometimes communicate with the living. She was certain that the ghostly figure was attempting to tell her something, and as she had appeared before her so many times, Merryn was convinced that the message must be important in some way. What was difficult for her to process, however, was the vision of herself in the arms of Nix. At least she was almost certain that it had been him. The one doubt in her mind was the fact that he had not been wearing his Banas Mihtig uniform. He was dressed simply in dark trousers and a shirt, open at the neck.

At that moment, Merryn heard a rustling in the grass behind her. She was swiftly brought back to reality, and she swung round to see what was approaching. Through the mixture of darkness and mist she saw Xance coming towards her from the direction of the Koyt, carrying her jacket.

"Merryn?" he said, "Oh, thank goodness that I've found you!" He sat down with her and pulled her in to his chest. He held her so tightly that she thought she would stop breathing for a second. Then he relaxed his hold on her, and moved her away slightly so that he could look at her face.

"Xance, is it really you?" Merryn spoke nervously, eyeing his face carefully. Her heart began to beat too fast again as her nerves kicked in.

"Of course, it's me. I was so worried about you. What's going on? Are you alright? What on earth are you doing out here alone?"

"I don't know how to explain, Xance," Merryn said. She felt so embarrassed. She knew that she had let him down.

"Merryn, I got to the party and Chloe said that she thought she had seen you leave ... *with me!* What happened?" Xance sounded concerned, "Who were you with?"

He stroked her hair and she felt comforted by his touch, although inside she was anxious to make sure that this time it was really was him.

"Xance, tell me where you were when you first saw me," she said grabbing his hands and squeezing them far too tightly.

"What ... why?" Xance questioned.

"Please! Just tell me!"

"Ok. I was in art class. I knew it was you, the second I saw you."

Merryn began to sob. The relief of knowing that she was actually with Xance was too much for her. Her shoulders juddered up and down as the tears streamed down her face. Xance pulled her in to his chest once more. She could feel his heart beating against her cheek. He smelt so good and she felt safe in his strong arms.

Eventually, she wiped away her tears and spoke, "I don't know how to tell you what happened, Xance. I'm so ashamed. I thought he was you!" she blurted.

"You thought *who* was me?"

"Nix."

"Nix? He was at the party?"

Xance's voice had dropped low, and Merryn was

scared that he may lose control again and go after Nix as he did before.

"Yes, but this is the bit that I don't understand … he looked like you! I mean, *exactly like you. He was you.* I don't know how, but he fooled me. I thought it was you, so I left the party with you to go for a walk."

"The evil, conniving … I'll …" Xance stopped for a second before continuing, "Merryn, are you ok? Did he hurt you?"

"I'm alright, honestly. How did he do it? How did he make himself look like you? He even sounded like you," Merryn said.

"He's obviously been bestowed with the gift of magic. Some Nethergeards are given it as a reward. He's a Mathikoy. He'll be able to use a hex to shape-shift," Xance explained angrily.

"Shape-shift?" Merryn was still confused.

"Yeah, it means that he can become the shape of another person. He will look like them and sound like them – but he won't have their mind or their thoughts."

"I'm so sorry, Xance. I really thought he was you. Can you forgive me?"

"Forgive you for what?" Xance said, showing concern.

Merryn looked down at the grass. She knew that she had to tell him, but she desperately didn't want to hurt him. Taking a deep breath, she said quietly, "I kissed him. I'm so sorry."

As she said it, she looked directly into Xance's eyes. She wanted him to understand that she was truly remorseful.

Xance didn't say anything. He stared straight at Merryn, but he didn't seem to be focussing on her. It was almost as if he was looking through her. She watched anxiously as he ran his hand through his hair several times.

"It's ok, Merryn," he eventually said, breaking the silence, "Well, it's not ok, but it's not your fault. I'm gutted that it happened, I just hope that you're alright."

"Xance, I'm fine. Stop worrying," Merryn tried to sound as convincing as possible as she stroked his arm, but inside she was crumbling. She felt sickened to the stomach that she had been so close to Nix, and at this point, she was unsure how she was going to move on from what had happened.

"Xance promise me that you won't tell the others about this. I'm so ashamed. I couldn't face them if they knew.

"Of course, I promise. Don't worry, he won't get away with it. I will deal with him … it's just … I've had to promise the First Luminary that I won't do anything in haste or anger again. I need to think about how I'm going to sort this, but I promise you, I will."

"Xance, I'm not sure that there's anything that you can do to him that's going to take away how awful I feel. I can't believe that I was like that with him. I should have known it wasn't you."

"Don't blame yourself. He knew exactly what he was doing," Xance paused for a second or two before continuing tentatively, "He … *you only kissed him?*"

Merryn stared at Xance and gulped down her nervousness. She knew that she had to tell the truth, it was only fair, "Yes, we kissed ... a lot, and it got quite ... heated."

Xance questioned, "Heated?"

She could see by the expression on his face that he was distraught.

He continued, "Did you ...?"

"No! No! We just kissed. It was intense. Passionate. Nothing more happened. I ... I don't ever want to lie to you Xance, so I have to be honest and say that for a few minutes, I wanted it to be more. He made me feel so good, but you have to believe me that I only felt like that because I thought it was you! His touch felt so familiar – I don't know how. I truly thought it was you. I didn't have any reason to think otherwise." Merryn began to cry once more. Guilt was consuming her and she was desperate for Xance to believe her and understand what had happened.

"Right, yes, I didn't think of that," Xance muttered half under his breath.

"You didn't think of what?"

"Nothing ... I ..." he stopped himself from speaking again.

"Xance?" Merryn pawed at his arm then stroked his face, but he moved away from her hand gently, obviously upset and finding it hard to digest what she had told him.

"It doesn't matter."

"Please, Xance. I know that there's something that you're not telling me. What is it about Nix that you won't tell me? How could he know me when he's from Nethergeard? And why can't I remember?"

Xance looked into her with his deep, blue eyes. She could see the hurt and devastation within them, and her stomach turned over and knotted at the thought of causing him pain.

"Merryn, selfishly, I don't want to tell you, but the truth is that I can't. You're right, with what you suspect – there is something, but I cannot tell you. Just as before, when you had to remember me, you will have to remember this on your own. I can't tell you. It would have dire consequences for Sefwarian Nyss and our people. I can't bear the thought that you will remember one day, but it is almost inevitable that you will," Xance explained sounding defeated and forlorn.

"I see," Merryn said, feeling dejected.

Xance, glanced around at the cloak of mist that was eerily close to them now.

"This storm is really going to take hold soon, we should start getting back to the village," he said starting to stand. He reached out and Merryn took his hand and stood up too. She breathed in deeply as he pulled her into his chest and squeezed tightly. She felt so safe in his arms, and now she was slightly calmer, she was grateful of the warmth that they provided. Xance held out her jacket and she pulled it on over her cold, damp arms. Then, steadily, hand in hand, they made their way carefully back towards the harbour as the rain began to pour down.

29

She ran. She couldn't see more than a few feet in front of her in the dark, narrow passageway, but she knew she had to keep running. The ground was hard underneath her bare feet, and every few steps she would land on a loose stone and wince as the pain shot through her foot and up her leg. She used her hands against the walls on either side to guide her along. In places, the stone was wet and her hands stung and throbbed from the cold. She needed to catch her breath and so slowed her pace to a quick walk. The tunnel seemed to be climbing in a fairly steep incline, and she could feel the muscles in her thighs having to work hard to continue to carry her forwards ...

She was in a church. It was dark, but the bright moonlight that streamed through the large stained-glass window provided just enough light so that she could just make out the wooden pews in regimented rows, and the beautifully carved wooden pulpit sitting high above the seats. She ran along the aisle and up a small set of steps to the back of the church. Turning left, *she reached a large, heavy arched doorway. Pulling at the circular metal handle, she managed to swing the exit open. Then there was nothing but darkness...*

HER KNEES STUNG AND ACHED. Blood had seeped from her leg and mixed with the salt water that soaked the hard stone underneath her. She sat motionless and exhausted, listening to the sound of the sea in the cave moving against the side of the rock. It's lulling, rhythmical lapping, and deep, sparkling glow hid the truth of what was slowly sinking beneath its beauty. She knew that she had tried her best, but he had been too strong, and he had the advantage of the boat. She hadn't really stood a chance...

Links

Merryn arrived early at the harbour the following morning. She had spent a restless night falling in and out of sleep. It seemed as though every time she managed to drift off, her dreams would take her back to the Koyt with Nix. She kept reliving all the detail of their liaison. Strangely though, her memory of this episode put her at the Koyt with Nix – not Xance. She was moving her fingers through his dark, wavy hair as he kissed her. She looked into his deep, dark brown eyes and felt a quiver run down her spine. In her dream, she knew that she loved everything about him; the way he looked, the way he held her, the way he touched her. She knew that it was her mind's way of continuing the guilt. She was never going to forgive herself for not realising that it wasn't Xance.

But something else niggled at her, and she was struggling with this more than her feeling of foolishness. She couldn't bring to her mind any long-term memory of Nix. She was convinced that he had some part to play in her past, and Xance had mostly confirmed this (although he hadn't actually come out and said it), but she just couldn't remember. She had an underlying feeling that there was something about Nix that was familiar to her, and despite the fact that he was the enemy, being a Nethergeard soldier, she couldn't help being drawn to him in some weird way.

Xance had requested everyone to meet at ten o'clock at the harbour. Fortunately, the storm from the previous night had cleared up now and Merryn was basking in the warm sun that peeked from behind a few loitering, grey clouds. The harbour was bustling with activity. The Saturday morning shoppers were out in force, and there was the usual small queue outside the bakery next to Kitto's Cave. A few small boats chugged gently out of the harbour and disappeared off around the point of the headland.

The group of Nyss arrived in a fairly steady stream; first Carter and Chloe together, then Xance, who Merryn had witnessed talking to Emily on the corner by the harbour steps a few moments earlier, Bryn, Tom, Jason, Luke, (who appeared to be nursing a particularly bad headache and had his hat pulled down to shade his eyes from the sun), and finally, Harry. Merryn watched as they all made their way to where she was sat on the wooden bench opposite The Run Inn. She could see that the awkwardness between Harry and Bryn was palpable.

They arrived separately, and sat down on the cobbled pavement at some distance from each other. Save a cursory greeting to everyone, neither of them spoke.

Once they were all present, Xance briefed them on his meeting with the First Luminary. They all listened carefully as he explained to them what he had been told. The information that the Sefwarian Intelligence agents had found informed them that the Magister Worlega, of Nethergeard, had tasked a division of his Banas Mihtig army to search for and find a fortune of jewels and coins. He had apparently received knowledge of its existence many years ago, but they did not know why he had waited until now to begin the search. Xance continued to share that the Nethergeard's seemed to think that the haul was somewhere in Porthrosen, as the village is home to several hexed structures that provide a gateway to other worlds, and it seemed the most logical place to conceal something that you may later want to remove to somewhere else.

"So, what you're saying is that the Banas Mihtig have been coming into Porthrosen to find treasure?" Carter interrupted.

"It seems so, yes," Xance replied, "If our information is correct, they now know where it is located, and they intend to strike at midnight tonight so we don't have a lot of time."

"But, if that's true, that they're looking for valuables, it doesn't make any sense," Carter continued.

"I know what you're going to say ... I had the same thought," Xance smiled.

"They don't need any treasure or jewels. The Magister

Worlega is already spectacularly wealthy. It just doesn't make sense that he would risk a war with the Sefwarian Nyss people after all these years to merely add to his fortune." Carter was standing now and pacing up and down with agitation.

"So, it's got to be something else?" Tom questioned.

"Yes, definitely," Xance nodded, "We are going to have to assume that whatever it is they are here for, it's not simply the jewels and coins. We know that the Magister Worlega wants ultimate power. We know that historically, he has tried before to take control of other worlds, including our own. He knows that we are here, in Porthrosen, to provide protection for Earth. So, whatever it is that the Banas Mihtig are really here for, it must be worth the risk of stirring up trouble with us, and it will most definitely have dire consequences for Sefwarian Nyss, probably the end of our freedom, otherwise it wouldn't be worth it for them. The problem is, if they really are coming here tonight, we are going to have to think up a strategy quickly."

Just then, Merryn remembered that some of the visions that she had experienced contained images of jewellery and coins inside a wooden box. She knew that she had to share this information with the others, but felt slightly apprehensive to say it aloud and sound ridiculous. She could see that Carter was becoming more and more troubled as his pacing was quickening.

"Xance … I may know something," she started then paused. All eyes were upon her, and the group fell into silence, waiting for her to speak. Merryn's nerves sent shudders into her stomach. She knew that she just had to

244

tell them what she could remember, even if it didn't make sense.

"I've been having visions and vivid dreams. In these, I have seen treasure: jewels and coins – in a box. It sounds ridiculous, but a spirit girl has been visiting me, and enabling the visions. I think she is trying to get me to remember something … from before … from the past," Merryn explained.

"Remember what though? Where were the jewels?" Carter approached Merryn and stood directly in front of her in an agitated manner.

"Carter, take it easy," Xance said, ushering him to move away. Carter stepped back as Chloe pulled on his arm to encourage him to sit down next to her on the cobbles.

"That's the problem," Merryn continued, "I'm not sure."

"Well, what else was in your visions? Maybe that will help," Luke said.

Merryn took a couple of large breaths in and out as she tried to compose her thoughts.

"There was water," she began, "Someone was in the water. They were in trouble. Someone else was in a boat."

"Where, in the sea?" Carter asked.

"No, I don't think so. It was dark. It was a cave, with water in it. The wooden box was under water."

"Well, if it's in a cave, that narrows it down a little," said Xance sounding encouraging, "There's quite a few around this coastline though so we going to need something else to help us pinpoint the place."

"I'm sorry, I'm trying to recall what else there was," Merryn apologised.

"Hey, it's ok," Xance reassured her.

"However, if you could hurry this up that would be better. A whole world is depending on you to solve this," Carter added anxiously.

Chloe nudged Carter with her elbow and hissed at him to shut up. Merryn noticed Xance had given him a warning look.

"I'm sorry, Merryn. I'm not trying to make you feel bad. I just want to be able to stop them before it's too late," Carter looked rueful.

"I know, you do," Merryn said, "I want to stop them too, we all do. I had no idea the visions were so important. I thought they were personal to me. I haven't been able to make much sense of them."

"Just try to recollect what you have seen. Was there something to do with lights at night?" Xance said, placing his hand on her arm and rubbing it reassuringly. She was grateful of his kindness, and felt comforted by his touch.

"Yes, I saw lots of small lights moving on the headland at night. I have seen a long, dark tunnel, the white house, Perfect Haven and Porthrosen church," Merryn recalled.

"That makes me think that the jewels could be located not too far away. There are about four different caves that we know about under the headland, but only one that is really close to Porthrosen church," Carter said.

"Roche cave!" Xance cried. "Accessible only by boat," he added.

"Where is it?" Merryn asked.

"It's a little further round the headland – just west of Church Cove," Xance explained.

"Well, we seem to have made a link from the church to the cave, is it possible that they could be joined by an underground tunnel, and perhaps with the house too? Could that be what you have seen, Merryn?" Tom asked. "You said that you had seen a tunnel?"

"Yes, I suppose it's possible. I don't know though. I only saw everything as separate images. I didn't ever see them together so I don't know if they are linked. I have no idea where the tunnel is – I just saw a tunnel. To be honest, it could have been anywhere." Merryn felt exasperated. She was so frustrated with herself for not being able to connect what she had seen and help all of it make sense. Now she had the pressure that everyone was relying on her. What if they were wrong and the tunnel didn't link the church to the cave? What if her clues were going to make them look in completely the wrong place?

"We have very little choice but to investigate further tonight and see what we can find. Hopefully, the Banas Mihtig will be there and we can resolve this. One thing is for certain, we cannot allow them to have free rein in Porthrosen and take whatever it is that they are so desperately looking for. Sefwarian Nyss is depending on us to protect its people. I couldn't live with myself if we didn't try," Xance said.

"Absolutely, there's no way that we're going to let them get away with this! They obviously think that they have the advantage. That Maddox has been nothing but smarmy the last few times we have encountered him. He thinks he's got one over on us," Carter responded.

Merryn could see that he was clearly riled by the situation and his temper was flaring once more.

"We'll meet at the church at eleven thirty tonight," Xance instructed everyone.

31

Perfect Haven

As they approached Porthrosen church, it became clear that there was already movement inside. Xance had indicated that he had spotted one or two small, yellow lights flickering from within the ancient building. In addition, Merryn's Elkalind rune, along with everyone else's, had appeared and was tingling fiercely on her wrist – suggesting that whatever was inside the church was most definitely from Nethergeard. Merryn watched as Carter climbed up on to a stone that jutted out from a mound of grass close to the church building. He observed through an obscured stained-glass window, then jumped down and informed everyone that he could see the shadows of several people within the church. It was clear that the Nethergeard soldiers had arrived earlier than expected.

Without further discussion, the huge, wooden door of the building was pushed open by Carter and Xance, and they all stormed in, their cemp-edge swords held aloft, in a colourful display of solidarity; ready for conflict. Merryn did not have time to think about what would happen once they were inside – she knew that she would have to act on her instinct and rely on her skill as a fighter. The group of Banas Mihtig soldiers were clearly taken by surprise, but did not shy away from a fight. Immediately, Maddox and Nix ran towards Xance and the other Cempalli soldiers. They were swiftly followed by their allies, and a huge fight began in the half-dark of the moonlit church.

Merryn and Chloe fought side by side, focussing on one particularly awkward opponent, whom neither of them recognised. He was a skilled fighter, and showed excellent use of his spear, which he wielded above his head like a helicopter blade before lunging forwards towards them. Despite his accomplished ability, he was no match for the pair of them together, and Merryn breathed out heavily in relief as she nodded at Chloe to make the final kick and send him flying through the wooden door of the church to land in an unconscious heap on the grass outside.

There was no time to rest, however, as Merryn's attention was soon taken by Kai, who had leapt on her from behind and was attempting to wrestle her to the floor. She managed to push him off, despite the fact that he was incredibly tall and physically strong, and he slid across the stone floor of the church. Chloe shouted to Merryn, and pointed towards the back of the church, where Maddox could be seen sliding a large picture sideways across a wall to reveal a hidden exit. Without further delay, he disappeared through a small, wooden, arched doorway holding what appeared to be a girl by the hair. Merryn was shocked as she recognised her immediately, and couldn't fathom why she was in the church at all. *What on earth is Emily doing here?*

Chloe ran through the middle of the fray, jumping on to and then over one of the wooden pews in pursuit of Maddox. Merryn knew instantly that she should follow, but Kai had other ideas and he grabbed her as she attempted to run past him, and pulled her towards him; the blade of his spear dangerously close to her chest. Merryn froze. She held her breath, and surveyed the frenzied scene of aggression that was playing out before her, as the sharp point began to press against her body. Before she had time to think, she felt a thud from behind. She was forced to the floor where she rolled over and swiftly came back upright to see Nix standing there and Kai lying on his front on the floor. She moved backwards, edging away from Nix as she observed the altercation that followed. She saw Kai appear to threaten Nix with his spear as he stood up, thrusting his weapon towards him aggressively. Merryn was convinced that she heard Nix shout something that sounded like: "I thought you were one of them," before he turned away from her and strode back to the mix of fighters, wading in with a sideways kick to Xance's chest. Merryn was in a predicament now as she crouched behind the wooden pew. She could see that she would be of use in the fight here in the church, and she was ultimately stressed about the possibility of

Xance getting hurt and she wanted to be present to look out for him, but she was also aware that Chloe had gone off on her own in pursuit of Maddox and Emily.

As she deliberated over what she felt was an impossible decision, she had forgotten all about Kai. Now she found herself being grabbed from behind once more. He held her by her hair and placed the silver blade of his spear perilously close to her throat. Merryn dared not breathe nor grapple too hard to attempt to free herself from his hold. She felt that Kai seemed more determined this time. As he dragged her backwards, she squirmed as much as she dare, but it wasn't enough to release herself from his grip. They eventually reached the small, wooden door at the back of the church where Maddox had disappeared. Merryn saw Kai take one last look at the ongoing battle behind him, as he went through the doorway taking her with him.

As Kai pulled Merryn through another tiny door which was positioned low to the floor of the small corridor in which they were now stood, she saw that the ground began to drop away at quite a steep, downward gradient. He continued to pull on her hair as he dragged her along the muddy earth of the dark tunnel that now encompassed them.

The passageway was narrow and had very little head height. The only illumination was the moonlight that seeped through from the small window in the corridor of the church. Merryn was using both her hands to alleviate some of the pain in her head as Kai's hands ripped and pulled at her hair. It was at this moment that she remembered her ring. She placed her hand over the top of the large, blue lapis lazuli stone and focussed all her thoughts. Within a few seconds, Kai was subjected to an electric-like shock that crackled and spat at his hands with its brilliant light. Merryn heard him yell out. The shock and pain forced him to release his hold on her and he fell to the ground with a thud. Merryn turned to run onwards when she heard the noise of a scuffle behind her. Flicking her head round to look over her shoulder, in the dark tunnel, she spotted Kai back up on his feet and fighting spear to cemp-edge with Jason. Even in the dark, she knew it was him as he was a short, muscularly-built male with tight curly hair, which formed an unmistakeable silhouette. He must have followed after them! If he had pursued them in order to save her, then she knew she could not continue without trying to help, but as she made her way back towards them, Merryn realised that she was too late. Kai lunged forwards, and the tip of his spear met with Jason's arm. He went down hard to the floor, and Merryn could hear him writhing in pain. She could only imagine what damage had been done as there was too little light now they had travelled further into the narrow, black tunnel. She managed to strike Kai down the centre of his back with her cemp-edge, its deep blue-green blade searing the skin on his shoulder blade. Without warning, Kai used the blunt end of his spear to hit Jason hard on the head, knocking him unconscious immediately then he swung around to face Merryn, who gasped in shock and jumped backwards. She couldn't believe that her blow hadn't put Kai on the floor, and she was now certain that her fate was looking particularly troubled. Kai lunged at Merryn repeatedly with his spear. She managed to dodge the jabs that were aimed at her torso, but unfortunately, she was not quick enough to miss Kai's elbow as he lifted it high and smashed it with full force into the side of her head. Merryn felt the sharp pain travel through her skull, and she felt disorientated by the impact. Kai made use of her confusion and grabbed her around the throat using the crook of his arm to hold her. With his other hand, he managed to disarm her – snatching her cemp and placing it into his top jacket pocket. Once again, she found herself being dragged along the passage, this time she was struggling to breathe as his arm tightened around her throat. Merryn had no choice but to assist her movement, if she did not wish to lose consciousness.

After they had travelled uphill for several minutes, Kai swung open a heavy wooden door that allowed him access in to what seemed to be the small, barren cellar of a building. The walls were made of grey stone and the floor was dusty and dirty. In the corner, sat a battered, old lamp, without a lampshade, which rested on a wooden box. Mysteriously, the lamp was lit and therefore provided a small amount of light so that it was possible to see the room reasonably clearly. Merryn wriggled and writhed in Kai's arms. She was scared that he would hurt her, but had made the decision that she would prefer to go down fighting, if he was going to kill her, rather than make it easy for him. She reached her hand up, placing it over her other hand. She tried to gain her focus on her ring once more, thinking that she would be able to shock Kai again and either overpower him or get away. Kai seemed to notice what she was planning though. He threw her to the floor and yelled at her,

"I don't think so! You don't think that I'm so stupid as to let you do that more than once do you?"

He grabbed her hand and forcefully removed her lapis lazuli ring, placing it into his pocket along with her cemp. As he did so, Merryn scooted backwards in the dust away from him. Her mind was racing. She was trying to work out whether she would be strong enough to fight him alone, but she knew that the odds were stacked against her because Kai had taken her weapon. It would also be risky because she had no one to back her up if things went badly, but she felt that if she didn't at least try, then she was failing Chloe and Emily. Emily … Merryn had forgotten that she had been taken by Maddox. What was she doing here? Merryn knew that she had to do something: Emily was not a Nyss. She was in real danger, and Merryn knew that she had to try to help or she would never forgive herself if this ended badly.

Kai advanced on her and hit her hard with the end of his spear. Merryn tried to avoid it, but it caught her on the leg and she winced audibly. He swung the spear around turning it one hundred and eighty degrees and stabbed at Merryn with the speared end of the stick. Merryn kicked at it and the spear flew from Kai's hands and landed with a clatter on the hard floor. Wasting no time, having lost his weapon, he dived forcefully at Merryn, savagely placing both his hands around her throat. Merryn knew she was the weaker party without her weapon, but she was not willing to go down without fighting. They rolled on the ground. Over and over, with Kai trying to maintain contact with Merryn's throat. The dust from the floor was irritating her face and she was struggling to keep her eyes open. She managed to lift one of her knees and drew it up quickly, making contact with Kai just below his belt. Kai yelled out, falling flat on his back at the side of her. Merryn knew that she had managed to hurt him. She rolled over on the floor and tried desperately to catch her breath, but it felt that instead of air she was only breathing in dust. She began to cough and splutter which only made her inhale more of the tiny irritating particles.

Suddenly, Kai was upon her once more. His hands were on her hair again, and he pulled her to her feet with malevolent aggression.

"Get up, you bitch!" he spat at her, dragging her towards what looked like a small hatch on the far side of the room. Merryn yelled out as the pain threatened to overwhelm her. Kai opened the small door and pushed her through it before following quickly behind. Merryn rolled over and stood up as quickly as she could. A series of narrow, uneven stone steps stood before her. She moved her hair away from her face as Kai shoved her from behind. She felt the sharp point of his spear poking into the centre of her back and knew that she had no choice except to climb the steps. She felt physically exhausted and the muscles in her legs vibrated with fatigue.

On reaching the top of the flight of stairs, Merryn was ordered to slide open a solid, wooden gate-type structure. It was heavy and she had to use both her hands and put all her weight behind the action in order to get it to move. Once it was open, she was pushed over the threshold and found herself in a large room with a huge fireplace at one end. Moonlight streamed through three huge Georgian-style windows that were laid bare to the outside world as the battered, white, panelled shutters were all open. Merryn instantly recognised the window structure as that of the large white house that sat high on the headland overlooking the sea; Perfect Haven. This was the house that she had seen in her visions. The only furniture in the room was a huge, dilapidated, wooden table that stood central to the floor space at one end of the room. Kai slammed the blunt end of his spear into Merryn's shoulder blades, and she fell to her knees with a thud as the pain from the blow resonated down her back. He then proceeded to kick her and she fell forwards, landing on her shoulder awkwardly before rolling onto her side. Lying on the hard, stone floor Merryn could now see the door where they had entered the room. The structure that she had slid sideways was actually an empty shelf unit that reached from the floor to the ceiling in height, and was clearly a hidden doorway that linked the house via the passageways to the church.

Now he was on her. He straddled her body and she felt the full weight of him turning her on to her back and pressing down on her. She tensed her whole body and tried to push him off her, but he had her pinned down. She beat at his chest with her hands, but he placed the silver point of his spear to her throat and leant over her menacingly.

"I'm going to enjoy this," he hissed quietly into her ear as he stroked her neck then slid his hand down the centre of her torso.

Reaching the hem of her T-shirt, he began to slide his hand underneath. His hand was hot and clammy, and

Merryn closed her eyes and held her breath as the touch of his skin on hers made her feel nauseous. She didn't want to look at him, and she was trying her best to block out what was happening as his hand crept further underneath her clothing. Feeling helpless, without her cempedge or ring, she was certain that this was the end. She thought about Xance, and wanted his face to be what she was picturing as her world went black.

3 2

Roche Cave

Suddenly, a flash of bright orange, blinding light filled the room followed by the crackle of white sparks. Kai was thrown across the floor by what appeared to be an invisible force. With her body free of his weight, Merryn was able to scramble to her feet and back away from Kai towards the hidden doorway. It was then that she saw the silhouette of a figure standing by one of the windows. The form was that of a tall man. Merryn remained motionless, holding her breath as she watched the dark shape raise his arms. Immediately, another flash of orange permeated the room, and she saw Kai's body lift from the floor before it smashed down again into a heap by the fireplace. He made no sound as he landed on the hard floor, his crumpled body eerily lifeless. Merryn's heart thudded within her chest. She was unsure whether to take a chance and run back the way she had come through the tunnel or see if she could attempt to exit via the door opposite. Thinking about how quickly the assailant had dealt with Kai, it seemed unlikely that her escape would be successful. As she was deliberating her options, the shape began to move towards her in the darkness.

"Merryn, are you ok?" He spoke to her gently, and in a voice which seemed strangely familiar.

Merryn was still fixed to the spot. Her mind raced. She recognised the voice, but couldn't place who it belonged to.

"It's ok," he said, reaching out his hand and placing it reassuringly on Merryn's arm, "It's me."

She strained and squinted her eyes to see who this mystery person was as the thumping of her heart thudded loudly in her ears, and her whole body shook with stress. "Tyler?" she said hesitantly.

"Yes, are you alright?"

Without speaking, Merryn fell in to Tyler's arms. The relief that this was someone that she knew, and not another enemy was overwhelming for her. Merryn fought back tears as he held her tightly in his arms and stroked her hair gently. Once she had gathered herself together, Merryn pulled away from Tyler and spoke, "I don't understand. How did you do this?"

"Sometimes, things are not as they seem," he answered.

"Clearly! What was that? I mean, how did you do that – the orange light and throwing Kai across the floor like that? Was that *magic?*" Merryn's confusion was evident in her voice and she glanced across at Kai's unmoving body.

"Well, I suppose that you were going to find out at some point," Tyler said, "I'm a Thaumaturge … from Sefwarian Nyss."

"You're from Sefwarian Nyss too?" Merryn said in disbelief.

Tyler nodded.

"What's a Thaumaturge? Are you a magician?" Merryn questioned.

"Yes, amongst other things," Tyler smiled.

"I had no idea, I …" Merryn was lost for words.

"You weren't supposed to know. I was sent from Sefwarian Nyss to watch over you."

"Why?"

"I have no idea – I was just asked by the First Luminary to keep watch. He never elaborated. I knew that if he had asked me then it must be important. I have much respect for him and the Luminary Synod."

"Do Xance and the others know who you are?"

"No," Tyler shook his head.

Before they had time to continue their conversation, there was a scuffle of noise coming from behind where Merryn stood. Running up the stairs was Xance and the others, including Jason, whom they must have found on the way. As they made their way in to the room, Merryn was elated and relieved to see that Xance appeared to be alright. She noticed that Jason's arm was a swamp of dark, red blood, but he seemed to be ok and another wave of relief washed over her.

"Xance! Are you all ok?" Merryn asked anxiously.

"We're fine, just about," Xance grinned, "Are you

alright? I was so worried when I realised that you had gone."

"I'm ok," Merryn said.

"Great. *Tyler?* What are you doing here?" Xance said, noticing Tyler standing next to Merryn. The others gathered around to listen.

"Can we explain later?" Merryn interjected, "We really should go. Maddox has taken Emily somewhere. They must have come this way, and we need to find them."

Xance looked puzzled and stressed, *"Emily?* Why is she here?"

"I don't know. She's been a bit weird recently, and seemed to be everywhere that we are. I think she's obsessed with you. She must have followed us," Merryn explained quickly then added, "What happened to the Banas Mihtig? Are you being followed?"

"No, I'm pretty sure we dealt with most of them, but Nix got away. I think he must have left the church. He disappeared," Xance answered.

As a group, they headed for the door opposite the hidden entrance where they had entered the room. Just as they were about to leave, Merryn stopped Xance. "Wait, I need to get my cemp and ring," she said as she pulled him backwards by the arm. She ran over to Kai's body and retrieved her weapon, fumbling around a little longer in his top pocket for her ring. She found the idea of being this close to Kai again completely abhorrent; she didn't want to touch his limp, lifeless body, and she shuddered at the thought of what might have happened had Tyler not arrived when he did. Not wasting any time, she returned to Xance and they followed after the others.

Another sliding bookshelf, presumably left half-open by Maddox, and then Carter and the rest of the group, indicated where they needed to go next. They were now in a smaller room, situated on the far side of the house, which led the way into another underground tunnel. This time, it seemed to take them on a winding path downhill. Merryn held on tightly to Xance's hand as they moved quickly in order to catch up with the rest of the group. They alternated between running and walking as parts of the passageway became extremely narrow and the ground beneath them was uneven and difficult to navigate without stumbling. Having travelled for what seemed like an eternity in the pitch-black tunnel with the sound of their feet thudding on the hard earth, they began to hear another sound which hinted that they were reaching the end of their journey. In the distance, the thunderous, rhythmical sound of waves lifting and crashing against the rocks could be heard. In addition, up ahead now, they could hear the footsteps and voices of Carter and the others, and as they negotiated a large bend in the tunnel, they joined them. After another ten metres or so, the passage began to open up in to a much wider area completely encircled with rocks. It appeared that there was no way forwards and they had reached a dead end. Looking around her, Merryn conceded that they were trapped and that they would have to return the way they had come. She felt exhausted, and could see that the others were tired and dispirited also. Surely, there had to be a way onwards. She knew that Emily was in grave danger and that they must find her.

Just then, Carter shouted, "Over here!"

Merryn looked behind her and saw that Carter was climbing across a series of large rocks. They were mostly horizontal and flat, forming a makeshift path over the barrier of rock that was preventing their journey from continuing. He seemed to be crawling now in order to avoid the stones which formed the ceiling. One by one, they all followed him. Merryn was relieved to find that once she had reached the pinnacle of her climb, the way down the other side was much easier as the rock eased away in a gradual decline. They now found themselves standing in a cave. The dark, damp rock arched overhead, dropping sharply on the left side almost vertical to the ground. Before them was the sea, encompassed on two sides by a narrow stone path that joined the rocks of the cave. The movement of the water slapped against the edge of the pathway. In places, it breached the perimeter of the stones and smacked down loudly on to the floor, creating cold, wet, slippery areas. The mouth of the cave gave way to the roaring ocean which thrashed and crashed against the many rocks that lay in its path. One huge rock rose in a wide triangular point out of the sea just past the mouth of the cave. Moonlight streamed through the entrance and lit the water, shining majestically. In the centre of the pool of water, a small boat rested uncomfortably on the intermittent wild movement of the waves. Inside the boat, a figure, silhouetted by the moonlight, was attempting to start the small motor. The sound of the propeller attempting to spin echoed through the cave.

"Where is she, Maddox?" Xance yelled.

Merryn held her breath, desperate for Emily to be

unhurt. She didn't like the girl, but would never wish any real harm on her.

"She's here somewhere!" Maddox shouted back, "You know me, I'm not big on sentiment. I had no use for her; she wouldn't tell me what I needed to know!"

"She's nothing to do with this, where is she?" Xance persisted, sounding slightly desperate now.

Just then, Maddox achieved success and the boat motor whirred loudly into motion. Merryn could see the dark outline of the boat turning round before it glided away towards the mouth of the cave and out on to the open sea. In the slipstream, a floating shape drifted towards them. As it reached a pool of moonlight resting on the surface of the water, it became clear to see that the object was a body floating face down.

"Emily!" Merryn screamed.

Carter and Xance wasted no time. They dived almost simultaneously in to the cold water. Merryn grabbed Chloe and they hugged each other tightly as they watched the two boys retrieve the body and swim back to the path towing her between them. Luke and Tom knelt down on the hard stone and reached out, pulling the body out of the water and on to the path. Chloe immediately released her hold on Merryn and knelt down to examine Emily's body. Merryn stood motionless, her eyes wide with disbelief, as she watched her friend shake her head slowly.

Xance, having dragged himself out of the water, scrambled to Emily's side and proceeded to shake and agitate her body, yelling in obvious distress, "Emily! No, no!"

"Xance, stop," Chloe grabbed his arm, "It's no good. We're too late."

"Tyler, is there anything that you can do?" Merryn asked, looking at him hopefully.

"I ... I could try, sometimes it works, but I'm not sure it will do any good now. We needed to be here sooner," Tyler said.

"What do you mean, Merryn?" Xance questioned.

"He can do magic," Merryn said.

Xance was clearly shocked. "What?"

"There's no time, let him try, Xance!" Merryn said anxiously.

Tyler stepped forwards and stood over Emily's limp body. He closed his eyes. Within a few seconds, an orange, misty glow appeared above Emily. Nothing happened. Emily did not move. Her body remained limp and lifeless. Tyler knelt down next to her. He continued to produce the orange, mystical glow for several minutes, but it had no effect. The group hung their heads in desolation. Xance clung to Merryn, pulling her in to his chest. Carter and Chloe embraced each other.

"I'm so sorry," Tyler said, shaking his head as he stood up.

Bryn removed his jacket and placed it over Emily's body.

"She shouldn't have been here! Why was she here?" Xance said quietly.

"I think that she had followed us, Xance," Merryn said, sitting down beside him on the wet stones and placing her arms around him, "She's been doing it for a while now." Despite her own distress, she knew that she had to support Xance right now, "I've suspected for a while that she has been growing increasingly obsessed with you. You must've noticed that it was getting worse? She didn't deserve this though. I know you had warned us that Maddox was dangerous, but I had no idea that he was capable of this."

"He can't be allowed to get away with this!" Xance said softly, clearly devastated.

"He won't. We'll deal with him, when the time is right. He will live to regret this," Carter reassured Xance.

"He's obviously done this because he tried to get her to tell him where the jewels are," said Bryn.

"She didn't have a chance, poor girl," Chloe added.

"So, he's left empty-handed." Carter's temper was beginning to flare. "He's committed murder over these jewels. There must be something within them that will give Nethergeard ultimate power – we have to find them! Otherwise, they will return and who knows what atrocities they are prepared to commit."

The cave fell silent for a few moments. Nobody spoke. Nobody moved. Apart from Carter, who, with his anger building, began to pace up and down.

Eventually, Xance broke the silence. "You said that your vision showed a box under the water, Merryn?" he asked.

"Yes," she answered.

"Then the chances are it's down there somewhere," Xance said nodding and indicating towards the water in the cave.

"Think carefully, Merryn," Carter added agitatedly, "Is

there anything else you can remember that will give us a clue as to where it might be?"

Merryn was feeling the overwhelming pressure that everyone was depending on her as every single one of them stared expectantly at her. She had experienced so many visions recently, but it was difficult to remember the main elements. They were all a bit of a blur, and she had never been particularly good at recalling things that she had seen. She had compared her visions as being similar to watching film excerpts, but as always happened when she had watched a film, she could remember the main events, but always struggled to recall the minutiae of detail involved in the plot or setting.

She tried to recall what she had seen within the cave, "I think I remember the box being near the edge of the water, hidden in a crevice in the rock," she said eventually.

One after another, the boys took it in turns to dive into the freezing cold water and search for the wooden box, each one emerging from the sea shaking and shivering from the icy water. Merryn sat with Chloe on the water's edge watching anxiously. She could see the hazy colours of their cemp-edge swords moving around under the water as they used them to light their way in the dark sea-pool. They searched for as long as they could, but the temperature in the water eventually began to take its toll on their bodies, and now each of the boys lay cold and exhausted on the stone floor of the cave.

"It's hopeless," Xance panted, his chest heaving up and down as he tried to catch his breath.

"Let me look," said Merryn standing up and removing her shoes.

"No, it's too dangerous," Xance said, sitting up.

"If it's not too dangerous for all of you, then it isn't too dangerous for me," Merryn replied forcefully. "It makes sense for me to look. If we are actually looking for what I have seen in my visions, then I sort of know what I'm looking for."

"I'm really not sure about this, Merryn," Xance frowned at her.

"Let her try, Xance," Carter joined the conversation, "It's our only option."

The rest of the group nodded in agreement.

"I'll be careful, I promise." Merryn hugged Xance before sliding herself into the icy sea water.

She used the blue-green glow from her cemp-edge to examine the edges of the pool, feeling along the rough rock with her fingers searching for the hidden crevice. Visibility under the water was limited and she found it difficult to see anything in the dark corners clearly, even with the glow from her sword. Several times, Merryn came up to the surface for air. Each time she saw the eager faces of her friends leaning over the water's edge in anticipation. After she had emerged for the fourth time, Xance became agitated, his stress clearly apparent.

"Enough," he said. "You'll freeze if you stay in there much longer."

"I'll just try one more time," Merryn puffed. She was worn out, numb with cold and drained, but was determined to not give up easily. As she dived under the water once more, she heard Xance's voice faintly in the distance shouting for her to come back.

Merryn knew that this was her last chance. Suddenly,

in the water before her, she saw something white. She strained her eyes to try to see what it was. Swimming towards her, was the spirit girl. Merryn was sure that it was the ghostly figure; her long, pale dress swirled and ballooned around her as the water filled the material of the skirt. Her long brown hair was mostly loose and whirled messily around her face. Merryn was shocked at the sight of her underneath the water, but she was not afraid. She now knew that the girl had been trying to help her. She knew that, somehow, this ghost was trying to create a link between Merryn and the past. Merryn had no idea why she was doing this, how it was even possible or how this ghostly girl even knew who Merryn was. It was all very confusing.

The girl beckoned for Merryn to follow her, and they swam just a short distance towards the far left of the pool. She pointed to the edge where a piece of flat rock jutted out from the corner of the pathway above. It hung over the water and created a screen between the cave and the water. Merryn swam forwards and underneath the level piece of stone. She held up her cemp-edge and allowed the blue-green light that emanated from it to illuminate the small space. Reaching in with her free hand, she stroked and pressed the rock. She was getting short of breath, and so she swam out and made her way back to the surface. As she burst through the water in to the cave, she gasped desperately for air. Xance had run over to the edge of the cave and was leaning over the pool towards her. She thought he was speaking to her, but the water was swirling in her ears and that, along with her heart thudding loudly in her chest, was all that she could hear.

Once her lungs were full of air again, she disappeared under the water and back to the overhanging stone. Alone in the water now, with no sign of the ghostly girl, she continued her search. She began to feel along the rock once more, and this time she was fortunate enough to find the wooden box. *This is it!* She thought feeling exhilarated.

It was pushed in to a deep crevice within the rock, and Merryn imagined it would be positioned far beneath the path above her. She couldn't remove it with one hand as it seemed to be wedged tightly in its place, having been situated there for many years, Merryn thought. She placed her cemp in her pocket and used both her hands to pull at the box, whilst she pressed on the wall of the rock below it with her feet. After several strong pulls, Merryn was relieved to feel the box move slightly. One more huge tug loosened the box entirely, and she pulled it successfully from its resting place and held it tightly with both her hands. It was heavy, and she was grateful that the water made it feel lighter and easier to manage. Needing air quite desperately now, she kicked her legs hard and made her way to the surface. As she emerged, Carter grabbed at the box to secure it, and Xance took her hands and pulled her from the water. He hugged her tightly, and she had to push him away from her to remind him that she needed air. She sat down on the floor, exhausted but elated, and breathed in huge gulps of air. The group all sat down, gathering around Carter and the mysterious wooden box. It was about the size of a bread bin and was rectangular in shape. The lid was secured by a metal loop which had a small metal stick attached to a thin chain pushed through it to prevent it from opening. Merryn noticed a crack in the wood, and this triggered her memory of her visions and dreams: she was now convinced that this was the box that she had seen.

"Are you alright, Merryn?" Xance asked stroking her wet hair.

She sat upright. "Yes, I'm fine," she smiled at him, "I just need to catch my breath," she continued, shivering.

He placed his arm around her and pulled her in close to him and, despite the fact that he was wet through too, she began to feel some comfort from the warmth of his body next to hers. They all watched as Carter lifted the lid of the box. Merryn was shocked to see that, just as it had been in her vision, the container was full of jewels. It was packed so tightly with the colourful gems, jewellery and bright silver and gold coins that many of them spilled out on to the wet stone floor once the lid was opened.

"Merryn, I thought you were crazy when you said there might be treasure under this water!" Tom said, struggling to contain his excitement.

"I can't believe it, we're rich!" yelled Bryn as he eyed the gems.

Everyone laughed apart from Xance who spoke with a serious tone, "No, sadly, we are not."

"What?" Harry questioned.

"It isn't ours. We have to hand it in," Xance explained.

"You are joking, right?" smiled Tom.

"No, I'm sorry, but I'm serious – it isn't ours to keep," Xance said.

"So, we all risked our lives for nothing. Jason has

endured that injury and we have nothing to show for it?" Harry moaned.

"Jason will be ok!" Xance said firmly, clearly annoyed by Harry's attitude, "Emily has lost her life because of this box. We have to deal with this situation honestly. We have to hand it over to the First Luminary. It isn't ours to keep. Besides we have to assume that whatever it is that the Nethergeards want so badly, it is in this box. If we keep it, we could all be in danger."

"He's right," Carter agreed with Xance, "Tempting as it is, we have to hand it in."

Harry was obviously disgruntled and he spoke through slightly gritted teeth, "Well, if complete honesty is what you stand for, Xance, shouldn't that policy apply to *everything?*"

"Shut up, Harry!" Carter responded quickly with an angry tone to his voice.

Feeling slightly uncomfortable at the change in tone within the group, Merryn looked around to try to gauge everyone's reaction. She may have been imagining it, but it seemed that all eyes were on her at that moment. Apart from Xance, however, who did not respond verbally, but glared at Harry and leant forwards slightly towards him, obviously annoyed at his comment. Merryn had no idea what Harry meant by his remark, but she felt sure that she witnessed Bryn dig Harry in the arm with his elbow and the two of them exchanged knowing glances. It was great that they seemed to be on better terms with each other again, Merryn thought, however, she couldn't help feeling that there was a joke they were sharing and it was at her expense.

33

Pausing Honesty

A few weeks had passed since that night. It had been a time filled with conflicted feelings for Merryn as she had struggled to reconcile her emotions regarding Emily's death. She blamed herself. She had tortured herself for not speaking out about Emily's seemingly growing obsession with Xance. Merryn had noticed a change in Emily's behaviour, and she had witnessed her on many an occasion watching Xance from afar. Then there was the incident in the school library, when Tyler had intervened. Emily had become particularly nasty and venomous, and it was blatantly obvious that she was jealous of Merryn's relationship with Xance. Deep down, Merryn knew that she had no control over the events of that terrible evening, but she also knew that she was always going to feel responsible, at least partly, for what happened.

Together with her friends, including Tyler, she had visited Sefwarian Nyss. They had presented the wooden box filled with jewels to the First Luminary, and he had been more than relieved and grateful that they had found it. Having sifted carefully through the box, he had removed from the haul a delicate ring adorned with a large, square-shaped ruby. He had shared with them his suspicion that this was the object the Nethergeards were so keen to obtain. He explained that it was an ancient ring that had formidable, magical powers, and that it once belonged to the original First Luminary. If the Nethergeards had found it, they would have been able to use its powers to overthrow the Luminary Synod and take possession of Sefwarian Nyss. Merryn realised that, somehow, the spirit girl had known about the ring's powers and that Sefwarian Nyss was in danger. She had, for some reason, chosen Merryn to relay her knowledge of its whereabouts. Despite this, Merryn had a suspicion that there was more to it. She was convinced that some of her visions were her own personal memories. They felt too familiar to her to be anything else.

To show his appreciation of their honesty in relinquishing the jewels to the Luminary Synod, the First Luminary had allowed them all to choose one piece of jewellery each to keep for themselves. Almost everyone had picked a ring, including Xance, who had decided on one with small, round emeralds dotted equidistantly around its gold band. He had told Merryn that the emeralds reminded him of her green eyes and that this fact had swayed his choice. Merryn had been the only one of the group who had selected something other than a ring. She had perused the selection of jewels, taking her time to look through the collection, but from the very beginning her eyes had been drawn to a necklace and despite the fact that there were many beautiful objects to choose from, she kept coming back to this one piece. It was a large, oval-shaped crystal encased in an ornate, antique, silver setting and was attached to a silver chain. Its colours were a mixture of greens, blues and purples and Merryn had liked the way it sparkled in the light.

LIFE HAD STEADILY RETURNED to a version of normal in Porthrosen. Merryn had celebrated her seventeenth birthday quietly at home with her parents and sister. The following day, she had travelled with Xance to Trunow, the nearest town and they had meandered aimlessly for hours, visiting various shops. They had spent a huge proportion of the time in a large perfumery, spraying a multitude of different scents on to mini white cards and wafting them before their noses. Merryn had been left in fits of giggles as she had accidentally tapped Xance on the nose with one of the perfume sample cards, and he was left rubbing his nose with his T-shirt in an attempt to remove the scent from his skin. Merryn eventually selected a perfume that was her favourite, and Xance bought it for her. She had protested vehemently at his intended generosity, as he had already given her the lapis lazuli ring as an early birthday present, but Xance had been insistent and they left the shop with Merryn carrying a small white gift bag tied with a pink ribbon, containing her new designer fragrance.

Later that afternoon, Xance had treated her to a meal. Merryn was overwhelmed at how Xance was making her feel so special, and they had chatted and laughed non-stop as they ate pasta and bread in the romantically lit Italian restaurant. She had felt overcome with emotion; she knew that she loved Xance, and she couldn't imagine being able to feel any more content than she was in that moment as she sat across the table from him, looking in to his beautiful, deep blue eyes and marvelling at how captivating his smile was.

As SHE SAT on the blanket at the Koyt watching the boats on the sea in the distance, Merryn pulled her jacket together and snuggled in a little nearer to Xance. She knew that soon, it would be too cold to sit at their favourite spot. Autumn was upon them, and the cold winds from the sea were increasing in frequency high up on the headland. Merryn loved being with Xance, and she was convinced that they were meant to be together always. She was aware that she still had a long way to go in being able to remember their past and that there were still many more things to discover about their previous relationship. Unfortunately, she suspected that there was much more that Xance was not telling her about Sefwarian Nyss, Porthrosen and their previous time together. She knew that she had to trust him though, and felt sure that he must have good reason for not revealing what he knew. She did feel comforted because he had been honest with her and told her that there was more information that he couldn't share, but she was unconvinced that this wasn't his own choice and perceived that he *wouldn't* tell her not *couldn't* tell her. Deep down, she believed that he was keeping secrets from her. Important things that, for some reason, he didn't feel able to share with her. She knew that Xance was a good person, and she trusted that his feelings for her were genuine. She hoped that he would open up to her when the time was right. Or perhaps, eventually, she would be able to remember herself as her visions and dreams were still continuing, and she was recalling past events with Xance more and more.

Despite feeling uneasy about Xance's alleged secrecy, she knew that she had no real right to be upset, for she had not been entirely honest with him either. What she hadn't shared with Xance was that, in addition to the increased visions and memories of herself with *him*, she was also experiencing an increasing number of visions that included Nix. She would never want to lie to him or hurt him, but she had been unable to be completely honest with him. She feared how he may react and what he may do if she revealed to him what she was seeing and feeling in her dreams. She knew that she would have to be honest with him soon, and share with him the knowledge that her memories of Nix were returning and that they were making her feel confused and conflicted.

Xance had assured her that the difficult times were over now, and that they should look forward to a positive future together. But Merryn knew that there were still so many questions left unanswered and that this was only the beginning.

Printed in Great Britain
by Amazon

74213134R00170